Song for
My Father

Song for My Father

A WEST INDIAN JOURNEY

S. Brian Samuel

IAN RANDLE PUBLISHERS
Kingston • Miami
www.ianrandlepublishers.com

First published in Jamaica, 2023 by
Ian Randle Publishers
16 Herb McKenley Drive
Box 686
Kingston 6
www.ianrandlepublishers.com

National Library of Jamaica Cataloguing-In-Publication Data
Name: Samuel, S. Brian, author.
Title: Song for my father : a West Indian journey / S. Brian Samuel.
Description: Kingston : Ian Randle Publishers, 2023.
Identifiers: ISBN 9789768286819 (pbk).
Subjects: LCSH: Samuel, Darwin Fitzgerald. |West Indians – Great
    Britain – History – 20th century. |Immigrants – Great Britain. |
    Grenada – Emigration and immigration – 20th century. | Great
    Britain – Emigration and immigration – 20th century. |Fathers
    and sons.
Classification: DDC 920 -- dc23.

Cover and Book Design by Ian Randle Publishers
Printed and Bound in the United States of America

Dedicated to the memory of
Thomas Dougald Samuel: 1950–2014
This one's for you, Tom: more turgid prose

Life is what happens to you while you're busy making other plans.
— John Lennon

Contents

Prologue

'So, where's your mum then? Is she dead?'

'No.'

'So, where is she?'

'Um... she's not here.'

'Yeah but ... *where* is she?'

In the playground of Fitzjohn's Primary School in London, this kid just wouldn't let up. I'd invited him back to our flat after school the previous evening, big mistake, and he'd noticed there wasn't a mum in the house. The next day he was on me like a rash: where's your mum? But how could I answer the question when I myself didn't know? My brothers and I had no clue where our mother was, nor did we spend too much time thinking about it, to be honest. But ever since we'd landed in England, that's all everyone seemed to want to know: Where's your mum? *I don't fucking know, okay?* People never asked me this in Trinidad, why was it such a big deal over here?

It was August 1961, and we'd recently moved into a two-bedroom flat in 41b Arkwright Road, Hampstead, our home for the next two years. Our family consisted of me, aged eight, big brothers Tom and Gerry (yes, you heard that right), aged ten and eleven, and our father, Darwin Fitzgerald (Gerry) Samuel, a teacher. As I was beginning to realize, we weren't your typical British family. An all-male, highly nuclear family: no mother, no sisters, cousins, uncles, aunties, or grandparents – just the four of us. What's so strange about that?

Two years earlier, in Port-of-Spain, our mother simply hadn't come home from work one day, and that was that: she was gone. In West Indian families, then and now, children are on a need-to-know basis, and clearly: we didn't need to know. All we knew was 'Mummy's gone away … for a while.' A year later, we travelled by ocean liner from Trinidad to England, and after a succession of cold cramped council flats into the relative luxury of Arkwright Road. Not that we were suffering without a mum; mums did funny things like make you take your shoes off in the house and cut the crusts off your sandwiches – what was that all about? But there was always that nagging question: where *is* she? And was her absence the reason why we were always on the move, running from pillar to post?

To this day, I still love the looks on people's faces when I tell them my brothers are called Tom and Gerry. Actually, Gerry came first, born in 1950 in London, followed by Tom, born in Grenada in November of the same year. Then a gap of three years before I came along: the runt of the litter born in 1953. My big brothers, Tom and Gerry: so close in age, so different in nature. The Wild One and the Mild One! Growing up in their wake, I guess I subconsciously copied bits of both of them, so I've ended up a bit of a hybrid: generally mild, with a bit of a wild side. Or is it vice-versa?

In February 1942, the depths of the Second World War, my father, nineteen-year-old Darwin Samuel signed up for a scheme to go to Britain to work in the armaments industry. Even the real threat of U-Boats couldn't deter him, anywhere was better than small-island, no-opportunity Grenada. Via a harrowing Atlantic crossing, he was lucky to survive. Darwin disembarked in Liverpool, to a city reeling under the onslaught of the Blitz. He qualified as a machinist and worked the production line for the iconic Lancaster Bomber, at the Metrovicks Factory in Manchester, prime target of the Luftwaffe.

Throughout the war my father endured; failure was not an option, not then, not ever.

After the war, Darwin stayed on in England, one of the few and far between: Black immigrant pioneers enduring stares from children in the street and sceptical looks from landladies, wondering if he'd blacken her sheets. Although Darwin never achieved his dream of studying law, he qualified as a metalwork and technical drawing teacher, putting to use the skills he'd learned during the war.

In 1950, two years after the voyage of the *Empire Windrush* had given birth to a flood of West Indian migration to England, our father went in the opposite direction: home. He married Scottish nurse Helen Hogan, and in short order their first son, Gerry, was born. Full of hope and optimism, twenty-eight-year-old Darwin Samuel and his brand-new family took ship to Grenada. After eight hard years in Britain, he'd had enough and was excited to be going back home: a man on the up.

Pity it didn't last. Ten years later in Port of Spain, our mother vanished without warning, thrusting their three young sons onto the sole care of our ill-prepared father. To say he was unprepared was putting it mildly. He was in a state of shock. But there was one thing he would never do: abandon his boys. In seeking to rebuild his shattered life, our father decided to rejoin the Windrush generation and return to England; there was nothing left for him in Trinidad anymore but bitter memories.

When we disembarked on Liverpool Docks on that cold morning in August 1960, I'd just turned seven, and England would already be my fifth country; a nomadic pattern that endures to this day. Unlike most of the Windrush generation, our journey didn't end when we got off the boat.

That was just the beginning.

Endee Samuel – My Grandfather

1.   Stormy Crossing

My grandfather was one hard bastard. He must have been because in what was literally and legally a White man's world, he'd done what few Black men could claim: amassed wealth – in the form of land. By the sweat of his brow and the strength of his back, he'd built up Mount Rose Estate into a mid-sized farm, growing cocoa, bananas, cloves, cinnamon, bananas, nutmeg, and mace. My one surviving photograph shows a spare, elderly man with jet-black skin, sparkling eyes, and a ready smile. But don't let that smile fool you: Endee was an unflinching disciplinarian, who didn't suffer fools gladly and for whom idleness was the work of the Devil.

Nathan Dennis 'Endee' Samuel was born in 1884, one short generation after the end of slavery in Grenada. Conditions for the vast majority of the peasant population were dire: eking out a living on the subsistence wages paid by the estates or growing cash crops on small hillside holdings. Despite the extreme privations of Grenada's ex-slaves, Endee managed to succeed and become a respected 'Peasant Proprietor,' as his position was stated in his title deeds. He bought land wherever he could find it, which he could pass on to his heirs, in perpetuity.

His equal passion was learning; like all Black Grenadians he would have received only a rudimentary education, but he went on to teach himself what the schools hadn't. He was an avid reader, fluid writer plus master of mental calculations involving pounds, shillings and pence, dollars and cents, tons, pounds, ounces, discounts, and percentages – all without a calculator in sight. His dream was for one of his sons to become a lawyer, and for him to visit the Holy Land. His choice of names for his sons shows his admiration for the arts and intellect: Byron and Darwin.

There are two versions of how Perdmontemps got its name. One has it from the French *Perde Mon Temps* – 'Waste My Time.' But an alternative legend, from no less an authority than my grandfather, holds a different view. The town sits directly beneath a towering volcanic cone, called Morne Gazo, (Mongozo), and the true name of the area, as spelled on postage stamps of the day, was *Pied Montagne* – 'Foot of the Mountain.' I prefer that version. Whichever, then as now, Perdmontemps was no more than a few houses, one shop, two churches and three bars, strung out along the Eastern Main Road. Mount Rose Estate employed a dozen or so labourers, depending on the season, hard-backed men and women, who knew how to wield a cutlass. As kids we grew up with the rich smells of moist cocoa beans, drying in the sun on huge trays, pulled out each morning from underneath the shop. Inside the shop were stacks of cocoa, nutmeg, mace, saltfish, flour, and white rum: the unmistakable scents of every Grenadian country childhood.

By 1941, my father had passed his Certificate of Secondary Education at Saint Paul's Model School, and at age eighteen was looking to make something of himself. But in colonial Grenada there were few avenues for advancement for a poor Black boy from the country. Business and the colonial service were the sole preserve of the White and brown elites, and the plantations only hired unskilled labour. It was therefore common for young men to seek their fortunes abroad. Darwin's elder brother Byron had left Grenada two years earlier to try his luck in the oil fields of Trinidad. But it was far from smooth sailing; the colonial government in Port of Spain was clamping down on inter-island migration and Trinidadians were becoming increasingly xenophobic towards 'small-islanders,' sometimes violently so. After working in the oilfields, opening a school and other business ventures, Byron left Trinidad for the Wild West of the Caribbean – Venezuela.

Deep one moonless night, in one of the deserted bays that dot Trinidad's Gulf of Paria, my uncle, Byron Samuel, and a dozen other desperate migrants boarded an overloaded motorboat or pirogue, for a perilous voyage across the ten miles that separate Trinidad and Venezuela. It was a bold gambit: criminal gangs like the notorious Boysie Singh were known to routinely rob their paying passengers, and dump them, alive and bound, into the shark infested waters of the *Bocas del Dragón* – Dragon's Mouth. But Byron made it to Venezuela unscathed, to face his second, even greater hurdle: papers. For a couple of years, he'd had a torrid time, working illegal jobs and keeping one step ahead of the authorities. Until, somehow, he obtained a Venezuelan identity card, or *cedula*, in his new name: Alberto Breceno. The newly legal Byron, or rather Alberto, got a good job at the Orinoco Mining Company in Puerto Ordaz, a boom town on a bend in the mighty Orinoco River.

But Darwin didn't want to follow Byron to Trinidad or Venezuela; there was no doubt where his heart lay: England. The motherland, home of culture and learning, the spiritual heart of every British subject. But although Darwin was technically British, that didn't mean he could just pack his bags and go to England – he needed a plan. And that's what he lacked: a plan. But a certain Mister Hitler was about to change all that.

As 1941 dawned, Europe had moved from phony war to the real thing, with frightening speed, and now all everyone in Grenada talked about was war-war-war. Within days of the joint Declaration of War against Germany, announced by Britain and France on

September 3, 1939, the Grenada Legislative Council sent a telegram to the Secretary of State for the Colonies:

> *At this momentous hour when the Armed Forces of the Empire have once again been called upon to uphold the cause of righteousness, the people of the Colony of Grenada, through their chosen representatives on the Legislative Council, with their humble duty to Your Majesty desire to affirm their dutiful and abiding loyalty to Your Majesty's Throne and Person and unreservedly to offer Your Majesty their services in any capacity which may appear to Your Majesty's Ministers in the United Kingdom helpful to our common cause.*

Legend has it that Barbados's telegram was slightly more prosaic:

> *Don't worry, Britain. Barbados is behind you!*

The Caribbean's loyalty to Britain wasn't particularly surprising, given the effective job the Empire had done for centuries in brainwashing its subjects. In homes and schools, bars and churches all over the British world, there was an almost religious belief that the colonial power, personified by the reigning monarch, was indeed their 'mother.' Apart from the twin accidents of geography and race, young Darwin could be said to be just as British as the British – an even more so. Like every colonial schoolboy from Barbados to Bangalore, he'd been fed a constant diet of Britishness all his life. He studied English history, geography and literature; he learned by rote from the same textbooks as his English counterparts. My stepmother adds:.

> *Dr Joan Samuel, artist, teacher:*
>
> *I made this drawing to suggest the overriding Britishness of the educational environment in which your father grew up. It was based on a large, framed photograph which he must have removed from the family home when he was forced to leave with Nelleen (his first wife), which suggests how important it was. He is shown aged six, dressed in a sailor suit similar to those worn by the British royal princes and it was obviously taken to mark a special occasion. I*

believe the occasion being marked was that of changing his name and possibly being baptized with it. We know that his mother Irene Renwick was unmarried and that, originally, he went by the name Petrus Renwick, but later became Darwin Fitzgerald Samuel, which meant that Endee fully recognized him as his son who would become a legal heir to his estate. Endee's choice of names shows the breadth of his cultural understanding, admiration for the great civilizations of the world and high aspirations, not only for Darwin but for his brothers Byron and, extraordinarily, Lingham too (Lingham, a Hindu sacred symbol of masculinity). I hope it may be possible to retrieve the old photograph and use it to replace my later drawing.

For over four hundred years, the British Empire had effectively stamped every aspect of Britishness onto her far-flung colonies – except the weather. All facets of daily life: laws, language, culture, religion, government, sports were modelled off Britain. Every West Indian household had two faded photographs on its living room wall: Jesus Christ and King George VI. The newspapers everyone read, after a few weeks' impatient delay, were English. In the early days of radio, entire households and villages would be crowded around someone's wireless set, listening keenly to the BBC Overseas Service.

In Grenada, the first impact of the war was in food. Overnight there were shortages of staples like rice and flour, Lyle's Golden Syrup and Fray Bentos Corned Beef. But these shortages only affected the middle-class. Country folk had lived off the land and sea all their lives, war or no war. But rich or poor, young or old, town or country, everyone in Grenada was gripped with war fever; the whole island mobilized to do their bit, for king and country. Well, not everyone. Some people, including Endee, took the opposing view that Grenada had no business getting involved in Europe's interminable wars and that the so-called motherland hadn't done nearly enough to deserve the supreme sacrifice from its oppressed colonial subjects. In the 1930s, Grenada, like the rest of the colonial world had been swept up by the stirrings of Black Nationalism and the writings of Marcus Garvey and W.E.B. DuBois. Throughout the West Indies, this was a time of rising tensions between the entrenched planter class and the emerging trade union movement. Like a jungle telegraph the clarion call hopped from island to island, we want change, we need change, *we must have change!* Violent strikes and riots ensued, put down with fatal force by the British.

For a lot of people, you didn't have to look too far back to see what had happened to those foolish Blacks who volunteered to fight for the White man. During the Great War of 1914-18, thousands of West Indians volunteered to fight for Britain in her time of need. But when they arrived at the Western Front, the men of the British West Indies Regiment found themselves restricted to the most menial, demeaning tasks like digging latrines, transporting corpses, and clearing mines.

West Indian soldiers suffered the same injustices and racial discrimination they had experienced back home. The White officers felt they'd been dealt a rum hand, commanding a bunch of wogs on support duties, and took out their frustrations on their Black soldiers, treating them with contempt. White volunteers from Trinidad, sons of the planter class, even formed their own exclusive force – the Merchants and Planters Contingent, and were treated as equals in the British Army. In fact, all White colonial soldiers from the 'Dominions' – Australians, Canadians, New Zealanders, South Africans – were treated immeasurably better than their Caribbean, African, and Asian counterparts.

After the Great War, these West Indian, African, and Indian soldiers were unceremoniously tossed back to their homelands when Britain no longer needed them-unsung, unpaid, unemployed. The returning soldiers felt rightly that they'd been dealt a raw deal from their so-called Motherland. As a result, people with long enough memories looked askance at all this new-found patriotic hoopla: 'Now that England in trouble, dey want you – you think dey give a shit about allyu otherwise?'

Nowhere was this generational divide more evident than in the clash between Darwin and his father. They had vastly differing values and world views, but both men shared the same bull-headed determination. Endee was set in his strict Victorian ways and didn't take too kindly to any dissension, least of all from his own children. Unfortunately, his headstrong youngest son also didn't like being pushed around, even by his father. The stage was set for a clash of epic proportions: 'Two bull can't live in the same pen.' Their differing views on the war was a case in point: the son worried about it; the father worried his son would get involved in it. But Endee needn't have worried; Britain didn't want his son.

In the early days of the Second World War, coloured chaps weren't exactly welcomed into the British Armed Forces with open arms. War or no war, racial standards had to be maintained. The late Dudley Thompson, OJ, QC, ex-Jamaican Minister of National Security and Pan-African icon, tells a hilarious tale of his encounter at the Royal Air Force recruiting office, in England in 1940. Back home in Jamaica, Thompson had been so incensed after reading Hitler's *Mein Kampf* that he'd paid his own way to England, to volunteer for service in the RAF. In the recruitment office, there were many forms to fill out, one of which included the question: 'Are you of pure European descent?' Dudley, decidedly dark, ticked the 'yes' box, and calmly handed it over to the recruiting sergeant, who went through the form and paused, then asked Dudley if he'd properly understood the question.

'Yes, of course I did,' said Dudley. 'What made you believe I didn't understand the question, sergeant?'

This was clearly too much for the poor sergeant.

'Nothing, nothing at all. Welcome to the RAF!' Stamp.

Dudley Thompson went on to have a distinguished career as a flight lieutenant in the RAF, flying dozens of missions over Germany in Lancaster Bombers, perhaps one of them that my father had helped build. After the war, he studied law and moved to Kenya, where he made a name for himself, defending the Mau-Mau warriors and Jomo Kenyatta in their freedom fight against the British.

As the war progressed, and Britain's young men 'of pure European descent' were being annihilated by the Nazis, the British turned a blind eye to the race question – anyone would do. This was particularly true in the RAF, which needed a constant supply of pilots and flight officers to replace those being killed in alarming numbers during the long-running Battle of Britain. Many West Indians like Dudley Thompson, Julian Marryshow from Grenada, and Ulric Cross from Trinidad served with distinction, many making the ultimate sacrifice. A total of fifty-five hundred West Indians enlisted in the RAF, 103 of whom earned decorations. But in the British Army, in a despicable repeat of the Great War, most Black soldiers found themselves restricted to support roles like digging latrines and ferrying corpses, while the White soldiers got on with the real business of fighting.

In addition to soldiers, Britain also needed men to work in their factories to build the bombs and machines needed to defeat Hitler in Europe. Men to keep the home fires burning, literally. Colour or class didn't matter. What mattered was muscle; they'd give you the skills. So Whitehall decided to tap its Empire for one thing it lacked: manpower. Young men from the colonies were offered a deal: come to England, get trained and be guaranteed a job in the armaments industry. But in those dark days it was by no means certain who would emerge on the winning side. Britain was still reeling from the debacle at Dunkirk, desperately building up its inadequate military capacity, and fearing the expected imminent invasion.

Not long after the outbreak of the war, eighteen-year-old Darwin took the 'penny-bus' down to Government House, a grand Georgian mansion overlooking the beautiful town of Saint George's, to volunteer for military service, where, to his chagrin, he was given short shrift. After the customary wait, he was admitted into the imposing edifice, after answering what he considered rude questions as to the nature of his business. The disinterested bureaucrat curtly informed him that there were no protocols in place for recruiting volunteers from Grenada. 'We simply wouldn't know what to do with you.' If Darwin wanted to volunteer, he could travel to England – at his own expense – and apply from there like everyone else. Otherwise, he could join the Grenada Volunteer Service. Darwin scoffed at that suggestion. Some of his school friends were in the GVS, and all they did was march up and down endlessly in the hot sun, clutching wooden rifles. He wouldn't be seen dead with that bunch of jokers.

Darwin continued teaching, chomping at the bit. He wouldn't have long to wait. In January 1942, a British Merchant Navy ship steamed into the Carenage and dropped anchor. The next day leaflets were distributed across the length and breadth of Grenada, announcing the purpose of the ship's visit: men. Not men to fight; men to work. Under a scheme sponsored jointly by the Colonial Office and the War Office, West Indian men were being offered the opportunity of a free passage to England where they'd be enrolled in a technical training school, receive a stipend and then assigned a job in the armaments industry. Darwin jumped at this unexpected opportunity. To sweeten the deal, he was given an implied promise that after the war, those loyal British subjects who'd come to their aid would be first in line to receive scholarships. Not only was this promise implied, but it was also unwritten. But for Darwin it was enough: a one-way ticket out of Grenada. He signed up. I once cheekily asked him why he hadn't joined the Armed Forces. 'It was the first ship leaving Grenada,' he said. 'And I took it.'

Darwin figured that if he put in enough service during the war, he'd be able to pursue his dream of studying law after it was all over. For Black West Indians, law and medicine – the professions – were the only guaranteed means of advancement. A legal career was where a man, regardless of colour, could make a good living for himself. You weren't beholden to anyone, you just put up your shingle, and they would come. Like dentists and undertakers, sooner or later we all need a lawyer. Darwin's father was vehemently opposed to his son's decision to go to England and had no qualms in letting him know it. The way Endee saw it, if Darwin wasn't good enough for Britain's Armed Forces, then why should he risk his life in her bombed-out cities? Endee was a follower of the Black Nationalist Marcus Garvey and felt that Britain's colonies had no business getting involved in Europe's endless imperialist wars. None of which mattered one whit to his headstrong son: he was going to England. End of story.

Darwin and 520 other young men from the West Indies signed up for the work scheme. They were all super excited, with a strong overlay of fear: we're going to *England!* But regardless of the opportunities awaiting them, first of all they had to get there. At that time, Europe was in the depths of the Battle of the Atlantic, nowhere was safe from the German U-boat menace. Darwin's family and friends were aghast, that he could even think of making such a dangerous journey, to an even more dangerous destination. Endee didn't take well to his son's decision to defy him, resulting in a long-lasting rift between both men.

Even in the remote West Indies, war was being waged on and under the placid Caribbean Sea, with deadly consequences. German U-boats operating either solo or in wolf packs sank hundreds of Allied ships carrying valuable cargoes from South America to Britain, often within sight of land. Trinidad exported vast amounts of oil to the Allies and its departing tankers were a prime target for U-boats. The twin islands of Martinique and Guadeloupe were French possessions and fell to the pro-German Vichy Government. A U-boat base was built on Martinique, wreaking havoc on merchant as well as navy ships in the Caribbean. The Canadian ship *Cornwallis* was torpedoed in broad daylight in Carlysle Bay, Barbados. Six months earlier, two ships had been torpedoed in a single night in Castries Harbour, Saint Lucia: the *Lady Nelson* and *Umtata*, killing sixty-eight people.

Even the inter-island schooners weren't safe; U-boats routinely sank these local boats, after surfacing and giving the crews time to launch their lifeboat before strafing the wooden vessels below the waterline – they weren't worth a torpedo. The West Indian Schooner Pool was set up in 1943 by the US Navy to coordinate the shipping of vital cargoes within the Eastern Caribbean, involving about eighty-four boats owned and crewed by West Indian seamen, many of whom died at sea. As efficient as they were in sinking ships, one disadvantage of U-boats was they needed to spend hours on the surface, recharging their batteries. This involved running their diesel generators, which could be heard for miles around. The remote bays along Grenada's East Coast made for perfect hiding places, and many U-boat captains knew the local waters, having served on German ocean liners before the war. Late at night, high in the hills of Perdmontemps, our father told us that he would sometimes hear the unmistakable sound of the U-boats' generators, running at full blast. It was said that German sailors would even come ashore, seeking the delights of fresh food and female company.

Darwin was surprised and touched at how genuinely upset his father was, at his imminent departure into harm's way – not that Endee would ever show it. But Darwin's elder sister Laurina had no qualms about showing her feelings: she cried incessantly. His elder brother Byron was in Trinidad and didn't hear about Darwin's departure until after he had left. But his eldest brother Lingham had plenty to say. Decades later, our father chuckled at the memory of their parting conversation:

'Boy wha de *ass* wrong wid you? You doh read the papers? You doh see how the whole a England getting' bombed to shit? Oh, sweet Jesus, my little brother gone an' lost he mind!'

Darwin stood his ground.

'No, I haven't lost my mind, but have you? You really think this war got nuttin' to do with we? I can't believe you Grenadians can be so dotish, you see what those Nazis doing to the Jews? If they beat England, what the hell you think they'll do to we?'

'*You* Grenadians? Wait, you turn British now?'

'You know what I mean! And, actually, I am British – and so are you! I want to *DO* something with my life, I'm tired of this place. This ship to England is my first ticket out of here, and I'm taking it!'

Lingham looked at his little brother with new respect. 'Okay, brother. I hear you!'

The ship sailed at dawn, and as Grenada's lush mountains receded over the horizon, Darwin had a stomach full of butterflies, whether from seasickness or otherwise. He had reason enough to be nervous: at just nineteen he was heading into an unknown and dangerous new world, with neither family nor friend to greet him. But despite the dangers, this was his one opportunity to get away from Grenada and he grabbed it, with both hands. He couldn't continue living in his father's house, a young man was duty-bound to make his own way in the world. Or die trying.

When we were kids our father would have us spellbound with his war stories, starting with his very first night on the ship:

> *We were scared witless! At nights we slept on deck, or we tried to sleep,*
> *'cos we were forever on the lookout for torpedoes – which of course*
> *we couldn't see anyway. We knew that U-boats were all around the*

Caribbean, some of us had even seen them. And there we were, in a British ship: a giant, floating, bullseye! The crew thought we were all a huge entertainment.

The ship left Grenada and sailed northwards, stopping at other islands along the way: Saint Vincent, Barbados, St Lucia, Dominica, Antigua, and Saint Kitts. At each stop they picked up more young men, who all shared a common bond: Britain bound. After leaving its final stop in Jamaica, the ship passed through the stormy Mona Passage between Cuba and Hispaniola, leaving the sheltered waters of the Caribbean and entering the Atlantic Ocean, headed for New York. As the ship sailed northwards, temperatures sank southwards, and the ship's thin-blooded Caribbean contingent grew ever more traumatized. They were issued with second-hand winter clothing, but it could never be enough: the Atlantic in mid-winter was not the best place to have your first experience of cold weather! After the ship docked in a freezing cold New York Harbour, Darwin wrote to his father, on a postcard of the Empire State Building:

Dear Endee,
Sailed into New York Harbor this morning past the Statue of Liberty and docked at the Hudson River Terminal in Manhattan. Unforgettable!
Your loving son,
Darwin.

The ship stayed a week in New York, enough time for the West Indians, travelling in groups for safety, to taste the pleasures of 'the greatest city on earth.' Our father told us about going to the world-famous Apollo Theater and not understanding a word of what the Harlem 'hep cats' were saying to him. But the trouble wasn't onshore, it was onboard. On the voyage up from the West Indies, Darwin and three other lucky Grenadians had been allocated one of the best berths on the ship: an extra cabin bolted onto the deck, with portholes on all four sides. But in New York a group of British

Navy Officers joined the ship and immediately commandeered this comfortable cabin. Darwin and his friends protested but to no avail, and were unceremoniously turfed out, to find whatever rough berths they could, below decks. Because the ship was now full to the gills they were forced to sleep in cramped airless quarters next to the ship's heads or toilets, where the stench was unbearable.

But you know what? Karma is a bitch.

For the first two days the convoy settled into itself, each ship maintaining a zig-zag pattern in a vain attempt to shake off any lurking U-boats. On the third day, the weather worsened, the barometer rapidly falling as the seas rapidly rose. By the fourth morning, they were well and truly in the grip of every sailor's worst nightmare: a North Atlantic winter storm. Temperatures fell, winds rose, seas grew more mountainous and passengers more seasick. Every ship in the convoy fought its own grim battle for survival against the unspeakable power of the storm, battered by hurricane force winds that tore away anything – or anyone – not securely lashed down. Crew members on deck were in real danger of being swept overboard. With every wave, tons of ice-cold water crashed onto the decks, sweeping everything and everyone in its path.

All that night the petrified passengers remained tied to their bunks, clutching sodden bibles and praying with all their might. After every monstrous wave, the ship would slowly right herself, shuddering as the propellers broke the surface, before ploughing headlong into the next monumental wall of water. Below decks, thousands of gallons of water sloshed around from stem to stern, soaking and freezing everyone on board. In the morning the storm abated and the seasick passengers emerged hesitantly on deck, thankful to have made it through the night. Where they were met by a scene of utter devastation. The ship looked, quite literally, like a bomb had just hit it. Spars, cranes and rigging were twisted out of recognition, like broken toys in the hands of a malevolent child. The glass in the wheelhouse had shattered, leaving the crew to steer the ship exposed to the bitter elements. But it wasn't what was on deck that got my father's attention, it was what wasn't. His friend nudged him:

'Darwin – look!'

He turned around, and his jaw dropped. He looked at where his former cabin was – and saw nothing! A giant wave had washed the whole cabin overboard, leaving sheared-off bolts protruding from the deck. Our father's ex-cabin, and its four British occupants, were never seen again. The meek shall indeed inherit the *berth*.

Storms weren't the only danger in the Atlantic - far from it. In those early days of the war, Britain had no effective answer to Germany's U-boat menace. In response to the invisible threat of submarines, British naval planners resorted to a tried and tested military stratagem: safety in numbers. All ships heading to England would gather in US Eastern Seaboard ports, then set out together across the Atlantic in convoys, consisting of dozens or even hundreds of merchant vessels, protected by a few Navy ships. This was the North Atlantic Convoy System – otherwise known as a target-rich environment. In that terrible winter of 1941/42 when our father made his crossing, 15 per cent of all shipping across the Atlantic was lost to enemy action, principally U-boats.

The voyage was rough on all concerned: captains, crews and especially the passengers, unused to the rigours of the Atlantic. With almost zero visibility at times, ships had to stay within sight of each other while constantly zig-zagging. The U-boat attacks always seemed to come at night; both crew and passengers would be woken from a fitful sleep, first by the flash then the distant boom as another ship got hit. Everyone would silently cross themselves, praying for the departed souls – and thankful it wasn't them. But the convoy sailed on, never stopping, never slowing down.

Song for My Father

After a harrowing crossing, Darwin disembarked at Liverpool Docks in early 1942: cold, bleary-eyed and bewildered. Thrust from the tropical heat of Grenada, into grimy midlands cities like Liverpool and Ashton-under-Lyme, Darwin faced a stark choice: adapt and conquer – or die trying. Going home in failure was not an option. Not then, not ever.

Under the deal Darwin had signed up for, he would be given a place at a Technical College to study machine tool operating. He was assigned digs (food and lodging) at a boarding house run by a stern lady called Mrs Meldrum. He described the hilarious scene when he first knocked on her door. Her eyes nearly popped out of her skull at the sight of this Black man, standing on her doorstep! She stared at him in unbridled, wide-eyed wonderment, then burst out: 'Well I never!' She quickly recovered her composure, and admitted she'd never seen a Black man before. After the initial shock, the two of them got on like a house on fire. Every morning Darwin would greet her with a mock punch to the jaw. One morning he tripped on the rug and almost knocked her out!

Darwin was lucky, many landladies refused to take in coloured boarders, fearing they'd stain their sheets. You can imagine his culture shock, transplanted from tropical Grenada to mid-winter Liverpool. He felt it most in food. Having grown up on spicy West Indian fare like stewed chicken, fried fish, rice and peas, and plantain, he was suddenly faced with bland Northern English cooking, even blander with wartime shortages. But he couldn't pick and choose; it was eat or go hungry. His first meal on English soil would set the tone:

'On the ship it wasn't so bad because they gave us food and we cooked it ourselves in the ship's galley, and we'd all brought a good stock of spices with us. But in England I was at the tender mercies of Mrs Meldrum's culinary skills – or lack of. On that first day, I was hungry as hell, but when she brought out the food I was in shock. English food was awful at the best of times but with war rationing we lived on the bare minimum. The first course was some watery vegetable soup, boiled to within an inch of its life, followed by the main event, lumpy powdered eggs, hunks of bread with tiny bits of spam fried in dripping. I thought, 'what the hell is this?'

Darwin landed in a nation reeling under the onslaught of Germany's most destructive offensive of the war: the Blitz. Taken from the German word 'blitzkrieg' (lightning) and commencing in the summer of 1940, bombers of the Luftwaffe rained a barrage of destruction upon England's industrial heartland: London, Manchester, Birmingham, and Liverpool. 'You got so conditioned to the bombing, that as soon as the air raid siren went off, you dropped whatever you were doing and ran to the nearest shelter, like Pavlov's dog.'

Four months before Darwin landed in Liverpool, the city had withstood its most devastating attack of the war, the Christmas Blitz. On the night of November 28, 1940, the Liverpool docklands were hit by 350 tons of high explosives, thirty land mines, and three thousand incendiaries, killing more than three hundred people. It was terrifying, said our father, recalling his first few weeks in England.

> *I thought the Atlantic crossing was scary, but this was ten times worse: a vision of hell. On my very first day in England, in the tram on the way from the docks, I passed row upon row of burnt-out houses, shops and factories. I cried when I thought of how many men, women and children must have burned to death inside that inferno. For the first but not the last time in England, I asked myself: Who send me?*

In London, the most common air raid shelters were the Underground stations, but the midlands had no Underground so that meant sheltering in basements, churches, or any solid-looking building you could find. When you emerged the following morning it was a crap shoot as to what you'd find: peace and tranquillity –

or utter destruction. By far the worst, towards the end of the war, were the V-1 bombs or Doodlebugs, followed by the even more devastating V-2, rocket-propelled bombs that could level an entire city block. These were launched from occupied France with only a vague target area in mind. As long as you heard the drone of the bomb's jet engine, you were safe. But if it stopped...

In September 1942, Darwin enrolled at the Government Engineering Training Centre in Liverpool, qualifying as a machinist and lathe operator the following year. For a country boy from Grenada, subjects like metalwork and mechanical drawing couldn't have come naturally. But he persevered; failure was not an option. Upon qualification, he was given a job at Cornercroft Engineering Works in Coventry. Like all British heavy industries, Cornercroft had switched its production lines at the outbreak of the war, and now was a leading manufacturer of electronics, aircraft components, tanks, and gun parts for the Ministry of Defence.

After two years at Cornercroft, he got a job with the industrial giant Metropolitan-Vickers at their factory-city in Trafford Park in Manchester, which employed thirty thousand people at the height of the war. This was a step up, as he now worked as a supervisor on the assembly line for the iconic Lancaster Bomber, scourge of the Ruhr Valley. He was responsible for final inspections of components, ensuring that all parts were machined exactly to rigorous technical specifications. By the end of the war, Metrovicks had delivered 1,080 Lancaster Bombers to the RAF and the Canadian Air Force, and I'm proud to say my father would have worked on a fair few of them.

Regardless of the depredations of war – or perhaps because of them – Britain partied. They partied like there was no tomorrow, as indeed there may not have been. Every weekend thousands of men and women gravitated to pubs, working men's clubs and ballrooms to dance their cares away to the latest tunes imported from America. Off-duty British servicemen and American GI's flocked to these venues, intent on forgetting the horrors that awaited their return to active duty. Swing bands would come over on tour including Tommy Dorsey and Dad's favourite, the Glenn Miller Orchestra.

Having grown up knowing our father in his more mature years, I can only imagine what he must have been like in his twenties, his pomp. He wasn't a tall man, but he was solid, built like the proverbial brick shithouse. At college, he excelled at javelin and the shot put. In the rough Midlands factory cities, a man had to be able to hold his own, and I'm sure my father managed to do just that. And then some. Judging by yellowed photographs of a dapper young man in three-piece suit and calfskin gloves, I'd say our father managed to adapt to English conditions just fine. He told us that the only racial problems he had were from Englishmen; he never seemed to have any problems with English women ...

Dapper Darwin

Song for My Father

Darwin worked at Metrovicks until 1947, when he sought to make good on the government's implied promise of a scholarship. He applied to study law, but post-war Britain didn't need any more lawyers (who does?). What Britain needed was a skilled workforce to rebuild its shattered industries, and Darwin was a qualified machinist who fit that bill perfectly. The disinterested bureaucrat told him the same thing my equally disinterested careers master would tell me two decades later: 'Don't be silly, boy, you can't be a *lawyer!*' Darwin swallowed his pride and enrolled to study teacher training at Shoreditch Technical College in London. Although he was an excellent teacher for most of his working life, our father never quite got over his disappointment in not studying law. Nevertheless, his two years in London were liberating, and he enjoyed the student life, growing in political awareness and mixing with students from around the Commonwealth. He boasted that more than once, Kwame Nkrumah, future president of an independent Ghana, slept on the floor of his flat, after the two of them had been carousing at some student party. The girl who finally snared our father was a Scottish lass called Helen, but everyone knew her as Nelleen. Their backgrounds couldn't have been more different.

Helen Hogan was born in the small Scottish village of Larbert in Stirlingshire, on September 27, 1928, to Janet and Stephen Hogan, their second and last child after Helen's elder brother, Stephen. Their father was born in Ireland and moved to Scotland as a child. After being gassed in the trenches during the Great War, Stephen senior was never a well man, working as a bus driver when his health allowed. A committed Communist, he was the head of the Scottish branch of the Transport and General Workers Union (TGWU). Despite failing health, he would regularly make the arduous journey by train to London every year to attend the annual meetings, unfailing in support for his friend Ernest Bevin, future Cabinet minister and

The Hogan Clan

Nurse Nelleen

A Scandalous Wedding

stalwart of the early Socialist movement. After becoming bedridden, Stephen Hogan died in May 1939, another delayed casualty of the Great War.

Growing up in Scotland during the Depression could be summed up by that most pessimistic of philosophers, Thomas Hobbes: 'nasty, brutish and short.' To which could be added-cold. Shortly before she died, my mother started her memoirs, but unfortunately she only reached up to the year before she met our father – coincidence?

> *Nelleen's Drudge Days:*
>
> *We moved from Larbert to Falkirk and grew up in an attic apartment in Callendar View – a very large apartment building dating back to (probably) the early eighteen hundreds. I well remember the five flights of stone stairs leading to our wee house – seems to me I was forever trekking up and down these cold steps. The apartment consisted of one large room with recesses for the beds – there was no electricity of course – lighting was provided by piped-in gas to an outlet fitted with a mantle which I chiefly remember for its extreme fragility. Heating and cooking were provided by means of an old coal-burning cast iron stove – one of the earliest chores as I recall was scrubbing this monster and using steel wool on the shiny parts.*

After her husband died in 1939, Mrs Hogan soon remarried, not that it improved the family's economic standing any:

> *After a bit, we moved back to Gran's house at 116 Glasgow Road. More blooming drudgery for me – I swear to goodness NOBODY in that house ever washed a dish, cleaned out a fireplace, or scrubbed a staircase in that house, as long as I was there.*

After a couple years working at the British American Tobacco factory in Bonnybridge, sixteen-year-old Nelleen talked her way into a job as a student nurse at Camelon Cottage Hospital in Falkirk, the beginning of an arduous four-year course. She could handle any amount of work, the important thing was, she was free.

They met at a party in London when he was in his final year at Shoredotch Teachers' College, and she a newly qualified nurse. After a lightning romance, Darwin and Helen were married at Marylebone Registry Office, on July 13, 1949. Six months and four days later, their first son Gerald Hatley Samuel was born. It was only decades later, when Gerry compared our parents' marriage and his own birth date, that he realized our parent's sudden nuptials had been a shotgun wedding! Back in Scotland, Nelleen's pregnancy and subsequent marriage to Darwin were not welcomed by her scandalized family. It couldn't have been easy: a mixed-race couple in 1949 turned heads and set tongues wagging.

'Have ye not heard? Our Nell's getting married – to a *coloured* gentleman!'

The Hogan clan were singularly unimpressed with headstrong Helen's decision to marry a Black man and had no qualms about letting her know it; all she got from her mother was a hard slap that left her with a bruise on her wedding day. By the strict Catholic morals of the day, she had committed two unpardonable offences: first getting pregnant, second marrying a darkie. One was a mortal sin, the other a capital crime. The only member of Nelleen's family to attend the wedding was her brother, Stephen, after whom I was named (but not called). Speaking of names, it was around this time that my father changed his first name, in fact, if not in law. In England, Darwin was considered a surname, so he shortened his middle name Fitzgerald to Gerry, and henceforth went by that moniker.

In his marriage to Nelleen, Darwin was no different from many West Indian men in England at the time, who ended up marrying White women. In a practical sense, they had little choice as there were very few single West Indian women in England. It was like the lyrics of the popular calypso by Harry Belafonte (with my father's own lyrical twist at the end!):

Brown skin girl stay home and mind baby
I'm going away in a sailing boat
And if I don't come back
Throw away the damn baby!

Nelleen was not alone; many British women were similarly ostracized by their families because of their attachments to West Indian men or Black American soldiers. Then, as now, Britain wasn't quite the inclusive society it claims to be.

Turning heads: London 1949

Having graduated from teacher's college, gotten married and become a father, Darwin knew exactly what he wanted to do next: go home. In this, our father exhibited his strong contrarian streak: a lifelong tendency to swim against the tide. Two years previously, in 1948, the *Empire Windrush* made its fateful voyage from Jamaica to England, sparking off a tidal wave of West Indian migration. Not so for Darwin, after eight years in England he'd had enough. And so, in July 1950, the new family of Darwin-alias-Gerry and Helen-alias-Nelleen Samuel, plus six-month old Gerry junior, took ship from Southampton to Trinidad, thence by plane to Grenada. Before leaving London, Darwin had gotten a job as a handicrafts teacher with the colonial government in Grenada. With their first son just six months old and second already on the way, it would be going home for him and going to a Brave New World for her. Nelleen had been rejected by her family and was only too happy to leave England for a tropical adventure.

2. A Year in the Life of a Peasant Proprietor

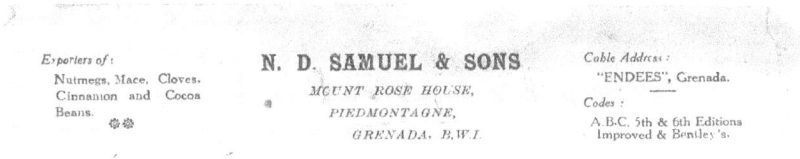

Sat 9 Jan., 1950: This diary was given to me by Byron.

So began the first entry in the Lett's Desk Diary of 1950, kept by my grandfather, Nathan Dennis 'Endee' Samuel. On that day, Endee also wrote that he had *'sold 2,055 lbs Cocoa without polish to V. E. Clarke at 43c per lb = $883.65'* plus other minutiae of running an agricultural estate in Grenada.

For over half a century, my grandfather's diary lay untouched in the bowels of the home he'd built, Mount Rose House, until building renovations brought it to light. And what a find it proved to be: priceless! I don't know if it was the first, last, or only year that Endee had kept a diary, but he couldn't have chosen a more eventful year than 1950. Tumultuous not only for his own family, also for the Crown Colony of Grenada, which became engulfed in a violent uprising against British rule. In his personal life, Endee wrote of the petty squabbles that afflict

any family: '*Wilson call and complain that Edith and Maud are making his father's house a brothel.*' He wrote of his stormy reunion with his youngest son, Darwin, who in mid-year returned home, after almost a decade in England. Most painfully, Endee wrote of a heart-breaking family tragedy, a cruel blow from which he never fully recovered.

In his business life, Endee was assailed by grasping merchants, thieving employees and a court case that just wouldn't go away. In the wider society, Endee wrote of political events in Grenada and the rise to power of one Eric Matthew Gairy, a brash young trade unionist and future Prime Minister (some would say despot) of Grenada. Finally, Endee wrote of the goings-on in the community around him; he was an avid courthouse attendee and inveterate gossip, relaying events both mundane and horrifying with the same detached, offhand manner: '*A girl made a child, kill it, cut off its head, 1 foot and 1 hand. She is arrested.*'

Endee wrote it all down in his neat, organized script, not flowery but solid, pithy. Hence his 8,930-word diary is long on trivia and short on emotion. It is only by reading between the lines, sometimes literally, that we get a glimpse of the real Endee Samuel: the passions and pain that even he couldn't keep hidden.

According to its letterhead, N. D. Samuel & Sons were growers and exporters of '*Nutmegs, Mace, Cloves, Cinnamon and Cocoa Beans*' plus, bananas, coconuts, breadfruit, pigs, chickens, white rum, saltfish, flour, and just about anything that could grow or sell. The centre of operations was the general store-cum-rum shop, located on the main road by the bus stop in Perdmontemps, across the street from Ooh La-La gas station. The shop still stands today, selling the same items to the same clientele. Long gone are the giant cocoa trays or *boucans*, rolled out every morning from underneath the shop, to dry the previous day's crop of wet cocoa. There was also a stone oven out back in which Endee baked fresh bread every day before dawn, rain or shine.

By all accounts including his own, Endee was a man of substance. By dint of hard work and sheer bloody-mindedness, he rose to become a substantial landowner in the Parish of St David's. This was no mean feat for a Black man of humble origins to make it in what was quite literally a White man's world. Such was Endee's status, that the governor of the Windward Islands would occasionally drive up to Mount Rose, to seek out his views on current affairs, as a representative of his emerging class of 'Peasant Proprietors.' Over tiffin and tea no doubt. Endee was also a leading member of the Holy Order of the Rosy Cross, or Rosicrucians, secret handshakes and all.

> *Wed 11 Jan: I sent a letter to the Nutmeg Pool protesting against account sale of nutmeg & mace, enclosing Debit Note. I refused to acknowledge this document, in which was stated my nutmeg was sold for $18.32 per lb and mace for 49c. I wrote & posted letter immediately.*

As 1950 dawned Endee's son Lingham was working as an Electrical Engineer at the Grenada Electricity Commission, his other son Byron was in Trinidad, doing this-n-that, and his youngest son Darwin was nearing the end of an eight-year stint in England. Endee was finishing off construction on his new home, an imposing edifice located on a breezy ridge, with panoramic views of both the Atlantic and Caribbean coastlines. Mount Rose was the biggest, grandest, and most visible residence for miles around. Where it still stands proudly, no hurricane can dent those two-foot-thick walls.

> *Sat 21 Jan: Byron on driving Lingham's car collided with Hessie's bus in Cosy Corner, car was badly damaged. Hessie's bus apparently at fault. Police may make a case. A police came here seeking to find the person who brought stolen Cocoa at La Femme.*

Endee's lifelong passion was land, and the acquiring of it. He bought land at every opportunity, and rarely sold. In addition to Mount Rose, he owned property elsewhere in Grenada, and beyond.

Like most men of substance, Endee had several children, with several women. Mount Rose Estate was no gold mine, but it provided a living for Endee and his family and employed a dozen or so workers at any given time. But Endee's economic achievements had its limits; they did not allow him a seat at the top table of Grenadian colonial society with the planter class – the White and brown grandees represented by the Grenada Employers' Federation and the Grenada Nutmeg Association. Endee fought back; he was vocal in farmers' organizations and was a main driver behind the breakaway Grenada Nutmeg Producers' Protective League, a grouping of Black peasant proprietors, seeking to force a fairer deal from the planters.

> *Sat 4th Feb: I sent a letter to the Nutmeg Pool by post demanding that a fuller a/c sale be given to me, else I will take legal proceedings.*

On Monday, January 23, Endee makes a seemingly innocuous entry: '*Gordon Etienne sold 212 lbs Cocoa I paid him at 1/- per lb, retaining a balance of four pence (4d) per lb until he brings his sellers book as arranged.*' Clearly, all was not right with this transaction, as Endee had held back a portion of the sale proceeds until such time as Etienne had produced his seller's book, proof that he had grown the cocoa in question, not stolen it. As it turned out Etienne had indeed stolen the said cocoa, and Endee and his daughter Laurina were eventually charged by the police with knowingly buying stolen cocoa. These court cases would drag on for the entire year, causing no end of grief for Endee and Laurina.

When he wasn't appearing in the courthouse in an official capacity, Endee loved nothing more than to sit in the public benches and watch proceedings:

> *Wed 15th Feb: I went to the court house and heard the case of a woman called Say-Say. The jury brought a verdict of guilty in her. The Judge Cools La-Digue (Sir Louis Cools-Lartigue, O.B.E.) pronounced the death sentence on her. I came home in Gibbs' bus. The above is called 'The Mango Poisoning Case.'*

The case of 'Say-Say,' from the town of Sauteurs in the north of Grenada, was a famous murder trial in 1950. She killed a Polish doctor with a poisoned mango, the rumoured result of a love triangle gone awry. The goodly man was one of several Polish refugees who had settled in Grenada after the war, only to meet a grim ending five years later. The courthouse was a source of free entertainment, not just for Endee but the entire society:

> *Fri 17th Feb: Yesterday I attended Court to hear the proceedings in the matter of the 8 men that murdered one man at La Sagesse, but due to the density of the crowd I could not get entry, hence I heard very little of what passed.*

Endee used the diary as his accounting book and would record in painstaking detail his financial transactions: *I went to St. George's, sold two bags even to V. E. Clarke. 269.265 lbs less 6 lbs at 43c per lb brings $227.04, he paid cash. The 2,518 lbs he has on hand for me we now agree 43c = $1,082.74, to this I owe him $362.00 therefore the net amount he has for me now is $720.74 to be paid to me on the 10th inst.* All without a calculator in sight. His major concern was the constantly fluctuating price of cocoa – it never seemed to fluctuate in the right direction.

Endee was an avid listener of the BBC Overseas Service; even in his remote corner of the world he made sure to keep himself abreast of news from around the world. He also appreciated fine wines. Every Christmas it was his habit to import a crate of South African wines and invite his friends over for a tipple. For Christmas 1950, his friends came over as usual but were disappointed to find no wine. Endee told them that in July of that year South Africa had passed the Group Areas Act, the foundation stone for apartheid, and that he was boycotting all South African products until such time as they stopped oppressing their native populations. This was long before the evils of the White regime had become widely known. Two of Endee's heroes were W.E.B. DuBois and Marcus Garvey. A third would have been King George VI.

Wed 22nd Feb: I did not go to Ash Wednesday Mass, I was engage in baking. Mr. Tom Otway call here and asked me to sell him some Cocoa. 2,518 lbs I have now drying at VE Clarke's store, he promised to pay 43c but I told him I would not accept that. He said in any case he will give me more if I decide to sell it to him.

Life in Perdmontemps dawdled along. Endee wrote to a Mr Miller, asking to buy a plot of land, for him to donate for the construction of the new Saint Dominic's Church, but Mr Miller wasn't selling. Plus, of course, there was the village madman:

Wed 1st Mar: John McMillan declared crazy, he went at Abraham Gabriel and did considerable damages. He is sent to the Lunatic Asylum this PM. Laurina and Rose Pascall accompanied Amy to the Asylum.

The court case against Gordon Etienne dragged on. Endee confronted Etienne and remonstrated with him, how he, Endee, was out of pocket and in trouble with the police because he had foolishly trusted Etienne over the stolen cocoa. He did not get the satisfaction he sought. Eventually, the court case came up:

Wed 15th Mar: Gordon Etienne Appeal case came off, he was fined $24. He came up here, giving me a lot of lies. He tries to borrow 20/- from me, he failed.

Having convicted Etienne, the dogged Royal Grenada Police Force now turned their gaze onto his alleged partners in crime: Endee and Laurina, but the case kept getting put off. In the meantime, village life continued:

Mon 10th Apr: Two boys drowned in Westerhall bog, one is called John, a brother of Evrice, another is a son of Dolphon Gulston, the body of Dani is found but the body of John is not found.

Endee loved nothing more than a good speech, preferably his own:

Tues 2nd May: I attended a meeting in St. David's on the subject of the Nutmeg Producers' Protective League, it was well attended. I obtained very strong applause by the people for my brilliant speech.

Song for My Father

On Thursday, May 4, Endee made a seemingly harmless entry: *Laurina went and sleep at her brother Lingham who is sick.* Until then Lingham had been in rude health: he'd recently taken his five-year old niece Brenda on a week-long business trip to the neighbouring island of Carriacou, where he was 'stringing wire.' Whatever was ailing him, Lingham languished at home until May 16, when he was admitted to the Private Block of the Colonial Hospital. Without ever saying what was clinically afflicting his eldest son, Endee recorded his frighteningly rapid decline, within the space of just one month:

> *Sun 21st May: I went to St. George's with Laurina and Brenda, to see Lingham. We remained 3 hrs with him, he is very sick with pains.*
>
> *Tues 6th Jun: I went to the Hospital to take home Lingham but the doctors Munroe and Gentle both disadvised me from taking him home. So I agreed and left him in the Private Block. In the morning he vomited blood twice.*
>
> *Fri 16th Jun: I took Lingham from Hospital, he spent 31 days there at 20/- per day.*
>
> *Sat 17th Jun: The Polish doctor visited Lingham today, he said that Lingham's case is worst now to when he last attended him. He strongly recommended him to Barbados, U.S.A or England because his case is dangerous indeed.*
>
> *Thurs 22nd June: Dr. 'W' came and visit Lingham, he said that his case is much worst than the last time, he spoke as if he meant that Lingham will not live, but will die. I paid him $6.00 for the visit, the last time I paid $4.00. (Plenty rain today.)*

Dr W was a well-known Polish doctor in Grenada, with a last name so unpronounceable that Grenadians had to make it manageable. On Sunday, June 25, Lingham left Grenada by air for Barbados, accompanied by his sister Laurina. On arrival, he was immediately admitted into Bailey's Hospital, but it was too late:

Sun 2nd Jul: I received a Cable stating that Lingham has got worse, but later he died at Bailey's Hospital at Barbados. Mr. Mason was with me in all my movements.

It's almost surreal, the clinical manner in which Endee recorded these devastating events, which must have caused him immense pain. It took my cousin Brenda, four decades later, to give me a true picture of Endee's agony on that terrible night she'd witnessed, as a frightened five-year old girl:

'I'll never forget that awful night, seeing Endee standing there, holding onto the window frame, just holding on, tight, like his life depended on it. He had a look of absolute agony on his face, he couldn't speak. That was the only time I ever saw him cry. It was a horrible, horrible sound.'

Endee tried to bring the body of his son home from Barbados, but bureaucracy got the better of him, so Laurina was forced to bury her brother there:

Mon 3rd Jul: I went to St. George, to radio to Laurina telling her to have Lingham's body photographed in his coffin and to mark a good mark on his grave that I may know it when I go there. I tried my best to bring over the body, but I will not be permitted to land it unless the body is embalmed, as no one can embalm at Barbados, the idea fell to the ground. Miss Glen was with me with tooth and nail, and ready to help me.

Fourteen days after Lingham's death, on Sunday, July 16, 1950, Endee's youngest son Darwin arrived back in Grenada, after nearly a decade in England. His timing couldn't have been worse: too late for his brother, too early for his father.

Darwin (who now answered to the more stylish name of Gerry) didn't return alone; he was accompanied by his wife Nelleen and their six-month son Gerry junior. They landed at the newly opened Pearl's Airfield on a flight operated by the fledgling British West Indian Airways (BWIA). During a short stay in Port of Spain, Darwin and

MR. and MRS. SAMUELS

'*Handicrafts Necessary In WI*,' *Says Grenada Teacher*

Trinidad Guardian, July 15, 1950

Nelleen had been interviewed by the *Trinidad Guardian* newspaper. All things considered, Darwin had done well for himself in his eight years abroad. He'd taken a huge gamble in going to Britain in the depths of the Second World War and had endured hard years in Britain's bombed-out cities. Our father told us of the reunion between father and son at Mount Rose.

'Hey old man,' says the cheeky son. 'I see you got a few more grey hairs, how are you holding up these days?'

Endee didn't say a word. There was a bunch of bananas sitting on the ground, weighing easily twenty or thirty pounds. Endee bent down, picked it up with one hand, raised it over his head, then gently placed it back on the ground again. He turned to his son.

'Now you do that.'

Which of course, he couldn't.

Compared to his son's flowery description, Endee's diary entry of the father and son reunion was more prosaic:

> *Sun 16 July: Darwin and wife and child arrived here today. Darwin kissed me but his wife did not kiss me.*

Clearly, this wasn't some proud father welcoming his son home after a dangerous decade in England – with wife and brand-new grandson to boot. Endee's reserve is palpable; he had not forgotten, nor apparently forgiven his headstrong son's defiance of him ten years earlier, when he went to England against his father's strong wishes. Mind you, for Endee it had been a torrid year thus far with the recent death of Lingham. It would not get much better.

Darwin, Nelleen, and baby Gerry moved into a spare bedroom in Endee's house, while building works on the new Mount Rose were being finished. The next day, Endee and Darwin went down to the Ministry of Education, where he was offered a salary of $720 per year as a handicraft teacher. This was not what he had expected, and he rejected it. Darwin's salary negotiations boiled down to a question of currency. Historically, the Eastern Caribbean had used British pounds as their currency, but in 1949 the Colonial Office created the British West Indian dollar, known locally as the 'Bee-Wee Dollar,' at a fixed exchange rate of $4.80 to the pound. For several years, until 1962, both currencies were used simultaneously, and Endee's diary refers to transactions in both pounds and dollars, which can be confusing. But Darwin didn't want to be paid in Bee-Wee dollars; he wanted pounds. The issue was soon resolved, and Darwin went to work as a handicrafts teacher, at a salary of £27 per month – almost twice the salary he'd initially been offered, in Bee-Wee Dollars.

Darwin and his family had arrived in Grenada at a time of rising political tension. Just two weeks after they landed, Endee noted:

> *Tues 1st Aug: Great demonstration at St. David's sponsored by Mr. Gairy, it was heavily attended.*

Eric Matthew Gairy was a brash young Grenadian trade unionist, who would go on to have a defining impact on the modern history of Grenada. Like Darwin, he too had recently returned to Grenada, in Gairy's case from Aruba, where he'd honed his skills as a trade union organizer. His rise to power was meteoric: in just seven months, he'd built his Grenada Manual and Mental Workers Union (GMMWU) into a major political force, despite strenuous and coordinated opposition from the colonial government and elite planter class. What they didn't know was that Gairy was just warming up.

On the domestic front, problems started from day one. A clash of wills between Endee and Darwin was inevitable. The father steeped in stiff Victorian morality versus his son, bursting with post-war notions of liberalism and equality. Toss one brash young Scottish lass into the mix, and you had the recipe for a perfect storm. Knowing our mother's tough, no-nonsense personality, (we got to know our mother later in life, as will become apparent later in the book). I can just imagine that the clash between her and Endee must have been immediate – and explosive! Endee was irritated, beyond measure, by his son's self-declared change of name. As recounted by our father: Endee was hugely put out at me calling myself Gerry, and refused to even hear it, let alone acknowledge it:

'So, the name I gave you, after the brilliant naturalist Darwin, isn't good enough for you anymore? I paid good money to give you that name, who is this *Gerry*, anyway?'

The second fight was the battle of the dog-doo:

> *Thurs 10th Aug: I went home and found dog-mess in two places in the house. I called Neillene and show it to her, she said the dog does not sleep in the house. Perhaps it was in the day the dog did it, I then said I always say I don't want the dog to sleep inside the house, and that was the end of it.*

But, of course, that was far from the end of it. Over the next few days, Endee records his increasing irritation at the brazen defiance of this young girl: the nerve! The battle rumbled along, until Darwin decided to put his foot in it. Not the dog-doo, the argument.

> *Tues 15th Aug: Darwin gave Laurina the same story of his wife about the dog, and again said how his wife was upset; that all this is dam nonsense. He used the word 'damn' to Laurina about me, because is not Laurina he damn, it is me. I am waiting for him to damn me when he is speaking to me. It will be our last day.*

I find it hard to fathom, such open hostility from Endee to his youngest son. When we were children, our father would regale us with tales from his own childhood, never once did I ever hear him utter a bad word about Endee. On the contrary; he adored his father.

Granted, Endee was still heartsore over the death of Lingham, but he seemed to have focused all his anger on his youngest son, and his wilful wife.

This was a time of rising political turmoil in Grenada:

> *Wed 30th Aug: As the result of a serious strike by one Gairy who is said to be a leader of an organization called 'The People's Party,' the strikers killed S. A. Francis' cow, took away its two hind legs and left the body on the ground. S. A. Francis is the owner of the cow, he was prevented from taking away the body, his life was also threatened by the rioters who are entering people's property and take whatever they want. One woman and two men are arrested for cocoanuts they took away without any permission.*

> *Fri 1st Sept: Rain fell almost all night and part of the morning. Mr. Rex Worme called here today, he left his house in fear of the Riot by the strikers. They burned a tractor and a copra house at Woodlands last night.*

Whether because of turmoil in the streets or turmoil at home, Darwin soon realized he'd made a huge mistake in coming back to Grenada and set about trying to rectify it. On Sunday, August 27, 1950, he took a plane to Port-of-Spain to try his luck in Trinidad. You can sense the glee with which Endee recorded the results of the trip:

> *Sat 2nd Sept: Darwin came back from Trinidad, he said that he hopefully expects to job by the UBOT (United British Oilfields of Trinidad). He is likely to get a salary of $700 per month if he gets the work.*

Darwin didn't get the job in Trinidad and for the time being was stuck in his glowering father's house. At this time, the finishing touches on the new Mount Rose House were being added. Mount Rose House was and remains a substantial dwelling, surviving two devastating hurricanes to hit Grenada, to date: Janet (1955) and Ivan (2004).

Mount Rose House

Mount Rose *by Dr. Joan Samuel*

> *Fri 8th Sept: Messrs. R. O. Williams, Jacobs and Gresham came and inspect my house to value it, they all seem to satisfy but have not given me the valuation. Mr. William told me the house would be worth £4,000. I served them with refreshments.*

For Endee to have built a £4,000 house in Grenada in 1950 is a staggering achievement, considering that the average house price in England at the time was £1,891. No bank would have lent money to a Black peasant proprietor; he built his house by the sweat of his brow and strength of his back – literally.

The next battle was over Lingham's car. At the time of his death, Lingham had owned a car, which along with the rest of his estate was being sold by the administrator, one Mr Green. Darwin wanted to buy the car. For whatever reason or probably no reason at all, Endee opposed the idea and a simmering feud ensued. Endee wrote of being most aggravated, when Darwin accused him of keeping him in 'a fool's paradise.' *If this is a fool's paradise, then who's he calling the fool?*

In the end, Darwin pulled a fast one, and bought the car from the administrator, without Endee's knowledge. Two days after taking delivery of the car, Darwin crashed it. Endee was livid. This act of open defiance crossed a rubicon in Endee's mind, some unseen last straw. The very next morning, Endee went straight to his lawyer's office:

> *Mon 25th Sept: I went to St. George's today and took my Will from Mr. Teka, Clerk at J. B. Renwick. I signed it in the presence of Mr. R. O. Williams and Mr. Protain, who also signed their names as witnesses of my name and signature.*

On that morning, Endee didn't just sign the document; he changed it. In his Last Will and Testament, Endee virtually froze his youngest son Darwin out of his inheritance. My brothers and I received more land from Endee's Estate than our father did. Even in death, my grandfather remained, by all accounts including his own, one hard bastard.

Endee continued to vent over Darwin's wilful wife Nelleen, heavily pregnant with their second child:

> *She sleeps all day ... The bathroom is stink with her child's mess clothes, she will not wash them nor remove them ... Neilleen is using a dish in washing sores on her feet, then it was use in eating ... I complained of Neilleen's ill-treating the cushion on the Morris Chair ... his wife is inconsiderate and greedy.*

The reality was that Nelleen was having a difficult second pregnancy, coming so soon after her first child was born. Added to this, she wasn't used to the tropical heat of Grenada in the height of summer. Not that Endee would have noticed any of this; to him she was just a lazy woman who ill-treated his Morris chair. There were strong racial and class undertones to Endee's dislike of Nelleen. He was a lifelong Black Nationalist, and it must have rankled him to have this obstreperous White woman parachuted into his household. The fact that she was 'only a nurse' would also have been frowned upon by Endee, with his old-fashioned notions of one's proper place in society.

The domestic civil war rumbled on, becoming increasingly uncivil with each new skirmish. The new Mount Rose House neared completion, strikes and demonstrations continued to rock the island, and Endee's court case gathered steam. When the case was finally heard in the Saint David's Magistrate Court, Endee was acquitted of the charge of knowingly buying stolen cocoa. Laurina wasn't so lucky and was found guilty and fined $4.20. Isn't it typical? The boss walks free while his lackey takes the rap! But Endee's freedom from prosecution did nothing to lighten his mood at home, not one whit:

> *Mon 16th Oct: From Darwin's insolent talk to me, he hold me an enemy. Very cold with me but this A.M. he spoke to me. His wife too is unusually cold with Laurina, yesterday Maury came and put the shower in the bath, Darwin and his wife first bathe in it.*

On November 11, 1950, Eric Gairy's newly formed Grenada

United Labour Party (GULP) led a huge demonstration in St George's, attended by an estimated six thousand enthusiastic supporters. For an island with only seventy thousand people, most of whom lived in the rural parishes, this was a stunning achievement for Gairy, within a year of his arrival back in Grenada.

On November 26, 1950, Darwin and Nelleen's second son, Thomas Dougald, was born, an event deemed unworthy of mention in Endee's diary. Two weeks later, you can feel his joy:

> *Thurs 7th Dec: Darwin finally left my house and took up charge of his at St. Paul's at a rental of $30 per month with half acre of land attached.*

Thus, ended Darwin's homecoming. It may not have been the 'prodigal's return' he would have wished for but now at least he had his own house, away from the unforgiving glare of his father. Darwin and Nelleen stayed in Saint Paul's for a year then moved into a wooden house called Eden located in Belmont, overlooking the picturesque lagoon, a house belonging to Darwin's best friend and my godfather, Linton Banfield. It was in Eden where, three years later, your humble scribe was born: the third and last son of Gerry and Nelleen Samuel.

> *Sat 9th Dec: Nelleen told me she thanked me for my hospitality for housing and boarding her since she came from England. She had ample time to thank me but she never did until Darwin told her to do so.*

Endee's last entry for 1950:

> *Route and itinerary:*
>
> *England thru France, Switzerland, Germany, Italy, Vatican City, Palestine, Jerusalem, Bethlehem-Judea. Back to England – America, Panama, Barbados – Trinidad – home.*
>
> *The above is the visit I shall make soon.*

He never did.

3.   *Pillar to Post*

What Darwin and Nelleen hadn't realized when they landed in Grenada in July 1950 was that they had landed on an island on the brink of rebellion. Darwin's decision to return home coincided with another Grenadian's decision to do the same, a man who would go on to play a central role in the affairs of Grenada over the next four decades: Eric Matthew Gairy.

Gairy was born in the parish of St Patrick's in 1922, the same year as my father, and like my father had left Grenada as a young man, in Gairy's case to the oil refineries of Aruba. Love him or hate him, no one can deny the incendiary and immediate impact that Gairy made upon his return in December 1949. Within months, Gairy founded the Grenada Manual & Mental Workers Union (GMMWU) and immediately set about making a name for himself on the labour scene. In other words: causing trouble. After a series of labour skirmishes in which he rapidly built up an avid and sometimes violent following, Gairy made his boldest move yet: a general strike. When addressing his adoring crowds, Gairy liked to refer to himself, with mock self-deprecation, as 'this little Black boy.' In other words: I'm from the same rural poor as you – cue rapturous applause.

'So those planters won't talk with this little black boy eh? Well, let them watch this same little black boy shut down this whole blasted island!' Which is exactly what he did.

Attempts by all parties to avert the general strike failed, and on February 19, 1951, the entire country came to a standstill as workers stayed home or gathered in demonstrations – which often turned violent. Two days later, Gairy and his second-in-command Gascoigne Blaize were arrested and imprisoned on a British battleship stationed offshore, the *H.M.S. Devonshire.* A contingent of British marines was sent ashore, plus extra police forces flown in from Trinidad and St Lucia, to restore order. This would not be the last time that Grenada would be invaded by a foreign power – with help from its neighbours.

Arresting Gairy was a bad move. This naked show of imperial power inflamed an already tense situation, engulfing the island in more fire and violence. Many estates and business places were torched, and in the capital, St George's, there were running battles between machete-wielding demonstrators, and local police and British marines. So many buildings were burned down that the riots became known as the 'Red Sky Days.'

Grenada's planter class, never known for its liberal thinking, immediately branded Gairy a Communist and wanted his blood, legally and literally. The Grenada Legislature sent an urgent telegram to London requesting reinforcements to put down the 'Communist insurrection.' One planter even went so far as to accuse the British government, then under the socialist Labour Party, of being in cahoots with 'that Communist rascal Gairy!'

Despite the bleating of the planters, it was clear that Grenada had become ungovernable and that only one man held the key to bringing back any sense of normality: Eric Matthew Gairy. With the vast majority of the populace squarely behind him, Gairy was now 'the king of Grenada.' Realizing the futility of the standoff, the British released him from detention on March 6, 1951. The following day, he met with the governor of Grenada, Brigadier Sir Robert Arundell. For a Black 'country-bookie-boy,' he'd come a long way.

In his politics, my father was a lifelong leftist, so it wasn't surprising that upon his return from England he immediately clashed with his Victorian-era father. Endee didn't appreciate his son's new-fangled notions imported from post-war Britain. Although Endee was a staunch Black Nationalist, he had very conventional notions about the natural order of society, which didn't include his workers dictating to him how much he would pay them. A notion that was about to be sorely tested. The general strike of 1951 lasted three weeks, during which the bare necessities of life became luxuries. All government offices and schools were closed, in addition to the estates and shops.

By mid-1951, the political situation had stabilized somewhat, and when the dust settled Darwin found that he had been promoted to supervisor of handicrafts, thereby improving his income and standard of living considerably. His new job involved travelling around Grenada, which suited him just fine as he now had to get himself a quality car – at the government's expense.

In addition to teaching, Darwin dabbled in various business ventures, none of which thrived. Topping this list of unthriving enterprises was his taxi business. He bought two cars on hire-purchase, recruited two drivers, and rented a small office upstairs on Market Square in St George's. One day he was in his office and heard the unmistakable sound of two cars colliding in the street below: ba-*dang!* He put his head out the window and to his horror saw two cars in a head-on collision – and both were his!

That wasn't Darwin's only driving incident, although in that case he technically wasn't driving. I'm not sure exactly how, but one of his cars ended up in the sea on the Carenage, which is easy enough to do as there is no barrier, even easier after a skinful of Johnny Walker. Another car of his ended up in a head-on collision in Sendall Tunnel, a one-way street. I think Johnny may have been involved in that one as well.

Not long after my father's return to Grenada in 1950 he met Eric Gairy and the two men became friends. Darwin helped Gairy set up his fledgling People's Party and wrote some of his speeches. Literacy wasn't Gairy's strongest suit. It was a natural fit: both were returning Grenadians with international experience, filled with post-war zeal for social change. After the success of the general strike, Gairy had become a hero among the working class, hailed with divine-like devotion at huge rallies across the island. The following year would see elections to the Legislative Council, for the first time under Universal Adult Suffrage, abolishing the previous property requirements. This would effectively place political power into the hands of the masses; into Gairy's hands. On October 10, 1951, Gairy's Grenada United Labour Party (GULP) won a sweeping electoral victory, taking six of the eight seats in the Legislature. It was around this time that my father and Gairy fell out. It was the king thing: Gairy had become a megalomaniac. Nothing epitomized this more than the GULP party anthem, penned by himself and sung during every political gathering:

> *We'll never let our leader fall*
> *For we love him best of all.*
> *We don't want to fight*
> *To show our might*
> *But when we start, we will fight, fight, fight.*
> *In peace or war, you'll hear us sing,*
> *God save Gairy, God save us all!*

Liberal-minded Darwin Samuel wasn't about to sing any such fawning tosh! In this regard, Darwin was not alone; several of Gairy's early stalwarts abandoned him around this time. These were largely his more educated supporters, who resented his increasing refusal to share or even delegate authority. Among the rural working class though, Gairy sat on the right hand of God the Father – a view he himself did little to dispel. His adoring fans called him as he called himself: Uncle.

My father never said what it was that sparked the rift between he and Gairy, but there was clearly no love lost between both men, as I myself was to witness, many years later. In 1972, when my father and I were on a visit to Grenada, we ran into Gairy at the Rock Garden in Tanteen, one of several he owned, where he would hold court and dispense favours. My father went up to greet Gairy.

'You' said Gairy, 'you're back.'

'Just for a couple of weeks.'

'Good.'

Behind that famous plastic smile, menace dripped like honey. As usual Gairy was resplendent in white suit, white shirt, and white tie, but despite the apparent bonhomie there was ice in his eyes. As he walked off surrounded by his inevitable coterie of hangers-on, I asked my father what that was all about? He explained:

Endee died in 1958, and I flew up from Trinidad to arrange the funeral, as did Byron from Venezuela. As you'd expect it was a huge funeral, with people from all over Grenada and beyond. We held the wake at Mount Rose and who shows up? Gairy, now the premier of Grenada. Which was no problem except that he never went anywhere without his bunch of hangers-on, which in future would turn into his feared Mongoose Gang. If that wasn't bad enough Gairy starts making political speeches, holding forth about how he was going to 'liberate Grenada from the shackles of the planters.'

I was livid. My father was a planter, for god's sake!

The last straw was when his bullyboys strolled into the kitchen and started helping themselves to the food, long before anyone else! Byron and I protested to Gairy who just brushed us off, like he was to the manor born. Well not to *our* manor he wasn't! We insisted that he and his boys leave the funeral, immediately. He turned those lizard eyes on me, just as he did tonight' 'You'll regret this.' Then stalked off, followed by his boys. Hasn't changed much, has he?'

In 1954, after four years back in Grenada, Darwin moved his family to Guyana, or British Guiana (B-G) as it was then. Perhaps our father had gotten the wanderlust again, or perhaps his falling out with Gairy had made it untenable for him to stay. He got a job as a woodwork master at the Teacher Training College in Georgetown the capital and the young Samuel family was on the road again. Dad went first to establish the bridgehead, followed by Nelleen and us children when he was settled.

Soon after he arrived in British Guiana, Darwin became active in the politics of decolonization. In the previous year, 1953, the British government had intervened in the politics of the colony of B-G, suspending the Constitution and forcibly removing from office the socialist Chief Minister Cheddi Jagan. In true gunboat diplomacy style, the Royal Navy cruiser *HMS Superb* discharged a battalion of Royal Welsh Fusiliers in Georgetown, further inflaming local passions. This crass display of colonial power stirred up far more discontent than the authorities had bargained for, and riots quickly ensued. Into this volatile mixture steps Darwin (Gerry) Samuel, full of naively optimistic beliefs in democracy and the Equality of Man – concepts not necessarily welcomed by the colonial authorities of the day.

It was in B-G that our father first tried his hand at writing, with some success. He was a regular contributor to the *Argosy* newspaper and was working on a novel, for which he would jot down ideas in his pocket diary:

Sun Feb 6, 1955: 'Dead Birds in the Morning' on BBC.

Fri Feb 25: Intense specialization is neither necessary nor desirable. The necessities of a successful professional career are a broad mind and wide interests. These foundations must be laid in the school. If narrowness lives in school, it cannot be cured at university, or anywhere else. It is in school and not at university that the budding scientist should be helped, for instance, to develop a taste for music and the arts, and the young historian an understanding and reverence for science.

Song for My Father

Fri 1 Mar: The same stick that beat the black dog beat the white dog.

Wed 6 April: Sweet mout' will buy a horse on credit.

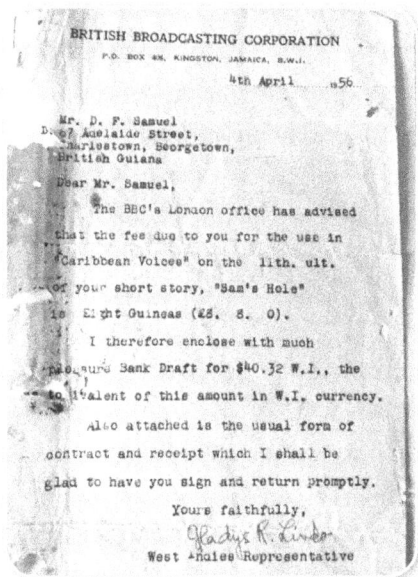

BRITISH BROADCASTING CORPORATION
P.O. BOX 4N, KINGSTON, JAMAICA, B.W.I.

4th April 1956

Mr. D. F. Samuel
D-67 Adelaide Street,
Charlestown, Georgetown,
British Guiana

Dear Mr. Samuel,

The BBC's London office has advised that the fee due to you for the use in "Caribbean Voices" on the 11th. ult. of your short story, "Sam's Hole" is Eight Guineas (£8. 8. 0).

I therefore enclose with much pleasure Bank Draft for $40.32 W.I., the equivalent of this amount in W.I. currency.

Also attached is the usual form of contract and receipt which I shall be glad to have you sign and return promptly.

Yours faithfully,

Gladys R. Lindo
West Indies Representative

BBC letter to my father, 1955
(with permission from the BBC)

He wrote a regular feature for the BBC Caribbean Service, entitled 'Topic for Tonight,' ranging from the Russian fleet sailing into the Caribbean (October 3, 1954), self-government for Nigeria (September 26, 1954) and the West Indian's desire to migrate to England (undated). He also wrote short stories and opinion pieces on West Indian Federation, the Cold War, and the role of the British Commonwealth.

The colonial authorities in Georgetown took a dim view of our father's inconvenient political commentaries. Perhaps as a result of this official displeasure, we only stayed in B-G two years. In 1956, the Samuel family was once again on the move: this time to Trinidad. In later conversation with my father, I got the distinct impression that our departure from B-G wasn't entirely voluntary.

Darwin's next job was in Port of Spain, as head of Technical Training at the Trinidad & Tobago Electricity Commission (T&TEC). We spent four great years in Trinidad, from 1956 to 1960, living first in Diego Martin then St Augustine, next to the University of the West Indies (UWI) Campus. Judging from old family photographs our parents certainly enjoyed life in Trinidad. In the colonial West Indies, having a White wife could be considered somewhat of a social coup – she could get you invitations to places where otherwise you may not. Added to which, in 1957 Nelleen got a job on Trinidad's Radio Guardian, hosting a daily show called 'Neighbour Nell.' Its sister media outlet, the *Trinidad Guardian* newspaper, gushed over their 'wee Scottish lass':

> *Mrs. Samuel believes that since today's woman is developing wide and varied interests, the old adage 'A woman's place is in the home' no longer applies. She is a personification of the fact that marriage, motherhood and a career may be successfully combined through intelligent application of common sense principles. Mrs. Samuel has three boys aged 7, 6 and 4 years. She is a trained nurse, dietitian, secretary and clothing designer.*

Radio Guardian even composed a calypso about our mother – I don't think it was a hit. Nelleen would do radio 'interviews' with movie stars like Bob Hope and Bing Crosby, when in fact they were no more than canned recordings sent out from Hollywood, with gaps in the soundtrack, where the local interviewer would ask scripted questions. Radio was the social media of the day, and overnight, Nurse Nelleen had become 'Celebrity Nell.'

Our father loved fast cars, his favourite brand being the iconic British sports car MG. Between Grenada, B-G and Trinidad, he bought, sold and crashed quite a few:

Morris Oxford MO: *A big black beast with rounded fenders, lots of chrome and a gear shift on the steering column.*

Vauxhaul Wyvern: *A four-door saloon with a Griffin on the front grille.*

MG Magnette ZA: *First of two models he owned in Trinidad.*

MG Magnette ZB: *It had a 'massive' 64 horsepower engine and came out in 1956. His was the Varitone model, with a two-tone paint job.*

Standard Ten: *A frugal little thing from the short-lived Standard Motor Company, the Ten was in reference to its diminutive* *horsepower. This was a big comedown for us kids after the luxury of his previous MGs, so we christened it the Standard Penny – we had high standards!*

Big Brother Gerry Looks Back on His Battles with Fondness:

My earliest memory, around 1955 aged five, was of me falling out of the rear left door of the MG Magnett. Luckily, the window was open as there was no A/C, and of course no child door locks. Dad braking like a maniac, me grabbing onto the open window for dear

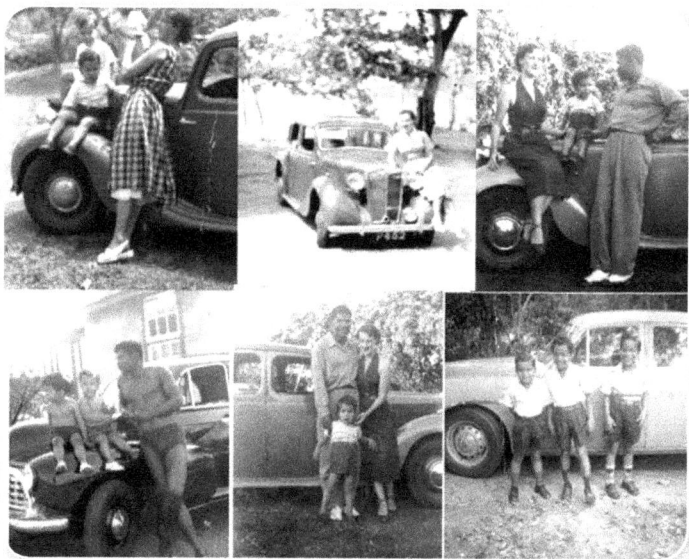

life, shoes (lucky I had them on as we loved going bare feet) scraping on the tarmac. Dad stopped the car, rushed round to me, gave be three whacks and threw me back into the car! We were both shaking.

I remember Guyana, where it rained. A lot. Dad telling us kids stories of Valhalla and Thor's hammer, which explained thunder and lightning. Have loved storms and thunder ever since. Fighting with younger brother Tommy was routine. As we were so similar in size, he was always challenging me for top spot, and of course, he had to be put down. Each and every time. Was an absolute rule. One memorable fight ended when with a furious barrage, I was making him retreat to the kitchen. Out of the corner of his eye he saw a kitchen knife, grabbed it and held it in front of him. 'Don't come any closer, or I'll stab you!' I rushed him – and he stabbed me! Luckily, I swerved to my right, so it was a cut on the left side of my waist, where I still have the scar to this day. Only a few stitches. Another time, Tommy was chasing me through the house and I slammed the door on him, he couldn't stop in time and ran straight into the door: bang! More stitches, another scar, on top his left eye this time. Now I know, this all sounds very dysfunctional, but it wasn't really, it's just what happens when brothers are close together in age. Usual stuff.

Trinidad in the last throes of colonialism seems to have been one long party: fancy dress fêtes, beach limes, Christmas parties, and country club soirees. Gerry and Nelleen Samuel were the talk of the town, 'the perfect mixed couple' as he described their marriage. We would love it when the speedometer on Dad's car reached a ton, speeding along the Churchill-Roosevelt Highway: 'Ninety ... ninety-five ... a ... *hundred!*' Sunday trips to Maracas Beach, Dad and Nelleen in front, three boys fidgeting in the back, competing as to who'd be the first to see the sea as we drove over the top of Trinidad's Norther mountains listening to calypsos about 'Jean and Dinah, Rosita and Clementina' and wondering why grown-ups thought it was so funny. But it wasn't all party central: bigger things were afoot. Like the rest of the British Empire, Trinidad and Tobago in the late 1950s was in the lead-up to independence, which finally came in August 1962. Led by the brilliant scholar Dr Eric Williams, all classes and

Neighbour Nell

races were firmly behind the drive towards independence. This was also the flowering of the Trinidadian intelligentsia, including Williams, C.L.R. James and V.S. Naipaul. In 1956, the People's National Movement (PNM) won a majority on the Legislative Council, thanks to hugely popular public lectures given by Williams in the centre of the capital, Port of Spain, dubbed 'the University of Woodford Square' and attended by thousands of enthusiastic listeners from all walks of life. Heady days.

And then it all changed; overnight.

High times in Port of Spain

4. *The Day She Left*

The only thing I remember about our mother is the day she left. I was six years old, and I remember that day with absolute clarity.

I remember snippets of life in Trinidad before then. I remember our two-storey house in Gordon Street, next to our friends the Fereiras. I remember Christmas 1958, when Gerry got a bicycle which Tommy promptly crashed and ended up in hospital. I remember sitting on my father's lap, steering his big MG Magnette. I remember him lifting me up onto a wildly rocking boat at night, scared witless. I remember us coming across a dead anaconda that some villagers had killed one night, as long as three cars in a row. I remember Sundays at Maracas Beach and our dog Simba getting run over by a car, and our father throwing him over a ravine on the way home. I remember being scared outside our house on Carnival morning, as the devilish Jab-Jab revellers came dancing down our street, hideously dressed in old rags, cow-horns, and daubed with black engine oil. I remember all these things – except our mother. We all have our defence mechanisms, and I guess mine was to forget. I simply don't remember her. I remember snapshots, but she's never in the frame. Where was she?

Growing up in Port-of-Spain was pretty close to boy heaven. We lived on Gordon Street, and the three of us boys would roam far and wide, playing with neighbourhood kids and getting into trouble. My best friend Brian Ferreira lived next door, and his little sister Gracie was my girlfriend, we'd even swapped chewing gum to seal the deal. And the skinny kid across the road who we called Skillinton. Every day an old man called Ripe Fig would ride past our house on his rickety old bicycle, with a gaggle of giggling children running after him shouting: 'Ripe Fig! Ripe Fig!' Then he'd slowly dismount, leggo a long fart, remount and ride off, leaving a gang of children dying in the road behind him!

Carbide is a raw material used in the manufacture of explosives and exists in abundance in Trinidad. So naturally most boys at some point will learn how to make a rudimentary mini-bomb. I forget the details but you needed an old tin of Lyle's Golden Syrup, a hunk of soft carbide, lots of spit, strike a match, stand back and...BOOM! One day a bunch of us were digging in the back yard, chasing a crapaud (toad) ever deeper into his hole. All I heard was:

'Brian! Watch out!'

I looked up, remember a nanosecond of pure terror, then blackness. The drainpipe, which had sat there along the side of the house for decades, decided at that very moment to give way. It spanned a wide arc, picking up momentum until it landed with a jarring thud, half an inch from my left eye. In the ensuing commotion our maid came running outside, to see me lying on the ground, unconscious, blood pouring down my face. She rushed inside and called Dad.

'Oh Gawd! Oh Gawd! Bri-Bri-dead! Come quick! Blood! Oh gawwd!!!' Dad could get no sense out of the jabbering woman, so he jumped in his car and raced home, heart pounding all the way. As he turned into our street, what did he see coming towards him? A hearse! Ah, but Bri-Bri didn't die! Between family, friends, and school, my memories of Trinidad can be summed up in one word: happiness. It was like the words to the Sparrow calypso: school days were happy-happy days.

Then it all changed. Overnight.

Every afternoon Dad would pick up Tommy and Gerry from Tranquillity Boys School, me from mine (which was so forgettable I've forgotten the name), then we'd drive to Radio Guardian on Maraval Road to pick up our mother. Dad would park in front of the building and tap the horn: bap, bad-dap-bap, bap-bap. Pretty soon she'd come bouncing down the steps, her light tropical dress blowing in the breeze (or so I imagine, I don't remember), then we'd all drive home.

Except on this day. On this day, she didn't come.

After a few more bursts on the horn, and still no sign of his wife, Dad went into the building, and emerged a short while later, alone, looking puzzled. We drove home in silence. She didn't come home that night, nor the next. A few days later, we were told that 'Mummy's gone away – for a while.' A few weeks later, I saw our father packing her clothes, and that was it: she was gone. I was six, Tommy nine, and Gerry ten, and our mother had just vanished, thrusting the three of us onto the sole care of our ill-prepared father. We never learned where she had gone, or why. That wouldn't come until many, many years later.

It wasn't as if our parents were constantly fighting; none of us could recollect a domestic shouting match or any kind of altercation. Kids see these things. Dad clearly hadn't seen this coming and was perplexed as to where she had gone – or what to do next. His mother, Irene Renwick, came over from Venezuela, to help out with us kids. None of us liked her. She had that old lady smell and pinched your cheeks too hard. Maybe at that point we wouldn't have liked anyone.

I guess it must have been pretty traumatic, losing your mother at such a tender age but, mercifully, I don't remember. We knew that she was gone, and we wanted her back, but I don't remember crying myself to sleep at night or getting into fights at school, 'cos I was some angry kid. Kids get over stuff, shrug it off, go outside, and play.

Strangely enough, Tom and Gerry also share this selective amnesia. I would have thought they would remember more of her, given they were older than me. They do, but not much. It's as if she's been airbrushed from our collective history, like a Russian dissident.

Where was she?

Even though I may not recall being emotionally traumatized by our mother's departure, that doesn't mean I've been immune to her influence. Strangely enough, the older I got the more she hurt me, a long, skeletal arm reaching out from the grave. Except that she was very much alive.

5. Brotherly Love – Sibling Rivalry

Timothy Anthony Byron ('Tabs') Samuel and his younger brother, Darwin Fitzgerald (Gerry) Samuel, were exceedingly close. Ever since their childhood days in Perdmontemps, they had maintained a remarkably tight bond. Despite many years and thousands of miles of separation, they kept up a constant and lengthy stream of correspondence in highly entertaining and personalized letters. The only ones that survive span the period from 1958 to 1961, when the brothers lived variously in Venezuela, Trinidad, and England. These were turbulent times for both men, including the death of their father, the breakup of Darwin's marriage, his subsequent migration to England, never-ending dramas in Byron's tangled love lives, and political meltdown in Venezuela.

Reading their correspondence, what struck me was how well my father's generation wrote. In the days when receiving a letter meant so much, you tended to put a lot of effort into the writing of it. You included all the news of the day: work, family, friends, world events, feelings, emotions, questions, advice – you wrote in the margins, to squeeze it all in. Our father typed all his letters (his handwriting was atrocious!) and kept a carbon copy, so you got both sides of the story: call and response. Good grammar was essential, and letter writing was something you only did when you had sufficient time; it couldn't be rushed. You sat down, thought about what you wanted to say (this could take a while), phrased the words in your head, did a mental grammar check – and only then, did you commit pen to paper – or finger to typewriter. If you made the slightest mistake, you used Tip-Ex to correct it. Your letter was your work of art.

As 1958 dawned, Byron was living in Puerto Ordaz, Venezuela, working at the Orinoco Mining Company in the Shipping Department. He'd been there for about five years since migrating from Trinidad, under a process that was 'unclear.' What was clear was that in Venezuela, Byron went by an assumed identity: Alberto Breceno. This naturally was a matter of great secrecy, as will become evident. My uncle Byron, after whom I was loosely named, was quite the ladies' man. No one knows exactly how many children he fathered between Grenada, Trinidad, and Venezuela – or with whom. Byron lived a complicated life, juggling angry baby-mothers and needy households in multiple countries, but he seemed to thrive on the confusion. Venezuela in the late fifties was beset by economic recession and deep political divisions, triggering crisis after crisis.

Byron   *Darwin*

Byron's letters, written on the distinctive Orinoco Mining Company letterhead, are full of current affairs, romantic escapades, humour, advice, and occasional big-brotherly upbraiding.

By contrast, Darwin seemed to live a charmed life. He worked as head of training at the Trinidad and Tobago Electricity Commission (T&TEC), and Nelleen was a celebrity, hosting a daily radio show called 'Neighbour Nell.' Trinidad in the 1950s was riding a wave of prosperity, thanks to a booming oil industry and the presence of two US military bases. Port of Spain was a society rising in self-confidence, high on the rhythms of calypso and steel pan; sustained by rum and roti. In such an atmosphere, a man would do well to keep his wife close by – especially a famous, vivacious, attractive white wife.

As idyllic as life in Trinidad appeared, Darwin was getting itchy feet again:

> *April 25th, 1958*
>
> *Dear Darwin,*
> *This is to let you know that I have not let up in my efforts to get you a position down here and apparently there is just the opportunity open right about now. ... Did Endee come down for the inauguration? He told me he would.*
>
> > *Yours very truly,*
> > *Byron*

The inauguration mentioned by Byron was for the short-lived West Indies Federation, a grand affair held in Port of Spain on April 22, 1958, attended by Princess Margaret. Endee did not make the trip, perhaps due to ill health, as he died of cancer on December 6, 1958, aged 85. Byron and Darwin took turns visiting their father in his final days, and both attended the funeral.

A year later, Byron was the first person to whom Darwin confided his devastating news:

Song for My Father

10th March, 1959

My Dear Byron,

It is a matter of much regret that I have to tell you – the first – that Nelleen and I have broken up in marriage, finally and irreconcilably. … Time and again I have been told that we had made the perfect mixed marriage – I trusted Nelleen implicitly and I can now say, unfortunately, that that trust has been broken on her part and all our plans for the future – house building, leave abroad etc. etc. have now all gone to naught. I feel as though the world has been knocked from under my feet and you can well imagine how much I am in the depths of despair, frustration – and bitterness. …

A beautiful thing, our marriage – and a happy relationship that weathered the storm of eight years – has been destroyed. You don't live ten years of your existence with one woman, sleeping, waking, cohabiting and procreating together, with her actually becoming a part of you which you miss desperately when it ends. If I said to you she's gone and 'happy riddance' then I would be lying in my teeth. But I have to brace myself and live for my children and in God's good time I have every belief that I would be infinitely happier. But the bonds have been strong and breaking it mentally as well as emotionally and spiritually is not going to be easy.

Please give my love to Gisela and for heaven's sake, don't feel sorry for me.

Your brother,
Darwin

We don't know Byron's immediate reaction to the news, but a year later he had clearly had enough of his younger brother's whining, telling him, in effect, to man-up:

I pray however, that when you write me, you'd make it your business to drop the sour sport and if you find it impossible to do so, then don't write.

Your brother,
Alberto'

It felt so strange, reading these letters describing in often aching detail life-changing events from our childhood. It took a long time for me to read them all, filled with so many powerful emotions on family matters, that went straight to my core. More than once, I had to pause to dry my eyes. Darwin and Byron's letters shone a light on decades-old family mysteries that had shaped so much of our childhoods; some would say adulthoods as well. Then, as now, West Indian parents weren't known for being inclusive with their children – *au contraire*, family secrets are the norm. Like: whatever happened to our mother?

Following the desertion of his wife, Darwin knew he had to leave Trinidad with its many ghosts constantly reminding him of a life now lost. After the torrid year he'd just endured, there was only one place he would go first: Byron. On January 10, 1960, Darwin flew from Port of Spain to Puerto Ordaz, Venezuela, returning on January 25. Darwin interviewed for a job at the Orinoco Mining Company, and the brothers celebrated their reunion by getting into several escapades, romantic and otherwise, the results of which continued to rumble on in subsequent letters.

But apart from having an awful lot of fun, the trip was a bust. Darwin didn't get the job at Orinoco Mining, mainly because he couldn't speak a word of Spanish. He therefore put into motion Plan B: England. In a lot of ways this would be like going back home for him. In hindsight, his previous stint in England must have seemed like halcyon days, compared to the year he'd just endured. The allure of a return to the mother country proved irresistible.

Before leaving Trinidad, he first of all had three little problems to deal with: us. He couldn't move to England with three hungry-belly boys in tow, so he needed someplace to park us for a few months while he went ahead to forge a trail. There was only one viable option: home. In February 1960, he took us by inter-island schooner from Trinidad to Grenada, to stay with his elder sister, Auntie

Laurina. Despite her protests that she was too old to look after 'those troublesome boys,' she appears to have had little choice in the matter.

> *Perdmontemps PO*
> *March 2nd, 1960*
>
> *My dear Darwin,*
> *I received your esteemed letter this afternoon and I could do or say nothing but to tell you that I will not be able to take care of any children at this stage. I am suffering with my nerves and if I should put pressure upon myself I will suffer the end. I think your mother are the right one to keep the children or you can take them to their mother but I cannot promise you to take care of them and people in Grenada is not what it used to be in the past. Endee died leaving not 1 cent so I have to work and pay all his bills. I am not happy as you all may think I am sick now, not a farthing. I am not making myself responsible for any children again.*

I remember standing on the heaving deck of the wooden schooner, holding Daddy's hand tight-tight-tight, squinting into the distant horizon, at the Dragon's Mouth, the narrow gap of water that separates Trinidad from Venezuela.

'Daddy, how will this big boat get through that little gap?'

'Just wait son, you'll see.'

And I did.

After getting us squared away in Grenada, Darwin boarded the Geest Line's *M/V Brunseck* in March 1960, bound for Liverpool, via the other Windward Islands, picking up bananas and passengers at each stop. Upon arrival in England, he bunked on a couch with his cousin Dennis Samuel at his flat in East London, and immediately started looking for a teaching job. But there weren't any immediate vacancies, so Darwin did what many West Indians did upon arrival in England: worked 'on the buses' – London Transport. Except in his case, he didn't actually work on the buses, but as a cleaner at a bus depot. Fortunately, a teaching vacancy soon appeared, and on

May 5, 1960, he started work as a metalwork and technical drawing teacher at Beethoven School, Paddington. A rough school in a rough neighbourhood.

Byron's last letter to Darwin in Trinidad arrived a few days before he took ship 'queenside':

> *March 9, 1960*
>
> *Dear Darwin,*
> *I figure by now you have returned from Grenada and the making of arrangements for the boys regarding their upkeep, education and other short-term plans covering your proposed 6-month stay in England. You must have thought seriously of the matter and I take it that your decision to follow this course is dictated by firm convictions. I see in it, though, the possibility or perhaps the subconscious design of reuniting with your wife. You will of course deny this, but ...*

What happened in Venezuela didn't stay in Venezuela. We'll never know the full details, but the brothers clearly had tussled over the affections of a certain Rita, an ex-girlfriend of Byron's, who took a shine to his younger brother. Both men seemingly came to a gentleman's agreement to suspend hostilities, in which Byron was seemingly magnanimous: *I have been informed that all intimate relationships between us must, and have been, discontinued. Good work!!!* A truce which, naturally, didn't last longer than it took not to write it. Byron took issue with some of his younger brother's tactics, and wasn't about to hold back:

> *But now, speaking quite seriously, I never could have thought that you, of all people, would discuss matters pertaining to my identity and documentation with third parties, let alone enter into details concerning my name etc., which I carry here. In that you have done but let me down flat. An explanation will be welcome, to say the least. After all, you ought to know that matters of this sort are strictly private, especially in a place like Venezuela. I am surprised you did not know how to divorce 'rival' from 'brother' and had to go all out to 'mauvais langue' me in the worst way.*

Song for My Father

Darwin had crossed the line by giving away his brother's greatest secret, in order to gain advantage with Rita, and Byron was right to upbraid him. But their strong affection was enough to overcome Byron's anger:

> *However, take care of yourself in this new venture, and whatever you do, try and make sure your future success is assured. For the time being I can offer no assistance, for which I am sorry. Yet, the knowledge that I am here and you are there is enough to brace us both up, and that means so much.*
>
> *I think this is as long as it should be, so I'd peter out with just a few more words, among which I'd again request the epic of your 'Two Nights with Mae-Mae' (too much biting). Now don't go and raise hell about this. I got it from between the lines under feigned duress. So you will understand. The woman is all yours. All I can do is 'cast an eye' on her from time to time on your behalf. Good luck and write before you go 'queenside.'*

Byron's next letter arrived just after Darwin landed in London. The sibling rivalry over Rita still rankled. Byron's magnanimous resignation in his previous letter was more apparent than real. He was still annoyed at his younger brother's caddish behaviour in the battle for Rita's affections, and as usual wasn't about to keep it on his chest:

> *1st April 1960*
>
> *Dear Darwin,*
> *I don't suppose you are so one-tracked so as to imagine that I too don't crash into situations wherein the multiplicity of your lies embarrasses me. ... Re Rita, you have used every trick in the bag to mislead, seduce and brainwash this woman.*
>
> *The merest ethics of guest to host, let alone basic respect to an elder brother, should have induced you to forego whatever enticement she had shown you. But never mind my talk about seducing. I am damn sure your methods would sooner earn you a bullet, if you don't knock*

off some of your rough edges. It is a pity you two iconoclasts have given rise to a state of tension between us two, and if I ever felt like giving her a cut arse, it is right now.

Which is stronger: the love of a brother or the love of a woman? Byron and Darwin's ongoing tension over Rita would suggest a tie: there was no winner – except Rita? This was just a year after Darwin's wife had shocked him to the core, leaving him 'in the depths of despair.' Was Rita a love on the rebound, desperately seeking solace? The fact that he and Rita had even talked about marriage would suggest so.

Byron's next letter was written on April 17, 1961, the day of the CIA-backed Bay of Pigs invasion, a shambolic attempted overthrow of Cuba, by a rag-tag bunch of anti-Castro forces:

April 17, 1961

Dear Darwin,

I like to time my actions with great events; that is why I write to you today, the date on which the imperialists have officially begun their vain attempt against the socialist forces of Fidel Castro in Cuba. They will be defeated.

By the way, do you remember Domingo Gascon? He was drowned about three months ago in the Orinoco River. He set out one night with a party of friends from the spot down the river called Los Castillos. Something happened and the boat was swamped and of the 13 persons on board Domingo was the one who lost his life. The body was recovered 36 hours afterward – a gruesome sight – half eaten by Caribe fish and other underwater creatures. It caused an uproar in Puerto Ordaz. Up to now people can't believe it. One of those things!

This would not be the last time that the mighty Orinoco River would claim the life of a loved one. Of course, no letter from Byron could be complete without a detailed accounting of his latest woman-worries:

I believe the most striking is that I have been able to shake off Maria.

She left the house about two months ago but not without taking everything she could lay her hands on. She even took my passport, with the result that I had to get another one. It was a good thing I carried my cedula with me otherwise it would have caused me quite a thing. The temperature began warming up just before Xmas last, or rather since I brought Amy this way. I finally told Maria to beat it, which she did, but now she is trying to make it difficult for me where Gisela is concerned.

Almost parallel with this episode I broke off diplomatic relations with Rita. I simply had my guts full of her egoism and uselessness as a woman except for one thing. And even in that regard she has become seriously handicapped – she had an operation for a womb malady and the whole organ was extracted. Up to now we still pass each other as Coolie pass Chinee.

And that was the saga of Rita, an ignominious ending if ever there was one. Byron's next letter was written towards the end of 1961, when Darwin and us boys were getting established in England. Byron still harboured hopes that his younger brother would return to the Caribbean at some point in the not-too-distant future:

So, what is England like by now, with all the restrictions on immigration and the like? Are you black Irish finding life any different as a result? You give the impression of being undecided as to whether to remain indefinitely in England or not. Clear your mind and make definite plans. It's good to hear your boys are doing well at school. My kids are doing satisfactorily both here and Trinidad. Bernard is entering technical school in January; Bernice goes ahead at high school, and here Alfredo and the others have benefitted immensely from their coming to San Felix. How's Phyllis? Marry the girl and 'done wid dat!

At which point we boys would have chimed in, 'Yes, pleeeeease!' We were living *en famille* with Auntie Phyllis, growing to love her more every day. After a year in a cold cramped council flat in Lewisham, we moved to a relatively spacious two-bedroom flat on

Arkwright Road in Hampstead. Life began to resume some semblance of normality again. Our father eventually didn't marry Phyllis, but that's another story …

> *So yes, what is this story about you buying a house? You say you want to borrow £100. I would not mind lending you, but that's a sizeable sum. But neither your present income nor your record as a debtor inspire confidence in the correctness of such an investment. If you are still of that opinion and wish to go ahead with the deal, which I hope is one that makes sense, I wish you would go into details in your next and we'll see what can happen. At this end things are neither bright nor hopeful.*
>
> *Happy New Year to all from,*
> *Byron*

That is the last letter between the two brothers that survives. Darwin and his brood stayed on in England, Byron and his in Venezuela; they would never meet again. In 1963, our father bought a house in Kenton, a boring suburb in Northwest London. Life was looking up. And then: disaster. A telegram arrived one Saturday morning. In those days, a telegram meant one thing: who dead? It was worse than anyone could imagine: Byron.

The news was sketchy and came in dribs and drabs, from telegrams and rushed long-distance calls. The story was eerily reminiscent of another tragic incident on the same Orinoco River, in which Byron's friend Domingo Gascon had died, recounted in an earlier letter. The city of Puerto Ordaz sits on a bend in the mighty Orinoco River, home to a number of deadly predators. Byron and family were on a boat trip when the boat capsized. Byron dived into the water and saved a number of children from the stricken boat, but an electric eel hit his son, shooting six hundred volts through his body and sending him into convulsive shock. Byron dived in once more to save his son and was hit by the same eel. Father and son perished.

The Orinoco had claimed more victims, and Byron died a hero.

Song for My Father

To this day, the tragic incident is still remembered in Puerto Ordaz. On that fateful Saturday morning when I walked into the kitchen, I'll never forget the terrible sight of my father sitting at the table, a crumpled telegram in his hand, tears streaming down his face, unable to speak. I fled.

6. *Second Crossing*

*A*untie Laurina was one of those old ladies who was old before she was old. She ran a small general store-cum-rum shop in Perdmontemps and supervised what remained of her father Endee's estate, which had largely been frittered away after his death in 1958. Some of my enduring childhood memories are the smells of that rum shop on a Friday night after the men got paid: white rum, saltfish, flour, pig foot souse, and sweat. We three boys would wedge ourselves into a corner and try to remain unseen, listening to the ebb and flow of ole talk. Because to be noticed by Auntie Laurina would mean being banished with a switch across your backside for sneaking around big people business.

But getting a lash from feeble Auntie Laurina was nothing compared to the real terror that lay ahead: the walk home. This was long before street lighting came to Perdmontemps, and on a moonless night it would be absolutely, totally black; you had to stumble down the road, feeling your way in the darkness. Our heads would be filled with folk tales of local demons like *Loup Garoux* (a werewolf), *La Diablesse* (a beautiful lady whose long dress hides a cloven hoof), *Sucuyant* (an old lady who peels off her skin and turns into a ball of fire), plus a host of other blood-curdling creatures. As we went stumbling down the path to the house, Tommy and Gerry

Auntie Laurina (left) and friend

would give me some new and terrifying piece of information then make a run for it, leaving me bawling in the dark.

'Gerryyyy! Tommyyyy! Wait for meeee!!'

To add to the terror, one day an old lady died, and they buried her just behind the shop. People said she'd died from sucking a penny. Despite our protests, the three of us were dragged to the funeral, trussed up in our good clothes, which in the West Indies meant dressing up little children like miniature adults, in ill-fitting jackets and tight ties. Hot, bored, and fidgety we endured the endless litany of hymns and sermons – Catholics take their funerals *very* seriously. Then comes the highlight of any West Indian funeral: the dead. What is it, this West Indian fascination with dead bodies? Every funeral is an open casket affair, no matter how ghoulish the sight, and all the deceased's family, each and every distant cousin ten times removed, friends and acquaintances, co-workers, church brothers and sisters, lodge members, plus the usual retinue of professional funeral goers, all sombrely file past the open coffin to say their goodbyes. Inevitably, some of these goodbyes are hugely dramatic, tear-filled, bawling, screaming, throw-myself-on-the-coffin affairs, where the mourner, usually female, has to be restrained by burly funeral attendants standing discretely close by, for just such an occasion.

Despite our pleadings, the three of us boys were frog-marched up to the coffin, where we saw to our horror that some people were bending over and *kissing* the corpse – lawdd! In any West Indian funeral, the file-by is the pinnacle of the event, where the undertaker smiles consolingly as he displays his finest funerary talents – his future income depends on it.

Over the next few weeks, in the wakes and rum shop gatherings that inevitably follow the funeral, after much crying, laughing, storytelling, and drinking of Clark's Court White Rum, a consensus will emerge on the success of the funeral and, in particular, the dead. 'He looked so peaceful, like he was sleeping.' Such complimentary comments would lead to the best of all conclusions: a good dead. But if the undertaker hadn't done his job properly, and the deceased didn't look 'peaceful,' there'd be no end of talk: who poison he?

Sadly, our Grenadian interlude approached its ending, and preparations began for our departure to England. We didn't know much about England except that everybody lived in skyscrapers and drove around in a 'limbozeen.' Our elder cousin Brenda gave us impromptu elocution lessons: 'Speak proper! You can't be shouting woy-yooooyy! every time you see a three-storey building. People will think you is a chupidee!' We flew on our own from Grenada to Port of Spain where we stayed with relatives. Before boarding the ship for Britain, I wrote excitedly to my father:

> Dear Daddy,
> I came by plane from Grenada to Auntie Phyllis, I got a nice ride. We are staying with Nen and Auntie Phyllis. I am coming on the Southern Cross. We land in Liverpool. I hope the boat do not sink.

On August 1, 1960, we boarded the Shaw Saville liner the *S.S. Southern Cross*, for a ten-day passage from Port of Spain to Liverpool. For the journey we were to be chaperoned by someone we had never met before: Phyllis Simmons, our father's 'new lady friend,' as snootily referred to by Auntie Laurina. We soon discovered that our new Auntie Phyllis was a wonderful, witty, warm-hearted woman who would become a much-loved mother-figure in our young lives.

We didn't realize it then, of course, but we were part of the Windrush Generation: the tidal wave of West Indian immigration to England that started in 1948, when a British passenger liner, H.M.T. *Empire Windrush*, found itself in Jamaica en route back to England, with a lot of empty cabins to fill. Its enterprising Captain John Almond placed an advert in the local newspaper, the *Daily Gleaner*, offering to take anyone to England for £48 one way. In those days, there were no restrictions on the movement of colonial subjects to England, and about five hundred Jamaicans took up the offer. The rest is history.

After the Windrush came the gold rush. West Indians, Indians, Pakistanis, and Africans flocked to Britain in the fifties and sixties, the vast majority of whom travelled by ocean liner. It was commonplace for liners to go on round-the-world voyages, picking up and dropping off passengers along the route, and the *Southern Cross* was on the return leg of such a voyage: homeward bound. But it wasn't cheap, Phyllis's ticket on the *Southern Cross* cost £75, equivalent to about £1,750 in today's money. Considering that his gross salary at Beethoven School was just £80 per month, it was a huge financial achievement to bring the four of us up from Trinidad, after being in England for only six months.

We were beside ourselves with excitement at the thought of our upcoming trip: ten whole days on this ginormous ship with swimming pools, cinemas, p l a y g r o u n d s, shuffleboard, and endless amounts of food – woy-yoooy!!

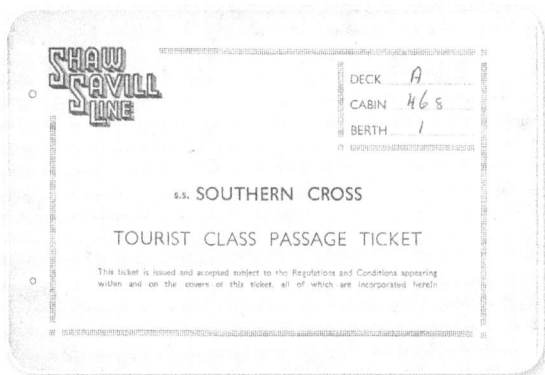

SHAW SAVILL LINE

DECK *A*
CABIN *46*s
BERTH *1*

s.s. SOUTHERN CROSS

TOURIST CLASS PASSAGE TICKET

This ticket is issued and accepted subject to the Regulations and Conditions appearing within and on the covers of this ticket, all of which are incorporated herein

By the end of the first day, the three of us had thoroughly explored every nook and cranny of the ship and had teamed up with other like-minded brats on board – we were primed and ready for fun and frolics at sea.

And then: disaster. On the second morning, Gerry woke up with a small spot, right in the middle of his (ample) forehead. Auntie Phyllis called the ship's doctor. The doctor took one look at the offending spot, shook his head, and muttered the fatal word:

'Quarantine.'

We didn't know what quarantine meant, but we soon found out. The doctor told Phyllis that Gerry had contracted chicken pox and that all four of us had to be moved 'to safer quarters.' Within minutes, a squadron of burly sailors arrived, to 'help us move.' Without another word, we were bundled out of our comfortable cabin and hauled off to the ship's quarantine quarters – a hot airless box, right at the back of the boat, above the constantly grinding propellers. They brought us three tepid meals a day – it was a long walk from the dining room to the arse-end of the boat. And there we remained, locked away for the remaining eight days: prisoners!

Song for My Father

You couldn't blame the doctor, there were 1,160 souls on board, including hundreds of kids. The last thing he needed was an outbreak of highly contagious chicken pox. Not that this helped us any; we were catatonic with boredom. Our only source of 'entertainment' was the BBC World Service, and we became avid if temporary followers of *The Archers*. The ship's captain came and spoke to us through the closed door, with his 'So sorry chaps, but do cheer up' speech, then left us a few *Hardy Boys* books. It was torture, to this day I've never read one *Hardy* bloody *Boys* book. Auntie Phyllis must have been going insane as well, not that we noticed. The worst thing was that this alleged bout of chicken pox only ever consisted of one accursed spot, and even that disappeared after two days. But no said the bastard doctor, we had to stay banged up on board.

I remember our joy at being reunited with our father on the docks in Liverpool, and the excitement of the drive down to London. Our father recorded the occasion in his pocket diary:

Wed 10 August 1960: Southern Cross arrived today. Cabin no 468.

The **Southern Cross** *docks at Liverpool Docks*

Our first few weeks in England were spent in the home of a vicar, in a sprawling house next to Clapham Common. We thought our new life in England was pretty good but were soon disabused of any such rosy notions. We moved into a tiny council flat in Grover Court, Lewisham, where the sole means of heating consisted of a coal fire in the living room. But by then we were under no illusions: this sure ain't Kansas, Toto!

Sun 11 Sept, 1960: Brian whistled for the first time today, a barely audible owlish whistle.

When I read that diary entry I sat up and did a double-take: I remembered that day, so well! I was pleased as punch with myself, for finally sort-of mastering the art of whistling, at which of course, my brothers were experts, and I annoyed everyone all that day with my *barely audible owlish whistle.* Until Tom and Gerry told me I'd better stop it, or they'd beat me up. Which they probably did anyway, just because they could.

Tues 4 Oct, 1960: Boys started school today.

My first school in England was St Stephen's Primary School in Deptford, which must have been unremarkable, as I have no recollection of it whatsoever. What I do remember is being most unimpressed with my new English school peers: grubby-faced urchins with constantly running noses and ridiculously long short pants. I was soon given the nickname 'chocolate-face,' which needless to say was immediate fighting talk. Being the youngest and smallest in class meant I usually lost, not that it stopped me.

It was infuriating, having these stupid English kids asking me if we wore grass skirts and lived in trees in Trinidad. It was bad enough to be missing home, but to have to put up with such ignorance as well? Complicit in this foolishness were the Catholic missionaries. I'd cringe when they'd visited my school and lectured us about how they were 'saving the savages in Africa' and show grainy black-and-white home movies of Black people who really did wear grass skirts – where did they get them from?

Mon 1 May 1961: Salary from today £967.13.0 gross. Technical Drawing and Metalwork Teacher, St. George's RC Secondary Modern School, Maida Vale.

But at least we had some semblance of family life again: Auntie Phyllis was a wonderful woman with whom we all immediately fell in love, as she did us. She had a piano and taught us how to play Für Elise. She was also a great cook, serving up delicious dishes that reminded us of home. We went to fairs, greyhound racing, stock car racing. This was a major improvement in affairs; all was going well.

And then, it all changed. Again, overnight.

Late one night in late 1962, the three of us boys were gently awakened by Auntie Phyllis, who with tears streaming down her face, told us that she and our father had decided to go their separate

Beloved Auntie Phillis

ways, and that she was leaving. We were shattered; we had grown extremely close to Auntie Phyllis, and for the second time in our young lives we were being robbed of a mother. Four sets of tears mingled that sad night when she walked out of our lives. A few weeks later, her piano disappeared.

We soon discovered that Auntie Phyllis had a replacement in our father's affections: an English woman called Irene. Oh, did we *hate* that woman! I don't know about Tom and Gerry, but with me it was feral. We were now old enough to know what was going on, and that this frumpy-dumpy Englishwoman was the sole reason why we'd lost our beloved Auntie Phyllis. This could mean only one thing: war.

I did my best to make that woman's life hell. Nothing she did could get a smile out of me. We were living in Hampstead, and one of the highlights of every summer was the Hampstead Heath Fair, with its roller-coasters, merry-go-rounds and everybody's favourite: bumper cars. But it wasn't cheap, which meant Dad would usually find some excuse for not taking us. This Sunday, lo and behold, Dad announces that we're all going to the fair. We all jump up: yaaay! Then he drops the dead cat:

'With Irene.'

We all answered, in unison:

'No thanks, don't feel like it.'

Unsurprisingly, Dad's face darkened:

'We … are … going … to … the … *fair!*'

We all piled into the old banger: Dad and Irene in front, three sulky faces in the back. It was torture: all the fun of the fair beckoning to us, but feeling duty bound not to enjoy ourselves. If *she's* here, we're not happy! She saw me cast a longing look at the bumper cars and offered me a ride.

'No thanks,' I muttered. 'Don't feel like it.'

Dad lifted me up and dropped me into the bumper car, hard.

'Go ... and ... have ... *fun!!*'

I drove to the centre of the ring, and just stayed there, crying. Bumper cars zoomed all around, bumping into me, still I didn't move. I just sat there and cried. *Why* is Daddy with this horrible woman? *Why* can't we have Auntie Phyllis back? *Why* are we in this horrible country? *Why?*

After that things got strange, but it wasn't until many years later that we discovered exactly how strange. I'm not sure how I know the following, and Gerry also isn't sure where we heard it, but 'this much we hold to be true':

It turns out that our father's new love, Irene, wasn't only frumpy and dumpy – she was also married. Our father had done the dishonourable thing by stealing another man's wife, then doubled the dishonour by not marrying her. Meanwhile in Phyllis's wretchedness at being dumped by Darwin, to whom did she turn for solace? Irene's jilted husband! They were two people sharing the same sad statistic: both cuckolded by my father. In fact, Phyllis and Irene's ex-husband grew so close – they eventually got married! It got stranger yet. When Phyllis left our house that sad night, she wasn't just heartbroken, she was also pregnant. I'm not sure if she knew it then, but several months later, Phyllis gave birth to a baby girl, in a discrete charitable home for 'single mothers of distressed circumstances.' Every West Indian family has its fair share of secrets and lies, and ours is no exception. In fact, we excelled. My father kept that secret deep within his chest; for as long as he was alive, we had no idea we had a half-sister.

Many years later, after my father had died, I needed to find a certain document, and decided to search in his files for it. I found far more than I'd bargained for. In my shaking hands was an old yellowed official document: *Certificate of Birth: Born to Phyllis Simmons on 2nd June, 1963: Jacqueline Simmons.* I was thunderstruck: we had a sister! I also found letters from Phyllis to our father, informing him of the birth of their daughter. Thirty years after the fact, I found out that my brothers and I had a sister, and not with just any woman, *with Auntie Phyllis!*

To this day, despite our best efforts, Auntie Phyllis and our half-sister Jacqueline Simmons remain lost to us. Phyllis must have changed her name when she married Irene's ex-husband, whose name we never knew, and they probably changed Jacqueline's surname as well. Another complication is Jacqueline had no middle name, a major limiting factor in the search. Gerry wrote to every single Jacqueline Simmons in the UK (a surprisingly large number): nothing. Countless Jacqueline Simmonses on Facebook have written me back: no, sorry, but I'm not your long-lost-sister. The search continues.

Dad's darkest deed.

And what became of Irene? I'm glad to say she didn't last long. Many years later after, we'd moved to Kenton, I answered the phone one Sunday afternoon; it was Irene. She hesitatingly asked for Dad.

'He's not here.' He was.

'Hello Brian! This is Irene, do you remember me?'

'No.' Click.

The Collins family was almost a carbon copy of ours: two West Indian single fathers bringing up children on their own, after their British wives had run out on them. Except that Lloyd Collins had two daughters as well as three boys. I met Paul Collins, and Tom met his elder brother Steve Collins on the same day, in the same school, in the same way. It was our first day at yet another new school: Fitzjohn's Primary, in Hampstead. As soon as Tom walked into his classroom, his teacher, the feared Mr Frost, said:

'Ah Samuel, a new coloured boy. Go sit next to Collins, the other coloured boy.'

At the exact same moment, I walked into my classroom, and my teacher said:

Song for My Father

'Ah Samuel, a new coloured boy. Go sit next to Collins, the other coloured boy.'

And so it turned out to be: I, Tom, Steve, and Paul Collins became an instant foursome, the only coloured kids in the class. Apart from meeting my future best friend Paul Collins, that first day at Fitzjohn's Primary was notable for another reason, one considerably more traumatic. I had just turned eight, still new to England and scared shitless. This was my fourth school in twelve months, and as usual my main concern was to draw as little attention to myself as possible. In the afternoon, all was going well, until...

I wanted to pee.

At first it wasn't so bad, I figured I'd just wait it out until the next break, except the next break never came. As the afternoon dragged on and on, my bladder grew fuller and fuller. I was too scared to raise my hand and ask to go and pee, inviting a whole classroom of stares my way, so I just sat there cross-legged in increasing stages of torture, willing my body to stem the increasing pressure upon my bursting bladder. And then, disaster! Someone bumped into the back of my chair. It was only a little bump, but it was enough to burst the dam. At first it was no more a trickle, a dribble of pee down the inside of my leg. But as that pent-up pressure released itself against my defenceless pee-pee, the dribble grew. In a heartbeat from trickle to stream, stream to river, river to flood. I just sat there, unable to control myself, shivering with relief.

'He's pissed his pants!'

The boy sitting behind me pointed to the rapidly spreading stain in my pants and repeated, louder:

'He's pissed his pants!'

The whole classroom turned my way – and erupted into howls of laughter. I disappeared in a welter of tears while the blushing teacher shepherded me out of the classroom to the toilets. As I walked my gauntlet of shame, that same little urchin behind me, some toerag called Raymond Rouch, shouted:

Samuel-Collins Family

'Bicky-Four-Two-Oh-Smell!'

Cue, more uproarious laughter: my shame was complete. I had no idea what he meant or where it came from, but that impulsive nickname, Bicky-Four-Two-Oh-Smell, clung to me throughout my three years at Fitzjohn's, like the bad smell from which it originated. I hated it with a passion. Even now, when my pesky nephews want to get a rise out of me, they'll cheekily shout: 'Hi uncle Bicks!' Grrr. Needless to say, from that moment on Raymond Rouch and I remained sworn enemies: war!

Every lunch break and playtime would be non-stop activity: football, cricket, or British Bulldog, a rough game that's since been banned in schools. Mind you it did result in plenty of grazed knees and bloody elbows. Miranda Wood was the prettiest girl in Fitzjohn's, with sparkling eyes, the cutest little button-nose and a tangle of ginger curls. Not that we boys were interested in girls except to run past and flick up their skirts, when they were playing hopscotch or some other silly girl's game. But every now and then, on those rare occasions when we weren't acting like pre-pubescent Neanderthals, Miranda Wood would flash us one of her special smiles, with a hint of a wink. And then, all of a sudden, silly girls didn't seem quite so silly anymore …

In three years at Fitzjohn's, there were many occasions when Rouch and I came to the brink of the all-out fight we both so dearly wanted, but always stopped short of actually engaging – until the last day of school. We'd done our eleven-plus exams and would be going our separate ways to secondary schools. Most of us would never see each other again, which was fine with me, except that there was unfinished business to settle: Rouch. He and I had agreed to have our long-awaited fight on the last day of school when our form teacher Mr Frost pretty much left us up to our own devices.

That was the mother of all fights! I amazed myself at the eruption of anger that came from somewhere I didn't even know existed. Unlike normal fights when some excited spectator would yell 'Bundle!,' automatically attracting teachers, this time nobody said a word – they were too engrossed with the fight! We rolled over desks and chairs, tumbled on the floor, flailing away for all we were worth.

Every time he hit me, I didn't feel a thing, nothing mattered. My split lip didn't matter, the pain didn't matter. All that mattered was I was going to kick … his … ass! For every time someone called me chocolate-face, I hit him. For every time he whispered 'Bicky!' behind my back, I hit him. For every other piece of shit I'd had to endure since coming to this godforsaken country, I hit him. I didn't stop hitting him until he yelled 'Okay, okay! I give up!' Then I stopped. Eventually. That was the best day of my young life – bar none! And to top it off, I got a kiss from Miranda Wood. I walked out of Fitzjohn's Primary School for the last time in July 1963, three feet off the ground!

Paul Collins was everything I wasn't. He passed his eleven-plus, I failed. He went to grammar school, me to secondary modern. He was on the football team, the cricket team, the boxing team, debating team, and every other damn team going. I wasn't even in the reserves. Dad used to say to me: 'Why can't you be like Paul?' Which no parent should ever say to their child. If it was meant as negative encouragement it failed dismally. Even though Paul was my best friend, I hated him. But fate is a helluva thing: Paul's perfection wasn't to last. Whilst I drifted through a succession of crappy secondary schools, Paul was the great brown hope: top of his class, school prefect, groomed for success. And then one day in fifth form, six months before his O-levels, out of the clear blue sky, Paul just … stopped. Stopped studying, stopped going to school, eventually stopped even waking up.

He'd get up in the morning, put on his uniform and go to school. After waiting in a café for his father to leave for work, Paul would go back home and sleep the whole day. When the letter came from school saying he was missing, he intercepted it. His father had no idea what was going on until it was way too late. Poor Mr Collins tried everything: talking, reasoning, begging, beating – nothing worked; Paul slept through it all. His bed was filthy, he slept in it, ate in it, did everything but shit in it – and even then, we're not sure. His O-levels came and went, Paul slept. No one could figure out what was going on inside his head. Paul Collins never worked a day, slept his whole life away.

Our respective fathers both remarried within a year of each other, to remarkably similar women. In 1970, Lloyd and Jill Collins moved to the South of France where they led a colourful life, including rabbit farming and other exotic ventures.

By the time I left Fitzjohn's Primary, we'd left Hampstead and moved to Kenton, North-West London. We missed our old haunts in Hampstead and had to make new friends all over again in the boring 'burbs. The 11-Plus exam determined whether you went to grammar or secondary modern school. The difference was an educational chasm, putting enormous pressure on eleven-year-olds to do well. At this the first of life's major hurdles, I failed miserably.

Lloyd and Darwin

Joan and Jill

My excuse was that I had whooping cough on the day of the exam. Well, it was a cough, and it whooped. Sort of. Mind you I was in good company: most primary schoolchildren failed. The 11-plus was abolished in 1977.

After Fitzjohn's, I entered first form at St Thomas's RC Secondary Modern in Stanmore, which has long since been bulldozed – probably the best educational service it ever delivered. This was the junior to St James's in Burnt Oak, where Tom went. Gerry stayed on at St George's in Maida Vale, where Dad taught. St Thomas's was a Convent school which meant that half the teachers were nuns. They would dole out equal parts punishment and prayers, teaching the Catechism by rote – and God help you if you were 'chosen' for the vocational stream, as I was. If you lived more than three miles from school, you were given a free bus and train pass. They had a big map on the wall, and when they measured my address I lived 2.9 miles away: pass denied. Oh, come on, that's just a few hundred yards! Needless to say, a free pass was used to travel to and from just about anywhere, and I'd missed out because of a few lousy yards. Just my luck.

So here I was – yet another new school, yet again the smallest kid in class, yet again one of three coloured kids in class. Vernon Johnson (Jamaica), Emmanuel Rocha (India), and Maurice Bigaignon (Mauritius) became my best buddies, hanging around together at playtimes and watching each other's backs, literally. There were some tough kids at St Thomas's, especially the remedial third formers. These yobs loved nothing more than bullying us first formers, so you had to keep your wits about you – and your fists.

7. *Bombsite Brats*

Until 1963, we lived in a two-bedroom flat at 41b Arkwright Road Hampstead, which even then was a pretty chic address. A bohemian community of West Indians, European émigrés, artists, poets, beatniks, and unemployed intellectuals. One such unemployed intellectual was Dad's pompous Barbadian friend, Torrey Pilgrim. He lived in a huge house just off Finchley Road, and every Sunday evening he'd host a debating society called the Creative Association, catering to the self-declared Hampstead intelligentsia. This eclectic group of bores would sit in his cavernous living room, discussing the important issues of the day: colonialism, anti-colonialism, imperialism, anti-imperialism, blah-blah endless blah.

For us kids it was torture, we'd end up in the kitchen with Mrs Pilgrim. Because Torrey was so busy being the self-appointed chairman of the Hampstead intelligentsia, it would be unreasonable to ask him to actually work for a living, so his compliant English wife did all the menial tasks like earning a salary and bringing up their two boys. Torrey later moved his family back to Barbados, where he became a yoga teacher and lifestyle guru. His wife still did everything else.

Sat 11 Mar, 1961: Took delivery of SLA 960 from Maines Car Sales.

Song for My Father

That day in Arkwright Road, Dad came home all excited.

'Good news boys, I've bought a car!' Ever since we'd arrived in England the previous year we'd been without a car, which was a big letdown for us spoiled kids. We ran to the window, looked outside, and saw a gleaming white car, parked in front of the house.

'Wow, a Jaguar! It's fantastic! Can we go for a ride?'

'Er, no, not that one. Behind it.'

We turned around and you could hear the sound of three tiny crests, falling. It was an old sit-up-and-beg Ford Popular, with tiny windows and dinky little rabbit-ear indicators. We put on a brave face, though by now we fully understood that the good old days of Trinidad were long gone, and that we had to make do and mend. But we still had great fun in that old banger. She gave us sterling service, ferrying us all over London and southern England for the next three years, seldom showing signs of her advancing years. They don't make 'em like that anymore. Thank God.

Our father was a great storyteller; he'd have us spellbound, recounting escapades from his boyhood in Grenada and in England during wartime. He also wrote short stories for the BBC World Service and would give us test readings before submitting them: 'Sam's Hole,' 'Dead Birds in the Morning,' and my favourite: the 'Rear-Admiral.'

Up until around the mid-sixties, most English homes were heated solely by coal fires, giving rise to outbreaks of London's infamous fog: thick, choking pea-soupers where you could barely see beyond the tip of your arm. When we got off the boat in Liverpool in August 1960, we thought it was freezing, not realizing this was the height of the British summer. As the months rolled by, we kept asking ourselves: it can't possibly get any colder than this – can it?

The English winter of 1963 was the coldest since time began. We were living in Arkwright Road, a snowball's throw from Hampstead Heath. When the blizzard came we had a great time, playing in the snow, skating on Whitestone Pond, and of course endless snowball fights. But what we liked best of all were toboggans. Hampstead Heath's steep slopes were ideal for toboggan runs, which they became the morning after every snowfall. We didn't have toboggans; toboggans cost money, but we had the next best thing: dustbin lids. If you flattened out the handle with a brick, an upside-down dustbin lid made a perfect one-man, unguided missile – only things missing were brakes and steering, but who needs them? You sat cross-legged on the lid at the top of the slope, someone would give you a shove and off you went hurtling down the slope: watch oooouuutttt!!!

But the Big Freeze wasn't all fun. In fact, it was torture: sheer, bloody torture. Every winter was cold, but our third was the mother of all winters. We slept in a bedroom with no heating whatsoever, you'd wake up in the morning to find ice – on the *inside* of the window. In the morning, your biggest dread was getting out of bed. You'd reluctantly wake up, snuggled under layers of blankets. Only when you absolutely had to, after Dad's final and most ominous wake-up warning, would you steel your nerves: three-two-one – GO! Jump out of bed, grab the first warm piece of clothing that comes to hand, run to the bathroom – invariably to find it occupied, hurry up in there! So long as it wasn't Dad, you couldn't tell him to hurry! If you were lucky, you had an electric bar heater in your bedroom, which of course you couldn't leave on all night, so you'd turn it on first thing in the morning and huddle around it, trying to get inside the bars.

Who send we?

93

Song for My Father

'Move from that fire, or you'll get chilblains!'

We never got chilblains, nor find out what they were. On one particularly cold night Dad took us to see the Christmas lights on Regent Street. Christmas was in the air, roasted chestnuts, Santa and reindeers, everyone was merry. Except me. I wasn't merry, I was freezing. Dad tried to cheer me up: look Bri-Bri, don't you love the Christmas lights? No, I don't like the lights. How can I appreciate lights when my shoes have holes, my socks are wet, my feet are blocks of ice, and I can't feel my ears? When are we going home?

When it came to his children's personal hygiene, our father had a hands-off approach, literally. I don't remember him once ever showing me how to wash my pee-pee, wipe my botty, or generally to keep myself clean, as any normal parent (usually the mother) would do. He just left it up to us, after drumming his motto into our heads: Keep Clean! But without going into the grimy details, such instructions are of little practical use. Dad wouldn't even know how many pairs of socks we had, let alone how often we changed them. We would wear the same socks for days, until they were stiff. And boy did they ever stink! Which was not a problem because we never took our shoes off, except when we went to bed.

My approach to personal hygiene was changed, irrevocably and for the better, after one particularly embarrassing episode. Timothy Dowling was a friend of mine at Fitzjohn's Primary, a poor little rich kid who lived in this huge house on Finchley Road. He'd invited me back to his house several times, but I'd always declined, until finally I relented. I should have followed my gut. On his front door, I was met by his mother.

'Hello Brian, I've heard so much about you! Would you like to take off your shoes? Timothy, please show Brian to the coat room.'

Huh? Take off my shoes? No thanks! But of course, this wasn't a question, it was that way that English people have of asking a question, when they're really giving an order (the police are masters at it). Slowly, I slid off my shoes, pulling my trousers down to hide the holes in my socks. But what I couldn't hide was the smell. Quickly the stench from my socks spread throughout the room, until Timothy's mum couldn't stand it anymore. She led me into the bathroom where she 'suggested' I wash my feet in the bathtub, then she gave me a new pair of fluffy socks, much nicer than the Woolworth wonders I usually wore. She threw my old ones away, with a pair of tongs.

I never went out with smelly socks on again, ever!

Both of Timothy's parents were busy lawyers who lavished their only child with toys, to make up for the one thing he really needed: their time. They had a nanny from Poland, and one day I noticed a number, tattooed on her forearm, and asked her what it meant. She quickly covered it up and hurried away, leaving me perplexed: what did I do now?

Timothy's pride and joy was his train set or rather his train room. This thing occupied an entire room, and not a small room either. There was every conceivable type and size of model train: engines, passenger carriages, freight cars, shunters, bowsers, stations, hills, valleys, mountains, tunnels: a whole train continent. He controlled it all from a central console in the middle of the room while the trains went choo-chooing all around him. Being an only child, he didn't know how to play with other kids, so the most I got to do was look on in wonder, only occasionally would he relent and hand me the controls. I was hooked.

I wanted a train set. I went down to Toys-Toys-Toys on Finchley Road and gawked at train sets in the window. They were awfully nice, but awfully expensive, even the starter kits. My birthday was coming up, so I put on my best smiley face and gently broached the subject with Dad.

'Daddy … (smile), can I have a train set for my birthday (bigger smile), pleeeease?' All I got was a grunt and a 'We'll see.' Which at least was better than an outright 'Are you mad?' As last my birthday came around, I wasn't so silly as to expect a present waiting for me when I awoke. Dad would only ever get around to buying your present on the day itself. That evening Dad came home with a box under his arm – a big box. And he was smiling: all good signs. I tore at the wrapping and before I could get it halfway off Dad proudly announced:

'It's a train set!'

'Yaaaay!!!' I ripped open the box, revealing my gleaming new train se…

'Huh?'

It wasn't a train set, it was a train: a dinky little clockwork choo-choo, with a smiley face on the front and a big key on top. You wound it up and it would go for half a lap before it huffed and puffed and died. Have you ever wanted to cry so badly you have to look skywards, to stop the tears from falling?

'Thanks, Daddy.' Sniff.

I gathered up my train set and shuffled off to my room, to 'play' with it. To the background noise of Tom and Gerry, falling over themselves laughing. Enjoy your train set, Prooglums!

We were baby-boomers, bomb-site brats. We'd play among the bomb-damaged buildings still scattered around London in the early sixties, rummaging through the debris, finding old newspapers, yellowed letters, and broken dolls. We would make up stories as to what had become of their owners, always ending with: Boom! We roamed around Hampstead, Finchley Road, Swiss Cottage, and Kilburn: a self-contained gang.

Your prized possession was your gun, preferably two. Every game was divided into cowboys against Indians, English against Germans. Nobody wanted to be Indians, nobody wanted to be Germans. In addition to toy guns, you had guns that actually fired things. With a spud gun you could shoot a lump of raw potato about ten paces, straight into your mate's ear. A notch above the spud gun was the pellet gun, a spring-loaded piece that could launch a plastic

Urchins

ball across the room, straight into your mate's eye. Later on, in the US, there were B-B guns, lethal for frogs and squirrels, and then the gold standard: the air gun. This fired a waisted lead shot that could penetrate tin cans, bottles, and as Gerry would learn to his cost, flesh.

When any group of boys get together their thoughts will soon turn to food, and the acquiring of more of it. We were eating machines; what we ate at home was just for starters. A group of us would get together in some piece of open land, someone would bring a pot and someone else some sugar, pilfered from his mum's kitchen. We'd light a fire, pick wild rhubarb, blackcurrants, and gooseberries that grew along the railway embankments, and bingo: a steaming pot of stew! We'd stand next to the tracks as trains whizzed by, screaming out loud and not hearing a word.

In 1963, we moved out of Hampstead when our father bought a house in Kenton. Like everything else at the time, we took it in our stride, but for our father on a meagre teacher's salary and four mouths to feed, it was quite an achievement. For weeks we drove all over London, looking at houses ('Please Dad, not the one overlooking

Willesden Green Cemetery!), until he finally made his choice: 24 Camplin Road, Kenton, Harrow, Middlesex.

It was a typical English semi-detached: two-and-a-half bedrooms upstairs, living, dining and kitchen downstairs, small front garden with a hedge, and a bigger back garden with apple trees. He paid £4,800 for the house, compared to his salary of £967 per year – a ratio that certainly wouldn't apply to London real estate today. Dad was pleased as punch, having beaten the seller down from £5,000, an Indian family who had migrated to Australia. I remember the day we moved in, Dad was all excited, rushing from room to room, directing traffic.

One immediate benefit was a significant increase in living space, and a big back garden. We even had a new luxury: a telephone, Wordsworth 9037. Dad had the front bedroom; Tom and I shared the back bedroom, and Gerry got the box. But although we now lived in Kenton, our schools, friends, and stomping grounds were still back in Hampstead, so we got to know the Bakerloo Line very well, schlepping between the city and the 'burbs.

I can't say we received a warm reception from our new neighbours. Before we'd even finished moving in a man from the house directly across the road knocked on our door, not to welcome us but to complain that we kids were riding our bikes on the pavement. 'I'm a policeman you know.' Policeman my arse. He was a British Railway guard! We'd laugh at him as he cycled off to work in the morning with his lunch pail dangling from the handlebars of his bicycle. This naturally set off a prolonged cold war between the Samuels and the Maynards.

Sadly, our suburban interlude didn't last. Eighteen months after we moved in, we moved out again, to a cold, cramped flat in Agamemnon Road, West Hampstead. Why? Didn't we just buy this nice warm house? We were told that we'd be moving 'just for a while.' We figured it out: Dad was in a financial bind, so he rented

Dad and his boys

out our house in Kenton and moved into a cheaper flat, and with the savings figured he'd pay off whatever debts were chasing him. If only it were so simple.

Agamemnon Road was the worst place we'd ever lived, which was saying something. It had two tiny unheated rooms, an unheated corridor, leading to an unheated kitchen, and an unheated bathroom. The landlady was this miserable Jamaican woman whom Dad christened the 'Gorgon.' He naturally had the bedroom to himself, while we three boys bunked in the living room-cum-bedroom. Gerry got a bed to himself, leaving Tom and I to share a bed.

Do you have any idea, the absolute *torture* of sharing a bed with your big brother? I'd be fast asleep when out of the blue: wham! Something hard would come crashing down on my leg. Ouch! I'd wake up, bleary-eyed: what? Tom would be lying there, calmly reading his Spiderman comic by flashlight.

'Your foot. It's on my half of the bed. Move it.'

Fortunately, our stint at Agamemnon Road only lasted one school term. But unfortunately for Dad his get-rich-quick scheme didn't quite work out as planned. True he rented out our house, but the question was: to whom? He'd put an ad in the local newspaper, which was answered by an exotic Martiniquan lady, resplendent in flowing kaftan, headwrap, dozens of bangles and bangarangs. I remember when she came to give the house the once-over, very picky: paint this, wallpaper that. So, we painted this and wallpapered that, and she moved in while we moved out, grumbling all the way.

I don't know what our father thought she did for a living, but Madame Martinique turned out to be … a prostitute! As reported by our scandalized neighbours, she used our house as her place of business and judging by the parade of Rollers and Bentleys parked outside, she had a very high-end clientele. But despite her high-rolling clientele she still didn't pay the rent, and after months of wrangling, she did a midnight runner, taking everything in the house that wasn't nailed down, including the curtains.

Worse was yet to come. When we got back inside the house, breaking down the back door to do so, we discovered to our horror that she had painted over our stained walnut mantelpieces – bright pink‼ I remember our first night, overjoyed to be back home but angry at how this woman had trashed the place. The next day Dad bought a dozen razor blades and handed them out, and for the next few weeks the four of us sat there for hours every evening, scraping off that damned paint until our fingertips bled. Great deal you did there, Dad!

Gerry Destroys a Relic:

Early 60s in Camplin Road. As a family we went to Portobello Market a few times. I for one got bored with Dad's absolute refusal to pay the asking price, which was of course the MO in any market, but which subsequently put me off haggling. Hate it. So anyway, there we were in the market, Dad in his element when for some reason his eyes alighted on a wind-up gramophone. A lovely mahogany thing with slats in the front for volume control. No classic horn on this superior model. Asking price was two quid (£2) but Dad being Dad, after a lengthy and to both parties enjoyable repartee about 'taking the food off my kids's plates' or some such, a price of 30 bob (£1 10 shillings or £1.50) was agreed on. Dad of course squeezed in a few 78 records into the deal. Great excitement when we got home. It was magical. No need to plug in, just occasionally wind her up and listen to her run! Fabulous. Among the records was Rimsky Korsakoff's Scheherazade which I've loved ever since.

Sadly, in the acts of wanton destruction that teenagers are prone to, I vividly remember the day it ceased to fascinate and entertain us, and we systematically destroyed that rather lovely thing. Not my finest hour.

Another time Dad took in a Grenadian friend of his, 'for a little while.' The problem was this friend came with his Danish wife and two annoying little girls who couldn't speak a word of English. All four of them shared one room, so overnight the population of the house had doubled. Which, with only one bathroom, one toilet, and one kitchen, quickly became a major pain. A little while turned into a long while, a long while into an eternity – the bloody people just wouldn't leave! Finally, it came to blows. One Saturday afternoon, I heard a commotion in the kitchen and when I half-opened the door I saw Dad and his friend, rolling around on the floor! I hastily withdrew. The upshot was that our unwanted guests moved out the very next day. Dad should've put the boot in sooner!

Although we lived in the 'burbs, we all went to schools in Inner London, and Dad would drive every day from Kenton down the Edgeware Road, drop me and Tom off at Fitzjohn's Primary then he and Gerry would drive onto St George's in Maida Vale. By this time, Dad had upgraded the old Ford Popular to a blue Hillman Minx, the first car on our street. English cars of the sixties were famous for, well nothing, and topping this list of non-attributes would be British motor electrics. In the depths of winter, after spending the night out in the cold, starting the car could be a nightmare. On particularly cold nights, Dad would put a small paraffin heater underneath the engine to stop it from freezing. On a frigid morning, we'd all run out of the house, jump into the car, praying hard. Dad would pull the choke, pump the gas, and turn the ignition.

Arr-arrrrr-arrwwww...

On a freezing cold morning, the saddest sound in the world is the sound of a car battery: dying. Dad tries again, nothing. Again, and again. By this point, you know it's not going to start, and all you're doing is flooding the engine. Everyone out! We'd then move onto step two in the winter starting ritual: the crank. You young 'uns don't know what a crank is – and be thankful. You insert the crank through a hole in the front bumper, where it connects directly to the driveshaft. In theory, one good turn of the crank handle would be enough to get the engine started – in theory. In practice, you'd yank on that crank in ever-diminishing lunges, as the engine just sat there: cold, unmoved. After failing with the crank, we'd move to step three:

the push. Of course, Dad couldn't push as he was driving, so the three of us boys would scrape the ice off the trunk (or boot, as the English called it), and bend our shoulders to the wheel. Dad would keep you pushing and pushing, and pushing, before finally flying the clutch.

Arr-arrrrr-arrwwww.….

We'd push the car all the way up Camplin Road, left onto Lodge Avenue, left again on Farrer Road, trying to start it at regular intervals. If all else failed it was onto the final solution: the hill. Around the corner from our house was a company called British Building Supplies, which had a sloping ramp down into their car park. We'd push and push and push, hitting the top of the ramp at maximum speed, then Dad would fly the clutch. Cough-cough … vroom!

And if the bastard still wouldn't start? Catch the bus – and get ready with the late excuses!

One morning, Dad came very close to having his car engine destroyed by an angry neighbour, because of me! A girl was the catalyst for this piece of high drama – isn't it forever thus? Her name was Annie, and she lived in the council flats around the corner on Kingsbury Road. We were both thirteen and had become 'friends,' in a thirteen-year-old way. Then one day, she told me with tears in her eyes that we couldn't be friends anymore. Her father had banned her from talking to me because I was coloured. I was devastated, and that evening told Dad about it. He exploded.

'What? This stupidness is still going on in this day and age? Who is this ignoramus?' I told him where the ignoramus lived.

'Come with me!' Uh-oh.

We went marching down the road. Dad in high dudgeon, me apprehensive. Bang-bang-bang! Dad hammers on the door. Ignoramus answers: fag in mouth, wearing a grubby wife-beater vest, clearly unimpressed.

'Yeah?'

'Did you tell your daughter she can't see my son because he's coloured?'

'Yeah, so?'

'So, you should be ashamed of yourself! What sort of an example is that to set your daughter, teaching her to hate just because of the colour of someone's skin? This is 1966, there's no place in this country for the colour bar. You, sir, are an ignoramus!'

Ignoramus clearly didn't know what an ignoramus was, but he didn't like being called one. I was worried things were about to get physical, but Dad wasn't a small man, and the ignoramus decided on another tactic: slam! Dad and I stormed off, that told him! The next morning, we got into the car as usual and drove the half-mile to the petrol station at Kingsbury roundabout. When the attendant took off the petrol cap, he called Dad over.

'Oi mate, 'ave a look at this. Someone's been tryin' to nobble your engine!'

There was sugar scattered around the petrol inlet. The ignoramus had come sneaking around at night and poured sugar into the petrol tank, guaranteed to ruin any engine after just a few miles of running. But fortunately, Dad caught it just in time. I can just imagine the speech he gave on the ignoramus's doorstep that evening, but I wasn't there to witness his command performance. And he put a padlock on his tank.

Our father took a belligerent attitude towards racism: he just wouldn't wear it. Neither would he accept meaningless platitudes from peripheral people. One day he was buying some meat, the butcher smiled at him and said:

'We're all the same, ain't we mate?'

'I beg your pardon?'

'Under the skin, we're all the same, ain't we?' Dad had heard this just once too often.

'Well, actually, no,' says Dad. 'We're not the same. I'm a teacher; you're a butcher. We're not the same, at all.'

You've never seen a face sour so quickly.

'Ere's your meat!' Slam.

Dad walked out the shop, chuckling. Maybe he had been a tad sharp with the poor butcher, but there's only so many times you can hear this kind of condescending crap, without (over)reacting. Our father instilled in us a clear sense that we were (a) West Indian, and (b) Black. Most of my friends were either West Indians, Indians, or Irish – who were Black like us. One night in Kenton, Dad woke us up at three o'clock in the morning. We looked at each other: who's done what now?

We followed him, sleepy-eyed, down to the living room where the grainy black-and-white television was on. It was February 25, 1964, the first Cassius Clay vs. Sonny Liston Heavyweight Championship Fight, and as usual BBC was showing it live.

'Boys, I woke you up, so you can witness history. Watch this fighter, Cassius Clay; one day he's going to be a great Black man.'

Never a truer word spoken. Another night he made us watch a BBC *Panorama* documentary on the Belsen concentration camp. We were horrified at the sight of thousands of emaciated corpses being bulldozed into mass graves. He told us: 'Never underestimate the capacity for man's inhumanity to man.'

One time in the US, Dad got some passport photographs taken. When he collected the prints, he complained because the photographer had made him look lighter than he was. The photographer was perplexed and said that's what his Black clients usually wanted: to look lighter. Well not this Black client.

In London during the sixties, thousands of West Indians worked 'on the buses': London Transport. The company even had recruiting offices in Jamaica and Barbados and offered subsidized fares to Britain. But this wasn't the case in all English cities. Bristol was home to a large West Indian community, centred around St Paul's. The Bristol Omnibus Company steadfastly refused to hire Blacks and made no bones about it. General Manager Ian Patey was quoted as saying: 'I understand that in London, coloured men have become arrogant and rude, after they have been employed for some months.' In April 1963, the West Indians of Bristol had had enough and boycotted the bus company. It wasn't easy to boycott the buses, but amazingly almost all the Black population and a good proportion of Whites maintained the boycott for months. The dispute gained national attention and even filtered into my ten-year-old consciousness. It was the first time I heard the term 'colour bar.' I thought it was some pub where Blacks weren't allowed!

In Hollywood of the sixties, Black people were portrayed as little more than stumbling, bumbling, big-lipped buffoons and 'Call Me Bwana,' starring Bob Hope was no different. Our father's Trinidadian friend worked as an extra on the movie, he told us he was doing a scene where he had to roll his eyes in that Black Sambo way, but every time he saw Bob Hope babbling in front him, he'd break out in laughter, as would Bob! It took them ten takes to nail the scene, and when I saw the movie, it was indeed funny. What wasn't funny was *Sammy Going South*, a 1963 film about some tousle-headed White kid travelling the length of Africa alone, hoodwinking the foolish natives. Because my name was Samuel, some kids thought they could then call me Sammy. Do *not* call me Sammy! Then there was the weekly TV series 'Til Death Us do Part,' with Alf Garnett regaling us with jokes about wogs and nignogs.

One of the problems with having a teacher for a father was that when you were on holiday, so was he. Dad would always have a list of holiday projects up his sleeve, to keep us busy. Every year something had to be done to that damned house: wallpapering, painting, moderations, or Dad's favourite: digging. He'd make flower beds but never get around to planting flowers. But we'd still have to turn over the sod, every sodding spring, for no apparent reason. His favourite gardening tool was the hoe, not the skinny little things they used in

England. Somehow he'd gotten a real West Indian hoe, a heavy blunt instrument that could batter the hardest earth. Sometimes he'd plant vegetables, but he wasn't really a gardener; he just liked to get his hands dirty.

And, of course, nothing in Darwin Samuel's house could be done by another man's hand. Oh no, we would do everything ourselves, under Dad's 'expert' direction. The bulb in the living room shorted out. Dad turned off the main fuse and stood on a chair, arms raised, re-wiring the light fitting. It was tough going. A few times he had to lower his arms and take a breather. Meantime, he's telling us how it's all done, how to connect the red wires versus the green ones, etc.

After half an hour of rewiring, Dad's done it.

'Okay Gerry – turn on the light!'

Flick – the light beams, Dad beams. See – that's how it's done! Then Gerry says:

'Dad, don't you need this?'

Dad looked down, to see Gerry holding the plastic cup that fits over the light fixture. The problem was Dad should have fitted on this piece *before* doing the re-wiring. Now he'd have to re-wire the whole damn thing again.

'Ahh, shittt!'

He yanked the light out of the ceiling, flung it to the ground, and stormed out the house in a steaming huff. We all fell about laughing. Gerry admitted that he had been holding the cup in his hand for a while, but thought he'd save it for the end. When Dad sheepishly returned an hour, later no doubt after a pint or two, Gerry had re-wired the light, and we were all quietly sitting there, grinning at nothing.

Dad decided to buy a garage. As the only house on the street with a car, it was only fitting that it should be housed properly, not out on the road. The company that sold the garage said they would assemble the prefabricated structure; so long as there was a concrete base, on which to place the garage. Dad contacted a local builder who said he could build us a concrete base for two hundred pounds. Two hundred pounds? Dad was outraged. He could build a concrete base for way less than that! So, we set about building a concrete base. Uh-oh.

Dad was in his technical element: drawing up plans, walking the perimeter, calculating how much sand, gravel and cement to buy, knocking little pegs into the ground attached with string. On Saturday morning, he assembled the construction team (us) and announced the plan.

'Boys, here's what we'll do. First, we'll build a retaining wall around the perimeter of the garage. Then we'll call the Redi-Mix truck, and they'll fill it in with concrete. QED: Quite Easily Done!'

'Yes, Dad.' (Gerry)

'Yes, Daddy.' (Bri-Bri)

'Whatever you say, Dad.' (Tommy)

Dad's retaining wall was to be one foot high, but before you build up, we were told, you've first got to dig down. So, we dug down: a trench, all the way around the perimeter of the garage; trying to keep it in line with the string, which kept getting trod on and quickly went wonky. When we finally finished digging the trench, we then set about building the retaining wall. For which we needed bricks. Problem: we didn't have bricks.

Dad looks around: bricks, bricks…? In the back garden was a disused coal shed. After we'd installed central heating the previous year (again first on the street), we had no more use for a coal shed, so we used it to store garden tools. But now that we were building a garage, we'd no longer need the tool shed, so we got the sledgehammer and set about breaking down the shed. There was only one catch: break down the shed, but don't break the bricks. How can you break down a shed without breaking bricks? Just do it.

Finally, we got the blasted shed dismantled, brick by unbroken brick, now it was time to build the retaining wall. For an entire weekend, the four of us toiled away on that meandering wall, first this way; then that. By Sunday night, the wall wasn't anywhere near finished, there was hardly a straight line to it, and we had run out of unbroken bricks. Dad was defeated. He called the builder the next morning: 'I give up, come.'

Which they did, the very next day. The foreman burst out laughing when he saw Dad's wonky wall.

'Which bleedin' idiot built that thing?'

Dad didn't know where to put his face. We guffawed! The first thing the real builders did was knock down Dad's wall with sledgehammers, none too pleased at the extra work. They then built a simple wooden enclosure, filled it in with Redi-Mix, and after the concrete dried the next day, they came back and removed the woodwork – QED!

Since Auntie Phyllis left in 1962, there had been several women in and out of Dad's life, with varying degrees of temporariness. Our father had evidently decided that he didn't need any female help in bringing up his sons; he'd do it on his own. Many times, we wished he wouldn't – like in the food department. Our father's cooking was truly, spectacularly, awful. He could destroy a boiled egg, so imagine what he could do with dinner. But it was a case of eat or get beat. He'd take off his belt, put it over the back of his chair, and announce with mock seriousness: 'Dinner … is served.' But he had no choice: with three hungry gannets to feed and not much money to feed them with, he couldn't afford the luxury of us liking it – just eat it.

Dinner could consist of fried eggs, bacon, baked beans, black pudding, and lots of bread. Our father's idea of frying an egg would be to drop it in the frying pan for ten seconds, then pour it onto your plate with all that half-cooked clear stuff around the yolk – yuck. Worse yet, in the winter our flat was so cold that the fat on your plate would coagulate in the blink of an eye. But you still had to eat it. Every. Last. Crumb.

Song for My Father

One day in Arkwright Road, Dad served up dinner of fried eggs and bacon, and I made the fatal mistake of not eating it straight away. Tom and Gerry had the right approach: wolf it down quickly. Within a minute, the mess on my plate had turned into this cold, coagulated pile of gook. So, there I was, faffing around and pretending to eat. You think Dad was fooled? Not in the least. He got up from the table and announced:

'I'm going next door to watch the news. When I come back, that plate had better be empty. Understood?'

'Sniff ... Yes, Daddy.'

Tom and Gerry grinned behind Dad's back, flicking their fingers in the signal understood by every Caribbean kid: licks like peas! The three of them trooped out, leaving me alone with this vision of culinary hell on the plate in front of me. I poked at it, prodded it, but it still didn't look any better. I forced a small piece into my mouth – and gagged. I looked around the room ... aha! On the mantelpiece was an empty vase. I don't know why we had a vase because we never had any flowers, but there it was – deliciously, beautifully, empty.

I tiptoed over to the mantelpiece, lifted the vase, and gingerly scraped the remains of my plate into its depths. I wiped the edges of my plate and even smeared a bit of fat around my mouth for effect. Five minutes later, Dad comes marching in, eagerly followed by Tom and Gerry. To be stunned by the sight of me sitting there, empty plate in front of me, making the appropriate face as though I'd just eaten something gross. Tom and Gerry slunk off disappointed, no licks tonight. I happily did the dishes, feeling immensely pleased with myself. The plan was that later that night I would go back and retrieve the bacon and eggs from the vase and dispose of them properly. Which of course, I promptly forgot all about.

Fast forward six months: it's Saturday morning, and Dad's corralled us for the annual spring cleaning. In the middle of the clean-up, Dad picks up the vase, looks inside it and says:

'What the hell is this?'

My sphincter tightened, it all came back to me in a rush: the bacon and eggs! I knew what was about to happen: Dad would look inside the vase, see the six-month old bacon and eggs, and would surely remember that night when I had miraculously eaten up my dinner. And if he didn't remember, Tom or Gerry would be sure to remind him. But when he looked inside the vase all he saw was ... fungus!

'Allayu – come here!'

By the tone of his voice, we'd know when we were in trouble, but whom? And for what? The three of us would engage in a shoving match: You go first! No, you go! As usual, it ended up with me getting shoved into the room first. Dad points to the fungus-filled vase.

'Who did this?'

'Not me, Dad!'

'Not me, Dad!'

'Not me, Daddy!'

He looked skyward, resorting to his standard comeback in stalemates like this:

'So, I suppose Prince Charles came in here and did this?'

Our father's signature dish would change every few months, depending on his girlfriend du jour. One girlfriend taught him a cheap and nutritious concoction called cornflour cake. He'd bake barrelfuls of the stuff, even Gerry could make it which was very handy when Dad was out, and we were hungry. When we went on school outings, I'd be jealous of the neat lunch boxes my friends' mothers would pack for them, with the crusts cut off the sandwiches and an apple tucked into the corner. But you know what? After they'd eaten all their cute little sandwiches, what they would end up begging me for? You got it: my big hunk of cornflour cake! Another girlfriend, Scandinavian this time, taught him some cheese fondue thing, and we gorged on that for a few months.

One time and I swear this is true, Dad fed us dog food. Or maybe cat, but definitely of the pet variety. We only discovered the fact after we'd eaten it, when Gerry saw the tin in the bin. Dad swore he didn't know it was dog food nor, evidently, that he'd picked it up in the pet food section of the supermarket. He'd fried up with onions and pepper and served it with rice and you know what? It wasn't half bad!

Our father was the product of his time, a time when all West Indian parents took the Biblical dictum 'spare the rod and spoil the child' very seriously. In that respect, he wasn't as bad as many West Indian parents, who went way over the top in flogging their children. Sadly, many still do. At least Dad never named his belt. But when he took off that belt – watch out! He'd make you go and get it from his bedroom, and God help you if you came back and said you couldn't find it. Oh, lord, how that belt stung. You'd literally bounce off the walls trying to dodge the next incoming blow. All of us got licks, but Tom got more than most. Mind you, he did his best to earn every beating he got! One morning in Camplin Road, I got a beating for something or other. I came downstairs in tears to be met by Pete Osborne, Tom's friend, laughing.

'Fuck off!' I said to him. Dad comes storming downstairs.

'*What* did you just say?' And promptly hauled me upstairs for another one! I remember being puzzled by my English peers, who'd be afraid of getting a telling off from their mum. What's a telling off, does it hurt? When they told me, it was just words, I was dismissive: wimps. Our father was a big man, not tall but stocky. He was an avid sportsman: in college he excelled in cricket, javelin, and the shot-put. As he got older, his muscle turned to bulk. One day, we were giving him a ribbing about his growing belly or as he called it his protuberance, and I patted it and came up the perfect geographical pun:

'Bag-Dad!'

The tonic that lifted every West Indian head with pride, at home but especially in Babylon, was cricket lovely cricket. Even as kids barely knowing the rules, we loved cricket. Not so much for the sporting contest but for the pleasure of sticking it to the English. In June 1963, our father took us to Lords Cricket Ground, just down the road from where we lived in Arkwright Road. After queueing up for what seemed like half a day, we entered the sacred home of cricket. No matter how much we may have liked cricket, a whole day of it for three hyperactive boys was a bit of a stretch. The abiding memory I have of that day is watching the great West Indian batsman Rohan Kanhai, down on one knee, as he spanked yet another ball to the boundary. Cricket may not have had the fan following of football, but it sure did feel sweet when we beat England.

Every summer Dad would play at the Kenton Cricket Club, which of course meant that the three of us would be dragged along, his reluctant cheering section. We'd be bored witless and usually find some diversion, inevitably missing Dad's rare moment of glory. The best part of the day was afternoon tea when we'd scarf the cucumber sandwiches and cakes from the players' pavilion.

In his early teens, Tom also started to play cricket and would occasionally partner with Dad on the pitch. Sharing the sporting field with your son should be a great occasion for a bit of father-son bonding, yes? No. On one such day, the team was practising in the nets, and Tom squared up to bowl to his father. Tom bowls the first ball: clean bowled! Tom grinned, Dad grinned, everyone cheered. Well done youngster – now do it again! Dad padded up to face Tom again. Second ball: clean bowled! Tom erupts, everyone erupts – Dad scowls. Everyone shouts, 'Do it again, son, make it a hat-trick!' Now everyone is taking a keen interest.

Third ball: clean bowled!!

The place goes wild; everyone rushes over to Tom to congratulate him. Everyone except Dad. What a wonderful occasion it would have been, for our father to say, 'well done son, I'm proud of you.' But did he? Of course not. He knocked down his stumps and stormed off in a huff, leaving Tom standing there – with the biggest grin you ever saw!

One of my most vivid memories of my father was his hair: thick, black, and curly. His mother was part Carib Indian, so Darwin's hair wasn't as kinky as most black men's. As a boy in Grenada, he had the nickname 'Dougla': West Indian slang for half-black, half-Indian. He brushed his hair straight back and kept it full-bodied and well-oiled, and he wore an afro, before afros were invented. He loved it when one of us would brush his hair, just as much as we loved brushing it. We were a tactile bunch, all four of us crowded onto his bed, me squirming under his armpit, while he regaled us with stories. He'd lie me on his chest and tap out a particular pattern with his big hands on my back, a percussive rhythm I still cherish. I also remember my father's smell: manly and musky.

Once in Chicago, Dad was giving Gerry a driving lesson in the Beetle when the brakes failed. The car ploughed through a snowbank and into a lamp post. Dad's head shattered the windscreen and for days he was combing bits of glass out of his hair. The doctor said his thick hair acted as a crash helmet, probably saving his life!

8. Three Brothers Bonding

John Wayne Gets the Wrong Hombre:

It was one of those long summer days, when the grown-ups were at work and we kids had the freedom of the house. We were in Pete Osborne's back garden, three doors down from us, a bunch of bored boys looking for trouble. Which was supplied by Tom who came charging in on his bike, grinning from ear to ear.

'Wait 'til you see what I've got!' He announced as he leapt from his bike, sending it clattering into a tangle of others. He reached into his pocket and furtively withdrew his latest acquisition: an air pistol! He explained how he'd swapped it with a school mate for a set of Campagnolo gears and a penknife. We gaped in wonder as Tom cocked it and reached for a bag of lead slugs. Gerry walked down to the end of the garden to put some cans on a wall for target practice. Then Tom said the fateful words:

'Watch me do a John Wayne!'

He swivelled round, gun in hand. Crack! A shot rang out. Gerry didn't immediately realize he'd been shot. He felt a slight tug on his hand, but it was only when he saw the blood oozing from the hole in his hand that the awful truth sank in.

'You bastard, you shot me!'

Amazingly, Gerry felt no pain. What he did feel was the lead slug, lodged just underneath the skin on his right hand, three inches away from the entry wound. Shit, this was serious. Tom knew he was in huge trouble; Dad would kill him, tear him limb from limb and bury his body: nothing less. Tom suggested that as the bullet lay just underneath the skin, couldn't he just use a razor blade and ...? Not surprisingly Gerry vetoed that idea. At which point everyone else in that back garden decided that now would be a good time to get the hell out of there!

Leaving Gerry standing alone, with a bullet in his hand. Which was now beginning to hurt, really hurt. So, he walked down the road to Dr Thompson's surgery on Kenton Road, our family doctor. Who took one look at Gerry's hand and decided he wasn't about to treat a bullet wound and sent him straight to Edgware General Hospital. It wasn't long before Dad got wind of it and the whole story came out, but it was one of those rare occasions when he flummoxed us by not exploding. Tom didn't even get a licking! Gerry eventually had to have two operations to remove the slug, leaving a big L-shaped scar on the back of his hand. The air pistol eventually fell into my eager little hands and got me into no end of trouble.

But that's another story ...

The three of us spent an awful lot of time with just each other for company, horsing around the flat or roaming the streets of London while our father was out and about. We were the original latchkey kids, almost every evening Dad went out, either to night school or selling *World Book Encyclopaedias* door to door. He specialized in West Indian communities like Kilburn and West Hampstead, where he naturally had a good rapport. All he needed was a foot in the door, literally. Occasionally, he'd take us along with him: willing props in his sales banter.

'Go ahead,' he'd challenge his intended victim. 'This is my son. He loves World Book, ask him to name the capital city of any country in the world – any country!'

Invariably, they would name an island in the West Indies and that was never a problem. Sold! Because of his sales prowess, Dad won a free set of World Books, a great help in the homework department. The concept of a babysitter was anathema to our father. Gerry babysat Tom; Tom sat on me. All our lives the three of us have remained remarkably close, a legacy from our formative days in the crucible.

The best month of the year was August, which meant two things: no school – and scrumping. In London's suburbs, every back garden has at least a couple of apple trees and every summer we would mercilessly plunder our neighbourhood. We felt it was our God-given right to eat as many apples as we could stuff into our capacious bellies – and then some. We wouldn't wait for the trees to ripen; we'd eat them green sprinkled with salt – bellyfuls!

We'd mark out gardens with the tastiest trees, remembering them for next season. Most back gardens were connected by an alleyway – perfect getaways. But you needed to be quick on your feet, you'd be up a tree, and some irate householder would come charging down the garden – and god help you if he caught hold of you. Grown-ups in those days thought nothing of giving you a hiding if you needed it, regardless of whether they knew you or not. Nowadays, they'd get arrested for abuse of snowflakes!

November meant Guy Fawkes and fireworks. Not any fireworks: bangers or firecrackers. Forget all the other twirly stuff. All that mattered were bangers. You could do amazing things with bangers: throw them at your mates or better yet girls, drop them through letterboxes and run away. A thrupenny banger was a mini-bomb. You didn't want that thing going off in your hand. The bravest trick required a banger, a milk bottle and a brick: (1) place lit banger in milk bottle; (2) quickly balance brick on bottle; (3) run!

Our father was a great believer in quality clothing; he may not have had much money, but we shopped at Selfridges. Well, some of us did. Being the youngest, most of my 'new' clothes were hand-me-downs from Tom or Gerry. Getting clothes from Gerry wasn't too

Two princelings and the hand-me-down kid

bad, but Tom! Dad would hand me some shapeless rag that Tom had abused for years, with scuffed elbows, torn pockets and a thousand stain marks down the front. Dad would look at it guiltily and say, it's not that bad. What part of that filthy rag could be described as not bad? While Tom giggled behind Dad's back: enjoy my rag, Prooglums!

One of the delights I was spared was attending the same school that Dad taught in; Tom and Gerry endured that torture for years. Dad would shout at Tom in class:

'Samuel! Have you done your homework?'

'No, Dad – I mean Sir!'

I don't think it was a picnic for Dad either. I remember overhearing (i.e., eavesdropping) Dad saying to one of his friends:

'So, there I was in the staff room at lunchtime, casually looking down at the boys in the playground. Then I noticed one boy in particular, roughhousing, wrestling on the ground, playing football, using his jacket as a goalpost. And I think: wait a minute, isn't that Tommy? And the brand-new jacket I just bought him?'

Tom hates that story. Among the 'I Survived St George's' Facebook group, Mr Samuel gets a passing grade:

> **Paul Murphy:** *He was my favourite teacher, an absolutely fantastic guy. I never really settled at St. George's, my only consolation I met a wonderful teacher who took me under his wing his name was Mr Samuel, I've never forgotten this wonderful man.*

> **Brian Carroll:** *I remember your dad well as our metal work teacher. A nice fella and you couldn't say that about a lot of the male teachers at the time 64-69.*

> **Joe Miller:** *Mr. Roddy Beare told your dad about Tommy not having his PE kit and that he would have to 'make a point.' Your dad said that boy has more than enough kit, you go ahead and make your point! Roddy was good with the leather end of the rope.*

> **Martin McGrath:** *Along with Mike Farnan, Mr Samuel was the best teacher I had.*

> **Eric Brown:** *My metalwork teacher. I was in Tommy's class. Dad gave him a hard time. He could swing a bat in the nets. I couldn't bowl to him!*

The main objective of Britain's secondary educational system in the sixties was to keep children occupied from 8:00 a.m. to 4:00 p.m. – and try to knock some learning into their thick skulls in the process. At St Thomas's RC School, the nuns walked around with a rubber strap ingeniously concealed in the folds of their habit, ready to dole out instant behaviour modification therapy for even the slightest infraction. Two, four, or six of the best – from straps made by the Dunlop Rubber Company. Whether for the good of our souls or to give her strength, the Headmistress Mother Bon Secours aka 'Bongo' would invoke heavenly inspiration at the precise point of impact: 'Jesus *Christ* and all the Saints! God *bless* your wretched soul!' Then she'd return the strap to its hidey-hole and walk on serenely, with a prayer in her heart and a smile on her face. She'd call out to me:

'Hey you, Blackie! Come here!'

Song for My Father

The most feared teacher at Tom's school was Mr Connelly, a hulking angry sadist who took out his life's many frustrations on the children in his charge. In his youth, he had been an aspiring rugby player until injury cut short his career. His talent for sport was replaced by a passion for anger. Tom would regale us with tales of what a hard bastard Connelly was and how 'He doesn't like me.' Mind you that was Tom's standard response to getting in trouble at school – which was often. Then to my horror, Connelly got transferred to my school, and I soon learned that you didn't cross Connelly lightly – and that sometimes you didn't even have to cross him, to cross him.

Connelly was on playground duty at lunchtime. At the end of the lunch hour, he blew his whistle, meaning get into lines. Hundreds of boys abandoned their games of football, cricket, or British bulldog, gathered up their jackets and slowly headed for their form lines. Too slowly.

Connelly blew the whistle again, meaning freeze! He barks out:

'All of you not in lines, come over here!'

About fifty boys, me included, shuffled across to form a new line. Connelly was furious, mumbling to himself:

'I'm tired a tellin' yeh, when I blow the whistle, you move! Well, you gonna learn today, that's fer feckin' sure.'

Most of the boys trooped off to their classes while we miscreants followed Connelly to the staff room. We were abuzz with curiosity: what's he gonna do? He can't strap *all* of us, can he? But that's exactly what he did. Connelly came out with his leather strap and gave us each six of the best. All fifty of us, three hundred strokes in total, and the last was delivered with exactly the same venom as the first, if not more.

After six of Connelly's lashes, you were in agony; I couldn't hold a pen all afternoon. Our respective form teachers were bemused when we finally got back to class, trying but not always succeeding in holding back the tears: what's gotten into Connelly this time?

That evening at dinner I still couldn't hold my knife and fork and foolishly told Dad what happened. He was livid and marched up to the school the next morning, to complain to the headmaster. As a teacher himself, he castigated the school for its shocking overuse of the strap. Not that it did any good – probably the opposite.

Then there was Mad Miss Duffy, history teacher and certified lunatic. One day in second form, class clown and hard-nut John 'Polly' Parrot was giving Miss Duffy his usual lip. She decided to give him the strap. He held out his hands and she flailed away, but all six of her blows were about as painful as a gnat on an elephant. Feeble Miss Duffy hadn't the strength to seriously hurt strap-happy Polly Parrot who just stood there, sneering. This enraged Duffy, who decided to give him six more.

'Whoa,' says Polly. 'You can't give me six more, it's against the law, innit?' Duffy flew into a rage.

'Put-your-hand-out .... NOW!'

Again Parrot refused. Duffy drew back the strap and THWACK! Slapped him hard, flush across his face, sending him tumbling backwards over a desk. She climbed over the desk, flailing away and screaming at the top of her lungs.

'Bundle!' Someone shouted the universal signal for a fight, and the whole classroom gathered around, watching Miss Duffy go mad and Polly screaming:

'Help! Help! Get this fuckin' madwoman offa me!'

Teachers from nearby classrooms came rushing in, closely followed by a gaggle of shouting shoving boys, craning their necks to get the best view: what's going on? The teachers finally managed to subdue Miss Duffy, panting and screaming incoherently, with flecks of yucky white stuff at the corners of her mouth. The ambulance took her away. She spent one term in Shenley Mental Hospital and came back: cured. Yeah right.

Song for My Father

School sports was a joke. The PE teacher would fling a football onto a soggy field and tell thirty-plus boys to go and play. Then he'd skive off to the bicycle sheds for a fag. I hated football, or any contact sport for that matter, because that's exactly what it meant: lots of contact. I was always the youngest and smallest in class, two fatal flaws in any schoolboy's life. One quirky Irish teacher decided to introduce us to Gaelic football; what a disaster! Let's give two dozen testosterone-fuelled teenagers a bunch of hard sticks and a harder ball, with zero padding or protection and see what happens. Carnage.

I liked cricket and being the West Indian kid was supposed to be good at it, but again, it's not much fun without the proper gear. Then there was cross-country running, when the sports master would conceal himself at devious corners to make sure no one took short cuts. And that was the extent of my sporting education, in hindsight it's amazing how I turned out to be the excellent sportsman I am today!

Then there were the (in)famous English school lunches or dinners as they called them. The menu never varied: meat, two overboiled vegetables, and lumpy mash – fish on Fridays. Why anyone would want to eat Brussels sprouts is beyond me. I'd try and hide them under my knife and fork but would invariably get sent back to finish them off. You couldn't leave anything but the barest scraps on your plate. The best part was pudding, apple crumble, and custard: yum.

One of the high points of boy life was Boy Scouts. What wasn't there to love? Cool uniforms, bonding with your buddies, sleeping in tents, playing with knives, lighting fires – boy heaven! At one point, three of the four patrol leaders in the Tenth Kenton Scout Troop were the Samuel brothers. I don't know who was happiest when we went away on camp: Dad or us. We went on Whitsun, Easter and Summer camps to Stanmore, Gilwell Park, and other campsites around London. The Scoutmaster was toothless old Skip Cullinane, who drove an old Bedford truck, still in its original army camouflage.

At camp Tom was my chief protector against the bullying of his mates. Only he could beat up his little brother – no one else.

At Gilwell Park, the bomb-hole was an old crater that had been filled in with water and used for swimming and canoeing. Correction, not water: mud. Tom's friend Lucien Pradere was trying to take away a canoe that was rightfully mine, and in the ensuing shoving match there could be only one loser: me. Up steps Tom.

'Oi, don't mess with my little brother. I won't tell you again.'

'Oh, yeah? Otherwise, what?'

'Otherwise: this.'

Tom executed the most picture-perfect punch in the world. Muhammad Ali would have written a poem about it. The right hook landed flush on Lucien's left chin, hard and unhindered, but even better than the punch was what followed. Lucien was standing on the edge of the bomb-hole, and he did the most graceful backward somersault imaginable, landing flat on his face in the mud: ker-splatt!!! The whole place erupted. Tom blushed; I beamed. Not for the first and certainly not the last time, I gushed: *thanks*, Tom!

Growing up in London in the sixties, there was no shortage of perverts. You'd find them in the shallow end of Finchley Road Baths,

offering to teach boys how to 'swim.' Even back then we knew: stay far. It was a Sunday night and I was thirteen, taking the last train home to Kingsbury from the Collins' house in Hampstead. It was summer holidays, so we were allowed out fairly late. At Neasden Station, a man gets on. I barely noticed him until he sat down directly opposite me. My radar beeped: why?

Clackety-clack, the train rolls on. The man is looking straight ahead – at me. I'm nervous as a cat, reading the ads, looking out the windows, anywhere except making eye contact with him. After a while, I run out of places to look, and I look ahead. To see him smiling at me, and stroking this massive, erect penis!

I jumped up and bolted down the carriage, not looking back. I left my bag on the seat, but damned if I was going back for it! I yanked open the interconnecting door between the carriages and stepped into the gap. The howl of the wind and clackety-clack of the wheels was deafening, but in my terrified state I didn't hear a thing. I jumped into the second carriage and slammed the door behind me.

About ten passengers were shocked to see this wild-eyed kid come running through the door, but even more shocked to see me run all the way down the length of the carriage and repeat the manoeuvre. I didn't stop until I'd reached the very last carriage, by which the train was pulling into Kingsbury Station. I was so terrified of seeing the man again that I climbed up the embankment and jumped over a fence into someone's back garden, skirted a barking dog, and ran all the way home, heart pounding. But that was nothing, compared to my next close encounter with a pervert.

Scout meetings were held in St Bernadette's Primary School, a ten-minute walk from our house. One evening after the scout meeting ended, I was heading out of the school gates when a car pulled up. A middle-aged man leans out the window.

'Excuse me, sonny. I'm here to pick up my son, his name is (whatever). It's his first night, have you seen him?'

There were quite a few newbies that night, and the name didn't ring a bell, so I told him his son must have been in another patrol, not mine.

'Okay, then, well he must have left already.' He started to turn the car around 'I'm heading down the road ... would you like a lift?'

'Sure.' I said and opened the passenger door. As I was about to jump into the front seat, Tom walks up.

'Brian, what the fuck are you doing?'

He yanked me by my left arm, hard. Then it dawned on me: what *am* I doing? I had one foot inside the door and as I looked across to the driver my heart leapt. To this day, I'll never forget that face, those eyes. I can't describe it, the only word I can use is ... evil. With the car already moving, Tom pulled me out and I tumbled onto the pavement. The driver gunned the engine, and the car sped off down Clifton Road, tyres squealing. I stood there, shaking. I had been this close! I got a real cussing from Tom: what kind of fucking idiot are you?

'Please,' I begged him. 'Don't tell Dad!'

But that's exactly what he did, the minute we got home. To his credit, Tom said he was telling Dad to let me know how serious this was. That pervert knew exactly what he was doing, and God knows what horrors he had in store for me. For a few days after that, Tom could do no wrong in Dad's eyes. Just a few.

Thanks, Tom!

But big brother Tom wasn't always made of such heroic stuff, trust me. He could also be an absolute terror, inventing new and ingenious ways of torturing me, like the dead-leg, the semi-suffocation, and his favourite: the nose-pull. Because Tom and Gerry were only eleven months apart, they rarely got into an all-out scrap and when they did, Gerry always prevailed. But the physical difference between Tom and I was three-plus years: a fatal disadvantage for a pesky little brother.

Song for My Father

Have you ever seen male goats on National Geographic, rearing up and head-butting each other, over and over for no apparent reason? They're probably brothers. Tom and I would fight for every reason imaginable – or more likely none at all. Of course, these weren't real fights, they were play-play fights. Well on Tom's part they were play-play. I was deadly serious! One time we were fighting, and I was so mad that Tom eventually had to run away, to stop himself from beating me anymore! I was like a knock-down doll: the more he hit me, the more I bounced back. Tom said he gained new respect for me on that day and even eased up on me a bit. Just a bit.

'Let's play slaps!' Gerry would suggest. Oh, shit. Because this wasn't a suggestion. It was an order; an order that was sure to end in pain – mine. Actually, slaps weren't so bad; it was when he'd 'suggest' we up the ante and play knuckles instead – major pain. Being the eldest Gerry was also strongest and quickest, so he'd get in a dozen hard raps across your knuckles before you could get off one. By the time you finally cried off, the top of your right hand would be red and swollen.

A bicycle is an inalienable right of boyhood. Not long after we'd arrived in England, Dad bought Gerry a bike from the second-hand shop. It was way too big for Gerry, so we all learned to ride standing up on the pedals with our legs through the frame because we were too short to sit in the saddle. At Fitzjohn's Primary, I entered a competition where you had to identify ten things wrong with a bicycle in a picture. It was easy, and months later I heard that I had won. I was over the moon, especially when I learned what the prize was: a guinea! The undreamt-of fortune, of one pound plus one precious shilling!

On the appointed day, we all walked the hundred yards down Arkwright Road to the Hampstead Public Library for the prize giving. I was ecstatic, lording it over Tommy and Gerry: 'I won a gui-nea! I won a gui-nea!' When my turn came, I proudly walked onstage, beaming. The man announces my name and hands me my one guinea – Premium Bond. Huh? What's that? Where's my guinea?

'It's a form of savings, you can open an account with it.'

Savings? Account? I don't want no damn account; I want my guinea! Just then: whip! Dad relieves me of said Premium bloody Bond. 'I'll take care of that for you.' And that was the last I ever saw of my guinea. Oh, did Tom and Gerry laugh!

After a while we started 'acquiring' bikes on our own. No, not stealing them! We'd make them up from discarded bits and pieces we'd trade with friends or scavenge at the Welsh Harp dump. It's amazing the things you'd find at the dump: entire bikes that just needed some tarting up. We could do anything on bikes, strip and rebuild them in a day. Gerry was the best. He had a beautiful grey ten-speed racing bike with Campagnolo gears and Wymann centre-pull brakes, which he eventually bequeathed to me – thanks G.

One of Dad's girlfriends du jour, no doubt trying to worm her way into his affections, bought me a bicycle for my birthday – a brand new bicycle! Tom and Gerry were sick with envy, which turned to hilarity the moment they saw the thing. It was one of those old, sit-up-and-beg bicycles with upright handlebars, sprung saddle, three-speed Sturmey-Archer gears, and even a basket at the front! I was aghast. I couldn't ride that thing to school; they'd laugh me to scorn! Tom and Gerry fell about themselves: happy birthday, Prooglums!

You, stupid woman. Why didn't you just *take me with you*! It was a mystery where she even found the thing. They'd stopped making bikes like that decades ago. The salesman must have been ecstatic to offload the last of his old stock: 'Oh, yes madam. He'll love it. It's all the rage among teenage boys.' Fortunately, we soon left for the US, and I managed to sell the blunderbuss for a pittance.

You needed a bike to have a paper round, which we all did the day after we reached the magical age of thirteen. The pay was fifteen shillings a week, from which Dad deducted five shillings as a 'voluntary contribution.' But we didn't mind; that still left the undreamt-of amount of ten bob spending money for the week, which could buy a treasure trove of sweets, cakes, and comics.

In addition to paper rounds, over the years I worked at Woolworth's, a flower shop, transformer factory (do you have any idea how *heavy* transformers are?), fishmonger's (the smell was overpowering, I lasted half a day), greengrocer, the milkman, and lastly at Sainsbury's. Tom and Gerry worked at Sainsbury's Kingsbury, and I was at the Kenton branch. I was getting along fine until we got a new manager. Mr Conlon had been manager at Kingsbury, where Tom and Gerry worked. When he was introduced to the staff, he repeats my name.

'Samuel, are you Tom Samuel's brother?'

'Er ... yes.'

'Right, well, let me tell you this, laddie: I'm onto you. I'll be watching you like a hawk, you hear me? And from now on, you're off the cash registers!'

Oh, *thanks*, Tom!

The air pistol that Tom shot Gerry with eventually found its way into my eager little hands. I'm not sure if air pistols were legal but as we had found out, they were certainly dangerous. One night when Dad was out, my friend Kevin Corrigan and I retrieved the air pistol from its hiding place in the attic and decided to have some fun. Directly opposite our house on Camplin Road lived the Maynards. We hated the Maynards; it was a family feud that had started on the very first day we moved into Camplin Road. The cold war had simmered on a slow boil for years until that night, when I decided to heat it up a notch. I loaded the air pistol, stuck it through the letterbox, made sure no one was walking along the road, took aim ... and fired.

Pang! The slug hit the Maynard's front letterbox with a loud clang – great shot! Miserable Mr Maynard opened the front door and looked around – whassat? Kevin Corrigan and I peeped through our letterbox and collapsed laughing. Five minutes later, we decided to do it again. This time I let Kevin take the shot.

Pang, another direct hit! Once again Mr Maynard opens his front door, once again Kevin and I collapse laughing. Then after about two minutes …

Bang-bang-bang!

'Open up! I know you're in there! I saw you fire that gun through the letterbox. If you don't open this door right *now*, I'm calling the police!'

Shit-shit-shit! I turn to Corrigan in desperation: what're we gonna do? I dunno he whispers. It's your house! Slowly, I pushed open the letterbox, to be met by a pair of angry eyes.

'Hand over that gun – now!'

Not wanting my prized possession to fall into the hands of Maynard's idiot son Paul, I removed the firing pin, sheepishly opened the door and handed over the gun.

'I'll see you later, when your father comes home!'

As soon as Maynard stalked back across the road, Kevin Corrigan, bastard, decides to piss off home!

'I'm not waiting around for *your* Dad!' Oh, thanks a bunch!

An hour later, Dad duly arrives home. He hadn't even entered the front door when Maynard pounced, waving the air pistol, indignation steaming out of his ears.

'Look what your son did … dangerous weapon … could have killed somebody … blah-blah-blah!'

Dad fumed, profusely apologized, and promised to deal with the matter 'firmly,' then closed the door on our still ranting neighbour. Strangely enough, he wasn't so mad at me for shooting up the Maynards' house. He was mad at me for getting caught and making him have to grovel to Mr kiss-my-ass Maynard! I didn't even get a licking. I never got my gun back, though.

Song for My Father

I suppose our father felt obligated to look after his sons' religious upbringing – which is probably why he did such a godawful job of it. Or rather he let others do the godawful job for him. Apart from sending us to Catholic schools and church on Sundays, Dad never once said a word to us on the subject of God. I can only guess that he himself had given up on God some time before, and therefore felt no need to burden his sons with more than a passing acquaintance.

Sunday mornings were special for our father, a time when he could relax with his cup of Nescafe, read the *Observer* and *Times Educational Supplement*, and perhaps a telephone call with a lady friend. For which, he didn't need us pesky kids around. So church was a double coincident of wants: our religious upbringing fitted perfectly with his need for some me-time. He would make sure we were all scrubbed up and send us off to Mass, sit back, put a record on the gramophone, open the papers for an hour of his own 'peace on earth.'

We attended All Saints' Catholic Church on Kingsbury Road, where Father Brunning once threw Tom out for eating an ice cream. We hated church and would go walking around Kenton for an hour instead of attending Mass. Then we'd ask the departing worshippers what the sermon was all about, so we could report to Dad. One Sunday as we were supposed to be in church, Dad drives past us walking along the street. When we got home, all he said was: 'I tried.' And praise the Lord; no more church!

One day at St Thomas's RC School, Headmistress Mother Bon Secours alias Bongo enters the classroom.

'Which one a yous is having a vocation?'

Nobody spoke; nobody moved; nobody breathed. A vocation was every nun's wet dream, and every boy's worst nightmare: 'The Calling' to study for the priesthood. Each Catholic school had its quota, and Bongo was on a quota-filling mission.

She repeats, louder: 'I said: *which one a yous is having a vocation?*'

This wasn't good enough. She went walking down the aisle.

'Right then. You, you … and you. Blackie, come with me!'

That Blackie was me, so now I had a vocation, officially. The three of us unhappy vocationists had to suffer through extra Catechism and Latin classes, which ate into our playtime. No surprises then, that for the Samuel brothers, religion has been a non-factor all our lives.

A Clear Conversation:

Our father was never one to tackle a ticklish subject head on. Like the day in Arkwright Road, when he summoned all of us into the living room.

'Allayu, come here!'

We trundled into the living room: who's done what now?

'Yes, Dad.'

'Yes, Dad.'

'Yes, Daddy.'

He had us sit down on the couch while he took out one of those new-fangled 45-rpm records and placed it on the record player.

'Listen.' He puts the stylus onto the record. After a silly musical interlude this woman's scratchy voice comes across:

> *Hello there, boys and girls, today we are going to talk about something very important: the birds and the bees!* This tinny little voice went on to talk about, literally, birds and bees, flowers and trees, cats and dogs and then finally, your mummy and daddy. That's when I sat up. What's she got to do with this?

The record had scratches in it so every now and then Dad would have to jog the needle, skipping important bits. After about three minutes of this convoluted doublespeak the record came to an end. The only memorable phrase I took away from it was 'a teaspoonful of sperm.' What's sperm? Dad turned to us.

'Right boys, any questions?'

'No, Dad.'

'No, Dad.'

'No, Daddy.'

'Fine, off you go then. Glad we had that chat!' We all trooped out.

As soon as we got behind closed doors, I whispered to Tom:

'Tommy, what the hell was that all about?'

'Booming, you idiot!'

'What? You have to boom to have a baby?'

'Yes, idiot.'

Queen Elizabeth had recently given birth to Prince Andrew, and all of England was agog over the spare heir.

'Even the Queen?' I asked, incredulous.

Like almost everyone else in Britain at the time, our father was a staunch royalist. We would religiously tune into the BBC on Christmas Day for the Queen's Christmas Message, encouraging words of hope and upliftment, and then like everyone else forget all about them. In 1969, the BBC aired the first of its kind: a fly-on-the-wall documentary on the daily lives of the Royal Family.

In hindsight it was cringeworthy, watching uncomfortable royals seated around the table, dressed to the nines, and attempting to make small talk about corgis and horses. But we were still awed: 'Oh look, they've got our same red kettle from John Barnes!' Our father did voluntary work for the Royal Life Saving Society and would hobnob at official functions with the likes of the Queen Mother and Lord Mountbatten, often at Buckingham Palace.

The first television programme I ever saw was 'Danger Man,' starring Patrick McGoohan, subsequently a cult classic. It was at the house of a friend of Dad's not long after we'd arrived in England, but it was several years later before we got our own set. In those days, a television was a major piece of furniture: a big wooden cabinet encasing a small, grainy black-and-white screen. We were overjoyed when Dad brought a second-hand set home – finally!

Not that there was much to watch; television programming in the sixties wasn't exactly child friendly. Most of what we watched were boring grown-up programmes like Panorama and the satire TW3: That Was The Week That Was. It may have been way over our heads, but through osmosis some of it filtered through. Dad was ambivalent about television: he wanted it for himself but not for us. When he would go out in the evenings, he'd leave strict instructions:

> *I'm going out to see a man about a horse, be back soon. Do your homework. Read a book. Don't watch television!'*

To enforce his prohibition, Dad would remove one of the valves from the back of the television set (stay with me here, children, we're talking prehistoric tech) and hide it somewhere in the room. Of course, it wouldn't take long to find the valve, and off we'd go, knowing we'd have at least two hours of TV time before he came back. On Saturday nights, the BBC had a horror series, and the three of us would sit there in the darkened living room, scared shitless. Problem was the television would stay warm for about ten minutes after you turned it off, so we had to estimate what time Dad would return and turn it off in good time. Amazingly, we never got caught, not that he let on anyway.

A couple of times we'd come home to find the television gone.

'I've gotten rid of it. We've been watching too much lately.'

We knew the truth: he'd pawned it. For a while it would be torture, not being able to watch our favourite shows like 'Ready-Steady-Go' and 'Top of the Pops.' Our number one TV show was 'Bonanza,' a western about a single father bringing up three sons Adam, Hoss, and Little Joe Cartwright, all of whom bore (in our minds at any rate) a striking resemblance to … us!

Without television we'd turn to the radio and books, becoming avid followers of 'The Archers' and the 'Goon Show' plus BBC radio plays that would have all four of us glued around the Rediffusion, lost in our own worlds of imagination. Then one day we'd come home and lo and behold: the television's back. We'd almost be disappointed. Almost.

Song for My Father

London of the so-called Swinging sixties was a decade of two halves, and the first half wasn't swinging at all: stuffy, dull, and dour. Too late for the post-war optimism of the fifties, too early for the radical change that came later. In 1960, English people went to church on Sundays, came home to roast beef and Yorkshire pudding. Men wore ties and women knew their place. All of which was about to be torn asunder, starting in the summer of 1964.

England's middle classes were shocked out of their post-war comfort by an explosion of mass violence that became known as the Battle of Mods and Rockers. That whole summer saw running street fights between hundreds of marauding youths: mods dressed in parkas riding tricked-out Italian scooters, versus leather-clad rockers on café-racer motorbikes. Brighton, Margate, Bournemouth, and other sleepy seaside towns became deluged by screaming, drinking fighting opponents. Could this really be happening – in England?

This was the first time that baby boomers, now in their teens and early twenties, had made their appearance on the world stage. The old days of war and privation meant nothing to them, and musically they had little in common with their parents. Not only that, but teenagers also had money in their pockets. Post-war Britain was on an economic boom and they relished their new-found spending power. What the world didn't realize then was that we baby boomers were only just starting!

In 1964, an unknown Jamaican teenage girl called Millie Small released a hopeful single, 'My Boy Lollipop.' This bouncy ska number was aimed at the émigré Jamaican population in the UK, but unbelievably it caught on among the general population and in no time, it rose to number one on the UK charts. All of a sudden, English people heard about Jamaica, and us non-Jamaicans had to be constantly telling people: no, I'm not a Jamaican!

It was Saturday morning, and I woke up as usual around ten and made my way downstairs, to be met by a strange sight. Dad was in the living room and spread around him on the table and floor were what seemed like dozens of newspapers, all open. He had an expression on his face I'd never seen before: extreme sadness and pain, holding back the tears. I thought, oh God, who dead now? It was November 23, 1963, the day after JFK's assassination. I was ten years old and only had a vague idea who Kennedy was, but I knew his death made my father cry, and in a sense that was the beginning of my political education.

Two years later, on a freezing cold day in January 1965, our father hauled the three of us to the South Bank of the Thames to watch a massive coffin containing the body of Winston Churchill being loaded onto a Royal Navy barge on the other side of the river, for its short journey to the Tower of London. It was bitterly cold, but the three of us boys cheered with the rest of the crowd when sixteen RAF fighter jets zoomed overhead, flying in an arrowhead formation as the boat chugged off. Cool!

There were two kinds of people: Beatles fans and Stones fans, and never the twain shall meet. Despite the enormous musical and cultural impact that the Beatles went on to make, in their early days they were pretty standard pop fare: mop-topped Liverpool lads singing cheery tunes your parents sang along to: yeah-yeah-yeah. The Stones weren't like that; they had an edge to them. In the early days, I was a Stones fan; then I straddled the line. But it was always close; I loved them both.

The first rock song that resonated with me was the Stones' '(I Can't Get No) Satisfaction.' For the entire summer of 1965, this catchy riff bombarded the airwaves of Britain, instantly connecting with a generation of unsatisfied youth. Those were the early days of pirate radio, listening on your transistor radio to the scratchy sounds of Radio Caroline, broadcast from a ship anchored in the North Sea. That summer I worked for two weeks at the annual fair put on by a travelling troupe of Gypsies on Kingsbury Common.

Song for My Father

I worked on the coconut shy, picking up balls and hawking for punters when things got slack. At the end of the first week, I asked for my pay, but the boss told me he could only pay me for both weeks together, at the end of the second week. I wasn't happy but okay. At the end of the second week, he said he would pay me the next day, Sunday, after the troupe had done the final reckoning. I went back on Sunday to be met by you guessed it: an empty field. For the rest of that summer, 'Satisfaction' had a bitter edge to it!

9. *Our American Dream*

By 1966, we'd been living in England for six years, and our father's wanderlust was beginning to grow again. In this respect, Darwin was certainly consistent: ever since he'd left home as a nineteen-year-old for wartime England, he never stopped moving. The move we were about to make would be his sixth country in twenty-four. He had won a fellowship from the Fulbright Teacher Exchange Program, to teach at an American high school in Illinois for the 1966/67 academic year. But there were three little problems in the way of this grand plan: us. It would have been a financial strain for all four of us to go to the US, especially as he would still be earning his paltry English salary while there. He applied to a boarding school, St Augustine's College in Ramsgate, begging them to take all three of his boys for a year – on full scholarships of course.

In his application letter, our father laid it on thick:

> *All three of my boys have been emotionally scarred by the departure of their mother: Gerry, the eldest, has become distant and aloof from me; Tommy the middle boy, is headstrong and rebellious; while Brian, the youngest, clings to me overmuch.*

Said it all.

Unfortunately for our father, his sons weren't too enthused at the idea of being parked in some toffee-nosed boarding school while he

Ramsgate 1966: Not happy

swanned off to America to have a ball. So, we deftly heaved a spanner into his carefully laid plans. When the headmaster interviewed us boys – without Dad present – we quietly confessed that, actually, we didn't really want to go to his school, nice as it was. We'd much rather go to America with our father. Application: denied!

And thus, in August 1966, all four Samuels boarded the Cunard liner *RMS Sylvania* for a week-long passage from Southampton to New York City. Thankfully, none of us got chicken pox this time, and we had a ball on the boat. On the second day just after lunch, a seasick passenger came running up the stairs and burst through the doors, heading for the ship's railing. An old sailor shouted.

'N-o-o-o!'

Too late: the passenger hurled the contents of his stomach over the side, where the wind took it in a graceful arc – straight into the faces of passengers further down the railing! The old salt couldn't resist a chuckle. 'That'll larn ya: a sailor never pisses to windward!'

Tom won the senior table tennis tournament, and me the juniors. One source of fun was bingo, and one night I won five pounds, from which Dad promptly relieved me of four. 'I bought the card; you only filled it in.' Ah well, one pound was better than none.

On a perfect summer's morning in August 1966, the *Sylvania* sailed into New York Harbour after a seven-day passage from Southampton. Under the towering Verranzano Narrows Bridge, past Ellis Island and the Statue of Liberty then docked at the Hudson River Terminal in Manhattan's West Side: unforgettable! We stayed in the Hotel Dixie in Times Square, on what seemed like the hundredth floor. We'd spit out of the window and count how long it took to reach the ground – and who it landed on! It was the first time we'd experienced air conditioning and couldn't understand why anyone would want to deliberately make the room cold, until we felt the heat of a New York August afternoon.

Song for My Father

All the exchange teachers stayed in a group, chaperoned by the Fulbright people. In three hectic days, we did New York: Empire State Building, Statue of Liberty, a boring baseball game at Yankee Stadium, and an even more boring museum. Then we boarded a Greyhound bus for Washington DC and stayed at the famous Hotel Washington. I, Tom, and Gerry had a great time on the rooftop terrace, filling our pockets with cashew nuts and looking down at the White House, across the road from 15th Street. Two days later, on August 25, 1966, we were actually in the White House, where President Lyndon Johnson gave a speech to the Fulbright exchange teachers in the Rose Garden. As he moved down the line, he squeezed my hand in his giant maw:

'Welcome to Amurca, suhhn.'

We were at the White House on the same day as Indian Prime Minister Indira Ghandi, according to the LBJ Presidential Diaries:

I always liked LBJ. He passed an incredible amount of domestic social legislation, including civil rights, Medicare, and Medicaid. What broke him, and his reputation, was Vietnam. We'd see hippies chanting on television: 'Hey, hey LBJ! How many kids ya killed today?' Ironically, thirty-two years later in 1998, my brother Gerry also went on a Fulbright Exchange Programme from England to America, in his case to Denver, Colorado. He never got to meet the president though.

11:15a		To the Flower Garden for	
Secy Gardner requested		REMARKS	
the President see approx		to 200 foreign teachers	Commissioner of Eduation, Harold Howe
200 teachers representing			
19 countries who will		Following his remarks, the President went to the crowd to shake hands for	
attend the 21st annual		several minutes -- then he came into the office asking for pictures taken w/	
orientation arranged by		him and Mrs. Gandhi -- he took the pictures and handed them out to the	
the Office of Education to		students.	
help prepare them for			
teaching assignments in			
elementary and		an xerox copy of the attendance for this occasion has been sent to DT.	
secondary schools and		It will not be carded -- but a card should be placed in the files to indicate	
colleges in this		that it is not carded at this time. see mf or mjdr re this	
country. The teachers			
will spend the 1966-67			
academic year here			
under the Educational			
and Cultural Exchange Act			

From LBJ Presidential Library, 1966

President Lyndon B. Johnson

We took another Greyhound from DC to Chicago, for what seemed like a thousand hours of torture. At 3:00 a.m., we finally pulled into the Greyhound bus station on West 95th Street, one of Chicago's worst ghettos. While Dad dozed, the three of us boys decided to explore Chicago. A few blocks away this grizzled old Black man was amazed to see three little foreign boys out on the mean streets of Chicago at this time of night.

'Boys, y'all best hurry back where y'all b'long, y'hear?'

'Why?' We innocently inquired.

'Cos of the po-leece!!' He bellowed back. We got the message and fled back to the (relative) safety of the bus station.

We got to La Grange, a leafy suburb fifteen miles west of Chicago, staying at the YMCA for a few weeks before moving into 1009 West Cossitt Avenue, a sprawling ground floor apartment. America: that was the year that was! The best year of our lives, by far. After dour, dull England, America was a breath of fresh air. We were agog at the largesse: colour television, endless channels, air conditioning, sock hops, and best of all: girls! Teachers would chastise me when I called them sir. 'Don't call me sir; call me Jim.' How can I call you Jim, sir? And best of all – they didn't beat you!

My father's diary:

> *September 1966, La Grange, Illinois: Since arriving here in this pleasant and prosperous Chicago suburb 5 days ago, me, a Negro plus family, have found nothing but kindness and friendliness from the natives. Doubtless my English accent and my relative rarity as an exchange teacher from England are contributing factors, and both black and white are being enriched by the social interaction and cross fertilization of ideas and opinions.*

> *'Well dang, if you ain't the first coloured Limey I ever seen!' was what one less sophisticated citizen remarked, looking me over. But the unease, the nuances of disapproval of which the Negro is more or less always aware, is probably now more than ever the case with me. Perhaps I am not, after all, without my almost innate racial neuroses. I have wondered, for example, how my friendly colleagues would react to an attempt on my part to purchase the house next door.*

Chicago Tribune 1966

I enrolled in eighth grade at Cossitt Avenue Elementary School, just down the road from our apartment. Tom and Gerry attended Lyons Township High School (LTHS). On my first day of school, Dad sent me off in a jacket and tie, only for me to ditch the stupid tie the moment I entered the gate, but I still stuck out like a dork. I caused not one but two kerfuffles on that first day.

The first was when we all had to stand up and tell the class what we'd done over the summer. Yet again, I was the new kid in a class that had known each other for years. When it was my turn, I nervously said that I had come by ship from England to New York, then by bus to Washington where I shook hands with President Johnson in the White House, then another bus to La Grange then … She stopped me right there. For the new kid in class, this was quite some opening gambit, and one she clearly didn't believe.

It was only after she quizzed me on every aspect of my story that she finally believed me, then proceeded to go completely doolally. She made me come to the front of the class and hold up my right hand.

'Class, this hand, this very hand right here – hold it up higher – has actually shaken the hand of the president … of the United States … of America!'

With Dad in the Rose Garden at the White House

Song for My Father

The second kerfuffle was when I put up my hand and asked the teacher if I could please have a rubber. To howls of laughter and disbelief from the class. What have I done now?

'I think you mean … an eraser.' She said, blushing.

In the small Midwestern town of La Grange, Illinois, the Samuel family achieved minor celebrity status in 1966/67. Not much happens in these one-horse towns, so when the good citizens heard that an 'English teacher' would be coming over from London, England (they always said it that way: London, England – like there's another one?) to teach in LTHS for a year, they were beside themselves with excitement. A real live Englishman! And then who appears? Us!

In our first few weeks in America, the great and the good of La Grange were falling over themselves to invite the Samuels over for dinner; everyone wanted a piece of the English teacher. They'd call the house to welcome us, and on the phone, Dad sounded every inch the Englishman. I wouldn't say he had an affected accent, but he constantly drummed into us the importance of speaking properly: 'The word is buTTer, it has two Ts for a reason!' He fancied himself as a bit of a thespian and in London had once played the lead role in 'The Importance of Being Ernest.' So, these Americans were avidly expecting a cultured evening with Ernest, the Englishman, from London, England.

Ernest, the Englishman

And then came … us. The looks on their faces when they opened the door, to be met by four decidedly non-white 'Englishmen': priceless! Guess who's coming to dinner? La Grange in 1966 was a suburban bastion of 'Americana Blanca,' just a few short years after the end (officially) of segregation. You could just imagine the whispered conversations in the kitchen:

'No Mary-Beth, they're not nig- they're … Britishers!'

Dad's diary:

> *Sept 17th, 1966: I am wondering why is it that complete strangers call inviting me to dinner – as if their turn had come in the 'be nice to the Samuels' programme, or 'help feed the Samuels' programme, at the back of which, somewhere, was the organizational genius of Dr. Reber (Principal of Lyons Township High School). Today another faceless form called … we are to be expected at 'quarter of six' on Tuesday.*

> *Sept 18th, 1996: Got up and sang Happy Birthday to me etc. and waxed emotional in 'for I am a jolly good fellow, and so say all of me.' Just to shame the children, who had forgotten!*

For us boys, America was a liberating year, where we each prospered in the freer atmosphere of American schools, compared to stuffy old England. We all did much better academically than we had ever done before. When your teacher took the time to actually talk to you, instead of knocking it into your head with something hard, information tended to stay there rather than immediately fall out of the other ear.

Despite all the good times you could tell that, like in the Thunderclap Newman song, there was 'something in the air.' The Civil Rights Movement was in full swing; so was Flower Power and along with it the Anti-War Movement. One night in Chicago, soon after we got to America, we met a young Black soldier on furlough from Vietnam, who told us spine-chilling tales of the Viet Cong's ingenuity in setting booby traps and other horrors of this useless war. Tom and Gerry's friends at high school were terrified of getting the dreaded low draft number. They had good reason; body-bags had started to arrive onto American shores, in droves.

Our father clearly enjoyed living in America at this pivotal moment in its history, and made sure to record his observations, no doubt with an eye to future publication:

September 1966, La Grange, Illinois:

I attended my first Civil Rights march two weeks ago, in the Chicago suburb of Cicero – as a spectator. I 'spectated' not only because I am less than two weeks in town, but also because Rights marching is becoming a little less avante garde, I'm told. I, a Negro from the Caribbean via England, am living less than 5 miles from racially explosive Cicero, and for all that the race issue affects me I might as well be living in Finchley Road, N.W.3.

Observing the march from the relative safety of the pavement, I was left unmistakably with the impression that a good time was had by all. The military, with fixed bayonets and a variety of lethal hardware arranged around their person, looked splendidly fierce, as was intended; the local plebeians came out to mock and jeer and cast stones as was expected; the television cameras concentrated where the soldiers and police were thickest, recorded the show with scrupulous authenticity; the marchers marched with as brave faces and as much élan as could be managed – and a good emotional binge was had by all.

Overhead the police and press 'choppers' hovered like crows, waiting to pounce on the ugly scene that would give meaning to their presence. To complete the performance, the fanatical Nazi 'leader' received national coverage of his torn poster, and his arrogant speech insulting Negroes, followed by the so-called Negro leader, loud and illogical making the expected anti police noises. At the end of it all, strike me pink if anything has changed.

The frequency of such occurrences in the American society leads one to wonder whether, indeed, there is a correlation between the severity of the violence, and the emotional response to the protest. My own feeling is that the unfortunate American tendency to crack the walnut with the sledgehammer; to 'put on a show' at the drop of a hat; the persistent frontier philosophy of solving all problems by pointing the inevitable gun; promotes rather than discourages occasions such as Cicero.

Dad got invited to a meeting of the National Association for the Advancement of Colored People (NAACP) in Chicago, and he took us along. All I remember was a lot of Black men talking very seriously and us kids being very bored. Civil Rights was beginning to morph into Black Power: tense times. Like all small towns, La Grange was segregated, with the Blacks living across the tracks, literally. The Samuel family defied such simple categorization (don't we always?) because we were supposed to be 'English' and therefore lived in the White side of town. But we weren't White. In the summer of '67, race riots erupted across the US. One night, a group of Tom and Gerry's White high school friends got caught on the wrong side of Chicago and got seriously beaten up. I'll never forget the sight of one of them puking up mouthfuls of blood into a bucket. Like LBJ said: Welcome to Amurca, suhhn!

Sept 17th, 1966: My initial impression is that an overwhelming majority of white people are sympathetic to the Negroes' demands for his share of the American cake, and there is no doubt that the Johnson Administration is determined that this shall happen with dispatch. Through the efforts of Dr. Martin Luther King, Roy Wilkins and other Negro intellectuals, the machinery of Negro advancement gained much momentum. However, splinter groups led by bitter and extreme men are emerging here and there – men on whom a lifetime of social and economic repression have left their psychological scars.

The Chicago blizzard of 1967 struck northern Illinois on the night of January 26, with freezing temperatures, high winds, and heavy snowfall for almost twenty-four hours. When the storm abated in the morning, we found that over three feet of snow had fallen, drifting higher. To this day, it remains the greatest single snowfall in Chicago history. The first thing we did, after we'd dug our way out of the house, was run down to the hardware store and buy snow shovels – we're gonna make some money! We spent the day digging out driveways all across La Grange, the three of us could do a driveway in ten minutes – cars cost extra. We thought we'd been clever in buying snow shovels, but some of those American boys really knew how to make money; they'd bought snow ploughs.

We only went to church once in America, but this was no ordinary church. Dad's Black American friend took us to a 'holy roller' Baptist church in Chicago's South Side: unforgettable. The first unforgettable thing was just being there: Chicago's most notorious ghetto looked more like a bombsite than a place where anyone actually lived: garbage strewn across the streets, derelict houses, derelict people but lots of liquor stores and Cadillacs.

Gerry: We drove in Dad's red-and-white Rambler station wagon, to this church in the South Side. The three of us all scrubbed up, the only kids wearing jackets. There was the heavenly choir, mainly women, in their long black graduation-style robes, singing away, warming up the congregation. Then after a few songs and prayers the pastor starts his sermon, fairly slowly at first, but imperceptibly, he began to get the rhythm, interspersed with loud amens from the congregation. Then he stops the sermon, 'cos it's time for the collection. 'I don't wanna hear the clink of coins, I wanna hear the rustle of notes!' The big bowl comes down the aisles, and of course the four Samuels' hands stayed firmly in their pockets!

Then he gets back into his speil, and you had these bouncers, big burly guys, interspersed in the aisles, who were there for the ones who 'got the spirit.' Someone would start yellin' and jabberin,' usually a woman, and these guys would hone in on her, one on each side and gently haul her off, to cool down. And then, to our great delight, one of the heavenly choir got possessed and started talking in tongues – and we saw her knickers!

I'll say one thing for Dad, he did make a point of taking us to experiences, like theatres, museums, or the Baha'i Temple, up on the West Side. In London he'd take us to the West End, of course we'd get the cheapest seats, the nosebleeds, way up in the rafters. For sixpence you could rent these little binoculars, he'd get one for himself and one for the three of us, which of course Tom and I would hardly ever pass to pesky Prooglums squirming next to us! We saw Fiddler on the Roof with Topol, Oliver! with Harry Seacombe, and Ginger Rogers in Mame! Another place he took us to a lot was the Commonwealth Institute, because he was involved with them, in some way. One experience we could've done without was the nudist camp! Took us to Hampstead Pond, some naturist bathing place where they had separate men's and women's bathing areas. I must've been twelve, Tom ten and you nine, and we're like: what? All these naked men, swimming and sunbathing, ginger pubes: what?

In La Grange, I was in a co-ed classroom for the first time since primary school. It didn't take long to make up for lost time. Jan Davies was the cutest girl in class, with sparkling brown eyes under a big fringe or bangs as they called them in America. Her dark hair turned up at the ends, touching the corners of her cute little mouth. Oh, did I have the hots for Jan! For the whole year, I was besotted. I'd sit behind her in class, so I could look at the back of that cute head of hers, and daydream...

As in any eighth grade, my classroom was divided into cliques: boys versus girls, geeks versus jocks, cute girls versus the rest. My best friend Rick Westman inducted me into the jocks clique, although I was far from one. If I didn't have a bicycle, Rick would lend me one of his, ditto air rifle, ditto anything else. In the spring we went for long bike rides: fishing, horsing around, and shooting anything that moved. I stayed at his house for weekends and had barbecues in his back yard with his family. They were so friendly and welcoming – in England I wouldn't say boo to my friends' parents let alone play games with them. So this is America, eh? I like. Never mind that I was seeing a very blinkered view of White middle-class Americana.

Song for My Father

4th Nov 1966

Dear Gerry,

Last night, the boys in the next apartment took us all out to dinner at an exclusive place in Washington, where Petula Clark was appearing. She was simply fantastic & I felt quite proud of being British – I even felt a bit homesick at times. Afterwards we asked if we could meet her. Again I did my stuff. Eventually all of us ended up in her hotel and I met her French husband. She was simply charming & so interested in what I was doing. She even asked me which places to go and see for sightseeing. We're still all in a daze over this!!

Love, Val (a fellow British exchange teacher)

My best night I had in La Grange was my last. I'd finally gotten over my painful shyness and let Jan know that, well, you know. She knew, and said she felt the same way too. This was not long before I was due to leave for England, so we both made sure that my last evening would be spent just the two of us, in her basement. And for the first time in his excited little life, little Bri-Bri got his groove on! Okay, it was only teenage stuff, but I was in kiss heaven. Then she chastised me:

'Iddy-boo! Don't you know? I've been crazy about you from that very first day, when you walked into the classroom wearing that dorky British jacket! We could have been doing this, a *long time* ago...'

Aaarrgghh! But how was I to know? Girls: isn't it forever thus? All too soon it was time for us to pack up and head back to London. We weren't enthralled at going back to fuddy-duddy England, not that we had any choice in the matter. For that summer our father got a job at Owasippe Scout Reservation in Michigan. Which of course meant that we got jobs too; nepotism runs in the family. We loaded up Dad's 1957 Rambler station wagon, a huge red beast with wings. Tom and Gerry were both driving by then, having been taught in school, lucky sods.

My first job was in the camp medical clinic, helping the nurse deal with bee stings, minor cuts and bruises. I enjoyed it immensely. The cute nurse took me under her wing; teaching me how to tie bandages, take a temperature and my favourite: make a hospital bed. As she'd bend over the bed, explaining how to fold the sheets firmly under the mattress, I'd look on behind her, enthralled. Then one day, it all went pear shaped. This scout came in not with a bee sting: he'd put an axe through his foot. The nurse was trying to keep him calm; I freaked.

'Jesus Christ, dude. I can see your bone! Hey, don't faint!'

Thus ended my short-lived career as a nursing assistant. After that I got a job washing dishes, but things improved afterwards with stints as a lifeguard on the lake and a tuck shop operator. The only downside of the tuck shop job was that my boss was Dad, a tough taskmaster, who ended up firing Tom from the same job at another camp. No perks for the boss's son!

Most of the scouts were White middle-class kids from the suburbs of Chicago, but one time we took in a troop of Black kids from the projects – Chicago's inner-city ghettos. These kids were hard as nails. They took one look at me and thought: who this Black kid think he is, actin' all White? I was nominally in charge of them, but they were more than nominally bigger than me. One night one of them broke into my tuck shop and stole the petty cash. I saw him clearly, and even half-heartedly gave chase until I came to my senses. My boss – Dad – insisted that I must have seen the perpetrator and ordered me to identify him to the police. Yeah right, do I *look* stupid?

After Owasippe, we drove in the big red Rambler up to Montreal for the 1967 World's Fair, where Dad pulled off some amazing acts of queue-jumping, with three boys in tow. There was a combined Trinidad and Tobago and Grenada pavilion, and it was great to see our twin homes represented on the world stage. The USA pavilion was the biggest, with a whole car park full of queue. We jumped that one too. After Montreal, Tom and Gerry, lucky sods, got to sail back to England on the *Sylvania* again, while Dad said I couldn't go with them – unfair! He and I flew back from Montreal on a BOAC VC-10, which was pretty cool, looking down at the clouds from thirty thousand feet; the beginning of my lifelong love affair with flying.

Daredevil Dad

10. *Back to Britain*

G oing back to England after America was a major bummer; none of us wanted to return, probably including Dad. We'd had a taste of the good life, the mid-American Dream, then had it snatched from our grasp. For one year, one glorious, eye-opening year all of us – I, Tom, and Gerry – had all experienced a transformation, exchanged the dank stuffiness of Britain for the boundless possibilities of the Promised Land. Where school was a place you actually liked being, rather than a cage you couldn't wait to escape from. Where your teachers told you that you could be anything you wanted to be, rather than what you couldn't be. For the second time in my life, I hated being in England.

I enrolled at St Gregory's RC School in Kenton, my third in four years. In hindsight, Dad's decision to take us to America for that crucial year wasn't the best thing for our education. When we got back to England, I'd just turned 14 and was supposed to be entering the O-Level stream. But because I hadn't done third form subjects like English Language and Literature, History and Geography, they instead put me into the remedial stream. I was deemed unfit to take the General Certificate of Education (GCE) O-Levels, and instead would sit for the Certificate of Secondary Education (CSE) Examinations. I was now an underachiever, officially.

Song for My Father

I slept through two years at St Greg's, a cog in a wheel. My best friend was Kevin Corrigan, a skinhead before skinheads became racists. One good thing about coming back from America was that we were cool: we had American accents and dressed straight out of an 'Archie' comic. But the accents quickly wore off and the clothes wore out.

The headmaster of St Greg's was John Drum, a roly-poly man with a unique way of administering justice, to me at any rate. He taught me a lesson I would never forget. Again, it was a girl that got me into this piece of trouble. Every evening after school, the students from St Greg's would gather at the corner of Kenton Road and Woodcock Hill, to await their respective buses home. I lived just around the corner from school and didn't take the bus, but still hung around with the rest anyway – where else was I supposed to meet girls?

'Brian, I'm starving.' Cooed this teen temptress. 'Can you get me a Mars Bar, pleeease?'

I didn't have the nine pence needed for a Mars Bar. That was a lot of money for a boy on a budget. But when she looked at me so pleadingly, eyelids fluttering, something stirred, deep inside me: I had to … satisfy her. Don't have the money to buy her a Mars Bar? No worries, I decided on the spur of the moment: I'll nick her one. There was a sweet shop on the corner by the bus stop, and every day hundreds of hungry kids would pile in after school, craving anything sweet and sticky. It was common practice for some boys to plunder the goodies sitting invitingly on the shelves, stuffing their pockets while the old man's back was turned. I don't know how the poor man made a living. I'd never done it before but figured that now was as good a time as any to start my criminal career – my honour was at stake! I walked into the shop and adopted the shoplifter's standard operating procedure:

'Hello, Sir. Can I have a thrupenny gobstopper, please?'

Even when robbing him blind, I was unfailingly polite. The old man looked skyward, muttered to himself, reached for the footstool, climbed onto it and reached up to the uppermost shelf for the jar of thrupenny gobstoppers, a huge ball of hard candy that took hours to dissolve in your mouth.

'What colour d'you want?'

'It doesn't matter.' I said, stuffing a Mars Bar into my blazer pocket, and for good measure a Lion Bar as well. 'Any colour will d...'

Clamp! Something grabbed me by the back of my neck and squeezed, hard. Like a vice.

'Gotcha, you bleedin' little toerag!' A hot, harsh voice breathed directly into my left ear. 'I knew you little sods was robbin' me dad blind. Now I've got proof! Dad, call the police!'

How I didn't shit myself right there and then, I will never know. The monster with the claw of steel was the shopkeeper's son, a boxer in the Royal Navy who'd been hiding behind the curtains at the back of the shop, waiting for the first little tea-leaf (thief) to try and steal from his father. And guess who that first little tea-leaf was? The old man fixed his kindly eyes on me and was surprised. He liked me. I was one of the few boys who was always polite. No, he says, don't call the police; call the school.

Thank you! I gave a silent benediction. Now if we can only keep this away from Dad! By this time, everyone had seen me get caught, and when I was frog-marched up the road to St Greg's, I did the walk of shame through dozens of chuckling schoolmates – bastards! When we got to the school, Mister Drum was still in his office, dammit. The giant and I sat in the reception, by which time he'd released his grip on my neck. A bit. He was determined to see justice done, and punishment administered. He led me into Drum's office, cowed, bowed, and penitent. Drum berated me for my deplorable lack of moral fibre.

'Stealing!' He fulminated, spraying me with a coating of spittle.

'Stealing! The most despicable crime a boy could commit! Worse than a crime: a sin!' More spittle. Then he got to the important part:

'I know your father.' I quailed.

'Your father is a teacher, just like me. I have a great deal of respect for your father. This will break his heart, to find out that his boy is guilty of ... stealing!' He paused for effect.

'Because I have so much respect for your father, I will not tell him of today's despicable episode.'

Thank you!! Because any punishment from Drum would be peanuts compared to what Dad would do to me. He'd kill me and bury my body in the backyard, nothing less. Mister Drum ordered me to pay restitution to the shopkeeper, in the sum of ten shillings. Ten shillings? Drum shot me a look. Fine. Plus, of course, the mandatory six of the best, with the owner's son watching the proceedings with grim satisfaction. And that was that: no police, and best of all: no Dad – phew! I went home and told Tom and Gerry about my close shave, swearing never to steal, ever again. End of story. Hah, if only.

The next morning, school gathered as usual in the hall for assembly. After hymn singing and information from various form masters, Drum took to the lectern for his usual morning talk. He came straight to the point:

'Yesterday evening, I was faced with a most unpleasant situation.' Uh-oh.

'One of my boys, one of our St Gregory's boys, was found guilty of...' Pause. 'Stealing!'

He went on and on, about the moral depravity of this boy, how he could stoop so low as to steal, especially from a poor shopkeeper. How this boy had brought shame on himself, his family, and the proud name of St Gregory's. I thought: proud name – this dump? Hundreds of faces turned my way, all of them breaking into barely suppressed giggles. I grinned sheepishly. Tough it out, Brian. Tough it out. Then Drum put the boot in. 'But the boy repented; he wept before me, went down on his knees, and with copious tears begged for forgiveness!'

What??? I was staggered, what are you talking about! Wept? Begged? No, I never! The whole assembly looked accusingly at me: you cried? Bawled like a baby? In front of Drum? You wuss! I mouthed my indignation: he's lying! As the assembly finished and the teachers filed out behind the headmaster, I could swear he smirked at me as he walked by. Bastard!

I never stole anything again – cured!

It was 1967, the Summer Love. I'd just turned fourteen, and London was in the midst of its Swinging London phase. Swinging my arse. This was another of those media inventions that had little to do with the lives of ordinary people. Twiggy, Lulu, and the Fab Four: you couldn't open a magazine without their mop-topped faces grinning at you. My friends and I would go window shopping in Carnaby Street and gawk at the girls in in their miniskirts and kaftans at the Biba Boutique: dry-land tourists.

There was always a societal rift of one sort or other: mods v rockers, hippies v skinheads, Stones v Beatles, and of course Black versus White. Not that it would ever get out of hand, with typical English understatement even rifts have rules. Immigration, hippies, anarchists, strikes, the pill, abortion, drugs, the IRA – there was a lot going on. Not that any of this affected us directly, it was what you saw on the BBC news. My brother Gerry says that he never experienced racism growing up in London. I don't know what London he grew up in because I had a ton of it. But we're all prone to our own selective amnesia, so the truth probably lies somewhere in between.

A few months after we got back from America, Dad calls a conference:

'Boys, as you know, ever since your mother left you three have been my number one priority. Well, you're getting older now and … I've decided to get married again!'

In the decade since our mother had run off, our father had had several girlfriends, some of whom harboured not-so secret hopes of one day becoming the next Mrs Samuel. When Dad made his announcement, our first thoughts turned to Eileen Gowdy, a feisty Irish teacher who had gone over to America with us on the Fulbright Exchange Program. While we were in La Grange, Eileen was in nearby Minneapolis and would often come down on weekends. Eileen and us boys got along like a house on fire; a fire which Dad immediately doused.

'No, not Eileen, Joan. Joan Danby.'

Who? That completely flummoxed us. None of us had any idea who this Joan Danby was.

'You remember her. She was on the *Sylvania* with us.'

Still, no bells rung. Dad continued:

'Anyway, the point is Joan and I met on the boat. She's an art teacher, and while we went to Illinois, she went to Hawaii. We've been in correspondence ever since; we met again recently, and I believe she is the right woman for me. I know this comes as a bit of a surprise to you, but don't worry, when you meet her you'll love her. I know you will.'

The Hawaii reference rang a bell, there'd been a regular flow of letters from there. I remember Tom, Gerry, and I chuckling afterwards: Dad's only gone and done it again: flummoxed us! Joan Danby lived in Stevenage, thirty miles north of London, with her mother and father, a stern retired policeman. We would drive up there for Sunday dinners, with advance warnings from Dad to mind our P's and Q's.

Dad and Joan got married on July 27, 1968, one year after returning from America. And overnight, we had a stepmother! This was a major change in domestic affairs, and one that took quite some getting used to. The first skirmish was over the fridge: Joan announced that henceforth, we couldn't just go and pillage the fridge when we felt like it. First we had to ask permission. But how can I

Samuel family, version four

ask permission when you're not here and I'm hungry? Another thing: old before new. Don't start a new bottle of milk if there's already an open one. Finish that first. We turned to Dad for support, which of course wasn't forthcoming.

Tom went to the fridge to make himself a cheese sandwich. Just as he was about to open a new pack of cheese, he noticed an already open pack in the back of the fridge. It was old and didn't look appetizing, but mindful of Joan's injunction against eating new over old, Tom thought he'd do the right thing and duly ate the old cheese first.

Joan comes home and looks in the fridge.

'Who's eaten my aged Chiltern cheese?'

Tom looked skyward. Damned if I do, damned if I don't.

It was common practice for us to open the fridge and guzzle a whole pint of milk, especially with the cream on top – then look for something to eat. If there was no jam or peanut butter, we'd make sugar sandwiches, the three of us could demolish a whole loaf of bread in one sitting. We would do what Dad called bored eating – why not? It took Joan quite a while to fully comprehend, the sheer volume of food that teenage boys consumed. But married life did have its upsides. We now got tasty meals every day – and even desserts! Joan also brought other radical improvements, like insisting that we all used separate towels, hitherto we'd all used the same damp towel – yuck! It couldn't have been easy for Joan, nominally in charge of three teenage boys who were unused to having a female in their lives, let alone one who gave orders!

After two uninspiring years at St Greg's, my father had the sense to realize that I wasn't going anywhere at that factory school. Any attempt at instilling the thirst for knowledge was a dismal failure. Career's day consisted of your disinterested careers master talking down to you:

'Right, Samuel, what do you want to be?'

'Er, well, Sir, my dad says...'

'Never mind what your dad says, boy, what do you want to be?'

'Er, well, Sir, a ... lawyer?'

'Don't be stupid boy, you can't be a *lawyer*! Now, let's see. Ah, I see you're studying woodwork, an excellent trade for a coloured boy. That's it then: you'll leave school at fifteen and enter a woodworking apprenticeship scheme – okay? Good. Next!'

Through his teaching connections (it certainly wasn't through my grades), Dad got me enrolled in a new concept taking root in England: sixth form college. Harrow Junior College was a brand-new school in Stanmore, the first sixth form college in England. They hadn't finished building it when I started lower sixth, in September 1969.

I'd just turned sixteen, an ambiguous time for any teenager but for me even more so. I was the archetypal late bloomer and being the smallest in class didn't add to my confidence. But now I was finally beginning to flesh out a bit. I'd never be beefy, but at least I wasn't a wimp anymore. Hitherto, most of my friends had been West Indians except for Kevin Corrigan, the wannabe Jamaican. But as I got older, race got to be less of a factor. My budding social status was also aided by, of all things, hair. Like everyone else in the late sixties, I let my hair grow long and shaggy which, in my own inflated opinion, resembled that of a certain Mr Hendrix.

Hair

There was no better time to be a teenager. All the music you liked your father hated; ditto clothes, movies, and just about everything else. We were imbued with a sense that we were making a distinct break with the stuffiness of the past. At college, I finally came into my own, in other words: I became a hippy. Slouching around in oversized Army Surplus greatcoats, clutching Pink Floyd albums, and going to Moody Blues concerts: the life of a teenage hippy in London. The shaggier the hair, the tighter the jeans, the bigger the flares, the cooler the dude.

For West Indians, the big issue was immigration. In the first half of the sixties, entry into England was open from anywhere in the Commonwealth: all you needed was a ticket and a relative in England to put you up for a while. Immigration was encouraged by the government, who depended on immigrant workers to fuel its growing economy. But then came the backlash: racism. Fed by right-wing politicians, large segments of the British population began to view immigrants as their competitors in the job market and a threat to the British way of life.

Song for My Father

The Joint Council for the Welfare of Immigrants (JCWI) was founded at a crowded meeting of immigrant and anti-racism groups at the Dominion Cinema in Southall on September 23, 1967. I'm not sure if our father was at that founding meeting, but he joined JCWI soon afterwards. Through the JCWI he also joined the Catholic Institute for International Relations (CIIR), formerly known by the much grander title of 'The Sword of the Spirit.' Dad and Joan befriended the eminent philosophers Sir Michael and Dame Ann Dummett, through whose influence in December 1969, Dad was sent on a fact-finding trip to the West Indies. In two weeks, he visited Barbados, Trinidad, Grenada, St Vincent, St Lucia, Guyana, and Dominica, compiling information on labour migration to the UK. That was his first visit back to the West Indies in nine years, and I remember the effect it had on him: rejuvenation – and a renewed thirst for home.

I guess some of Dad's activism rubbed off on me because I vividly remember, at a very early age, being aware the impact of race on my life. I felt it emotionally, intellectually, and sometimes physically. As far as I was concerned, non-White people couldn't flock to England fast enough. Then there was Enoch Powell; I hated that prick. In 1968, he made his infamous 'Rivers of Blood' speech in which he listed the dire consequences to the (White) English way of life that would result from unchecked immigration. 'It is like watching a nation busily engaged in heaping up its own funeral pyre.' I was an angry fifteen-year-old just returned from a liberating year in America, pissed off to be back in Britain – and now this?

The late sixties weren't only about pot-smoking hippies spouting flower power, it was also a time of radical politics. The Prague Spring, student riots in Paris led by Danny the Red, and the Anti-Vietnam Movement were all in full swing – heady days. On April 5, 1968, I got into a fight with my best friend Kevin Corrigan at scout camp because Martin Luther King had just been assassinated, and Kevin wouldn't stop acting like a jackass. A month earlier, Tom and Gerry were at the Battle of Grosvenor Square, a massive anti-Vietnam demonstration outside the US Embassy. With ten thousand protesters in attendance and heavy-handed tactics from the police, what started out as a song-singing protest march suddenly turned very violent. With bottles, bricks, and batons flying thick in the air they beat a hasty retreat, lest they suffer collateral damage. Of which there was plenty: over two hundred arrests and fifty people sent to hospital. Dad wouldn't let me go because I was only fifteen. Damn, missed the action, again! The Summer of Love was exactly that: one summer, and even then, largely confined to San Francisco and other hippy capitals in America. But in Europe these were the days of the 'Street Fighting Man,' the Rolling Stones' rock anthem to every anarchist the world over.

To my undying shame, the first time I ever got drunk was with my parents. I was fifteen, and we were at one of those boring family parties with Joan's relatives in Stevenage. I didn't know these people and was keeping myself to myself. Until I discovered Stone's Ginger Wine. It was the first time I'd seen it, and I loved its sharp ginger taste, not realizing it was alcoholic. Have you ever been drunk, without even realizing you're drunk? In no time, I was the life and soul of the party, dancing, laughing, and telling jokes. Dad even said he'd never seen me so outgoing before.

And then: disaster.

It's bad enough when you pass that tipping point, from pleasantly drunk to pukingly drunk, but when you don't even know there was a tipping point to pass – it's completely bewildering! It was only when I emptied the entire contents of my stomach onto the carpeted living room floor, over and over, that grown-ups started to ask questions. A big clue was the colour of my puke: a bright shade of Stone's Ginger Wine green. Then it clicked, and I was gently led to the bathroom to die. To this day, I hate the taste of anything ginger!

But at least I had a cast-iron excuse: I didn't know! I couldn't claim that excuse for my second drunk, but since I barely remember anything about it, I'll give Gerry the pleasure of retelling that one…

Brian Barfs Again:

Late one evening at Camplin Road, guessing summer of '68 when I was 18 and Brian 15, there was a knock on the door. I opened it to find a certain someone standing there, waving like a palm tree in a hurricane, too incapable of finding, letting alone, using his house key. In staggered in one Steven Brian Samuel, totally and utterly pissed. How he actually made it to the front door remains a mystery.

Staggering up the stairs he proceeded to puke on the steps, down his shirt, against the wall. He made it to his bedroom. He was so sick and poorly that even from Dad there was no recrimination but concern, for his well-being. This being the era of pop stars choking on their own vomit and dying in bed. Fortunately, B was on his side where he once again puked, into his shoes this time. Had to take them and wash them out in the bath. All's well that ends well and he lived to drink another day.

Vietnam: Background to Adolescence

I grew up with Vietnam, the first war to be brought into our living rooms through television. During our American year of 1966/67, we learned first-hand from returning GIs of the ingenuity of the Viet Cong in setting booby traps to kill American soldiers. Tom and Gerry's high school friends were rightly afraid of getting the dreaded low draft number, some of whom were subsequently sent to fight. By the time we returned to England the war was in full swing, every evening we watched graphic television footage of aerial bombings and deadly street-to-street fighting, in place names that would resonate through history: Khe Sahn, Da Nang and the Ho Chi Minh Trail – by eighteen I was a certified war junkie.

Just when you thought it was settling into a slow and deadly stalemate, North Vietnam pulled off its masterstroke: the Tet Offensive. Launched over the Vietnamese New Year in January 1968, North

Vietnamese regular troops and guerrillas swarmed across the South, catching the Americans completely unawares and capturing several key cities. Although the American forces regrouped and eventually beat back the invading forces, the Tet Offensive played a major role in shaping public opinion against the War.

The best part of the Vietnam War was the ending: America's ignominious defeat at the hands of 'a bunch of rice-eating Gooks.' After such a long, deadly and senseless war, there was something grimly satisfying about the sight of American soldiers, burning documents and desperately clinging onto the last chopper lifting off the US Embassy in Saigon, as the victorious North Vietnamese troops closed in. The word is: schadenfreude.

It was Sunday afternoon and our scout leader Skip Cullinane came for tea, with his wife and mannish daughter Kate. Skip had been scoutmaster of the Tenth Kenton for decades, a second father to hundreds of boys over the years. Not that he was a soft touch, you didn't mess around with Skip or you'd get a swift clip around the earhole. Skip was getting on in years and as a result of his lifelong smoking habit, had recently survived a bout of lung cancer. For which they'd had to remove all his teeth. He couldn't wear false teeth, so he'd gum his food to death before swallowing it – you didn't want to sit next to Skip at dinnertime around the campfire!

Tom and I were at home with Dad and Joan, so the two of us were drafted in to make polite talk. Joan could bake a wicked cake, and today's offering was a butter cake with vanilla icing and shelled almonds on top. Toothless old Skip gummed at the cake endlessly but couldn't chew the shelled almonds. So, he sucks them dry and discretely places them back onto his plate. Five minutes later, Gerry walks in. He sees a plate with almonds on it.

'Ah, almonds!' Gerry scoops them up in his hand and before anyone could say anything, pops them into his mouth! Jaws dropped; poor Skip didn't know where to put his face! Tom and I had to run out of the room to die laughing. In his usual unflappable manner, later on when Tom and I told Gerry that he'd just eaten Skip's gummed almonds he was unperturbed: no big deal. Yeah, right!

It was at Harrow Junior College that I had my first – and worst – motorbike accident. There was some guy who was selling a beautiful Lambretta scooter all kitted out with foglamps, ariels and racoon-tails. I told him I was interested in buying it, but first I had to give it a test ride. He looked dubious, and he had every right to be: I'd never ridden a bike in my life. And I didn't have the money either – I just wanted a joyride!

'You sure you know how to ride?'

'Of course, I ride my brother's bike all the time.'

He should have twigged when I asked him how to change the gears, but he still entrusted his chrome-plated steed into my care, for 'a slow ride' around the block. Sure, I said, a quick-slow ride. Then I zoomed off up the road. Shit, this thing is *fast*! I rode up to Stanmore Station then turned around and came back down the hill. I was so busy waving to all my friends that as I approached the corner, I was going faster than I should have; much faster. The corner rushed at me with frightening speed, and with my complete lack of experience, I lost control of the scooter. Ba-dang! The front wheel hit the curb, and I went sailing over the handlebars, hitting the ground face first. Then, mercifully: blackness. Later, I heard that the owner came running over, jumped over my prone body and shrieked:

'You fucking bastard! Look what you've done to my scooter!'

When I regained consciousness, I was propped-up on a low wall in front of school. The owner was screaming in my face. I barely remembered what had just happened. I felt no pain, which I thought was good. What wasn't good was everybody's reaction when they saw my face. I kept asking what's wrong, but no one would answer. Someone said call the ambulance, I said no. Because along with the ambulance would come police, and I had not one shred of legality.

I looked down at my feet. I was wearing desert boots: tan-coloured ankle-length suede shoes. In my befuddled state, it took me a while to realize that my left shoe wasn't tan-coloured anymore, it was red. Blood red. I moved my left foot and felt a squishy liquid feeling inside. I lifted up my sock and saw white – of ankle bone.

'Okay, call the ambulance.'

Two boys half-carried me into the school to wait for the ambulance. I got the shock of my life when we passed a mirror. Now I knew why everyone was recoiling! The whole left side of my face was a mass of blood, from forehead to chin. There was blood where my nose should have been, and bits of dirt and gravel were embedded in every cut. The shock wore off as the pain wore on. My face, ankle, and entire left side was a searing mass of pain. The ambulance arrived, by which time I began to seriously lose my mind. Shock is a hell of a thing. I couldn't even say my name. I just shivered uncontrollably. They laid me on the gurney and wheeled me into the ambulance, feeling like I wanted to die. I had done a lot of damage to this guy's scooter, had no means of paying for it, and worst of all, my father was going to *kill* me!

I was inconsolable, scarred for life and still a virgin! Then I remembered: there was a condom in my pocket! Never before in the entire history of condoms was there a more unemployed condom, but in teenage minds hope springs eternal. I still had on my jacket which was all torn up. I could feel the condom snuggled in the top pocket. I could just visualize the nurses handing my clothes to Dad, and him finding the condom ...

I needed to get rid of this damn condom – but how? The ambulance was speeding along with the siren on, two paramedics were sitting beside me. I made a motion to loosen my shirt and signal: I can't breathe. One of them got the message and opened the window. Straightaway I reached into my pocket, pulled out the condom, heaved myself up and threw it out the window, then collapsed back onto the gurney in agony. The paramedics looked at each other knowingly.

'Drugs.'

Edgeware General Hospital has long since been demolished, probably the best health service it ever delivered. Dad and Joan came a couple of hours later and were remarkably sanguine about the whole thing. I guess seeing your son all banged up on a hospital bed tends to soften even the hardest of hearts. The gash on my ankle was so wide they couldn't stitch it, so they put a big gauze bandage on it and treated the cuts on my face, elbows, and knees with some ointment which made them hurt even more. Then they left me to my own devices. This was now a few hours after the crash and despite all the painkillers, my entire body hurt. The nurse left a bedpan and said call her in case I needed help with it. Never in the history of mankind has one boy held in a pee for so long!

If I was feeling bad about myself, that was nothing compared to the poor sod next to me. He had tubes coming out of all parts of his body connected to a machine at the side of his bed, which sucked and wheezed as though it was breathing for him – which I guess it was. Despite all the machines, he still couldn't breathe properly and kept making this horrible gurgling sound.

At around midnight, the noise stopped. This must have triggered an alarm because the nurses came soon after. They took one look at him and the dials on the machine and shook their heads. One of them wrote something on the chart and that was it: dead. They started to disconnect the tubes, going about their business with practiced ease.

I pleaded: 'Excuse me, but couldn't you do that somewhere else?'

They shrugged and wheeled the corpse away. And *now* I'm supposed to sleep? In fact, thanks to all the drugs they'd dosed me up with, I fell into a deep, dreamless sleep. I awoke late the next morning, dying to pee. I tried to turn around in the bed and – ouch! The sheet had stuck to all the cuts on my elbows and knees, particularly the big oozing gash on my ankle. Every time I'd move, I'd pull off a scab. Trapped by sheets.

'Nurse!'

There's nothing nurses hate more than being summoned. A no-nonsense Jamaican nurse came over to my bedside.

'Yes?'

'Nurse, all my cuts have stuck to the sheets – ouch!'

She looked down at me, with that uniquely Jamaican mixture of sympathy and annoyance.

'Okay, here's what we're going to do ...'

Yank! Like a matador she expertly hauled off the sheet, taking with it all my half-healed scabs. Aaaaarrgghhh!!! She apologized and said that was the only way to do it – but did she have to smile? She asked if I wanted help to use the bedpan. I did but I couldn't stand the thought of Atilla the Nurse's hands on my gonads, so I declined the offer and shuffled off to the men's room, to painfully pee.

It was in 1970 that I first smoked weed, aged seventeen. Tom (who else?) was smoking by then, and I knew he had some pot in a film cannister, hidden deep in his bedside drawer. I dare not steal it, but I pestered him to give me a smoke, until he finally relented and said okay, let's go out back. It was a Sunday, and Dad and Joan were out. Tom rolled a joint; I was all excited. I'd finally be smoking pot! Tom lit the joint, took a couple of tokes, then passed it to me. I took a couple of tentative pulls, holding it down as instructed. He looked at me, curiously.

'How do you feel?'

'Fine.' I replied. 'Don't feel a thing.'

We shared a few more pulls. Five minutes later, we'd almost finished the joint, and I still didn't feel anything – or did I? And then, imperceptibly, it all seemed so funny. Here's me, wanting to get high, waiting to get high, wondering if I was high? I giggled; Tom smiled. I giggled some more. The birds sang. The sky was blue. We were happy; all was well with the world. In other words, I was stoned, or as Tom put it, 'kerpunkled to the bone.' And then: woosh! Up came my lunch, breakfast, and yesterday's dinner. As I stood there doubled over and retching in waves, who drives up? Dad and Joan! Ganja smoke was still floating in the air. Dad gets out the car and sees me puking onto the driveway, Tom standing next to me looking like he'd just been shot.

'What's going on here?' Dad scowls as Tom slowly backs away, crumbling the still-lit joint behind his back. I answered, between retches.

'It's nothing, Dad. I'm feeling suddenly sick. Must have been something I ate. Tom here is ... helping me.'

Dad looked at Tom, who mustered as much concerned innocence as he could. Yes, that's right. I'm just ... looking after my little brother!

'Okay then, clean up this mess!'

Dad and Joan marched inside. Tom always maintains that I saved his life that day. Dad would have killed him! What did he take me for – a wuss?

This was London at the end of the Swinging Sixties, and some of my friends were smoking pot – and more. I had an English girlfriend, Sharon, who every now and then would disappear for a weekend with her 'special' friends – and do LSD. She invited me to join their select circle, with the hint of cowardice if I declined. That was a step too far for me, and I wimped out. Not long afterwards, she had a bad trip, which almost killed her. She spent six months in a nursing home and upon her discharge the lively, vivacious girl I had known had been transformed into an empty-eyed zombie, shuffling around her living room in a dressing gown – a shadow of her former self. Phew, dodged that bullet!

Tom got a job at Harry Fenton, the coolest men's clothes shop in England. So, of course, he dressed the part. Every now and then he'd toss me a piece of clothing he no longer fancied, and all of a sudden Tom's hand-me-downs were worth having. One Saturday, he arranged for me and my mate Rob, both underage, to get into his favourite discotheque, the Purple Pussycat on Finchley Road, a major coup. Rob drove a Ford Anglia with a tuned-up Cortina engine that sounded like a low-flying jet. Rob and I got dressed in our most stylish duds and headed down to the club. As Rob was driving along Kenton Road, he overtook three cars in a row, nice! Then we heard the siren. The copper strode up to the driver's window, book in hand.

'In all my years on the Force, I have never seen such an exhibition of dangerous driving!'

As Rob began to stammer his apologies, I heard a tap-tap at my window. I looked around and – Dad! Talk about an unfortunate coincidence. He was driving past when he saw a car he recognized being stopped by the Old Bill. The only 'good' thing about this episode was that it wasn't my car, and I wasn't driving. But have you ever heard of the concept of vicarious liability? I did, that night.

Amazingly, Rob got off with no more than a flea in his ear, and we continued down to the Pussycat, a good deal more slowly. Once inside the famed nightclub, Rob and I began to relax. As we boogied to the sounds of 'Hot Chocolate' and 'The Equals,' my attention turned to a cute little brown girl sitting at the bar, all alone. Tom put me straight.

'That's Nancy, Big Boy's bird. Don't even think about it.'

'Who's Big Boy?' I asked.

'The bouncer. Didn't you see that big Black bastard on the door when you came in? He's crazy about Nancy, has her in here every night just to keep his eyes on her. Stay away.'

With such a clear warning, did I listen? Of course not. I still went over there and chatted up Nancy. An hour later, I was on the dance floor dancing with Nancy when I felt this hulking presence, breathing heavily at my shoulder. Big Boy, with clenched fists. Tom rushed over to plead my case: please, please don't beat him up. He's my idiot little brother; he means no harm…

Song for My Father

My first record player was a tiny Dansette I bought at Portobello Road Market for nine shillings, about two weeks' savings from my paper round job. I was over the moon, my own record player!! My eldest bother Gerry had just moved out and I'd inherited his tiny box room, privacy at last. The next week I bought my first record: the Jimi Hendrix single Voodoo Chile, I wore the grooves out of that record! Music was your everything: your identity, your expression, your late-night companion. But I soon found out that records were an expensive luxury, one I could ill afford. A long-play record cost about two weeks' wages, so you had to think very carefully about what you would buy. Fortunately, you could take each record for a test drive before you bought it; record shops had booths where you could listen to records – we'd spend hours inside those booths! For music lovers on a budget, samplers were great value: LPs put out by record companies including singles from their stable of artistes. Top of this list was Atlantic Records' "This is Soul!" plus Colombia Records' "Fill Your Head With Rock", lots of musical birds killed in one album. Records were a large part of your teenage budget, your growing collection a source of pride.

On May 26, 1967, the Beatles released their eighth album, *Sgt Pepper's Lonely Hearts Club Band,* and the world changed forever. Never, before or since, has one album made such an instant, monumental impact as *Pepper* and the boys: transformational. They followed up *Pepper's* with what to my mind was their finest work, *The White Album.* Inspired by their trip to India, meditation sessions with Maharishi Yogi, and copious amounts of mind-altering substances, this double album broke even more barriers than *Sgt Pepper's.* Not to be outdone, the Stones also released some of their best work around this time. Whereas the Beatles were more highbrow, confining themselves to their ivory tower in Abbey Road Studios, the Stones were more radical, epitomized by every anarchist's anthem: 'Street Fighting Man.' On July 5, 1969, Kevin Corrigan and I went to Hyde Park to a free concert given by the Stones, just two days after the death of their lead guitarist Brian Jones. We managed to wriggle our way close to the stage, where we saw to our horror that Mick Jagger was dressed in an outfit that looked suspiciously like – a skirt?

A few months after his marriage to Joan, Dad, ever the blunt instrument, says to Gerry: 'There are too many adults in this house.' Gerry got the hint and within a month had moved into a bedsit in Stonebridge Park. Dad's suggestion to Tom was a good deal more forthright. It was Sunday evening, and Tom and I were shooting the breeze in my bedroom. As usual, he'd been out partying all Saturday night and hadn't come home until Sunday afternoon. Equally as usual, Dad was angry: a ticking bomb on a short fuse. Tom was telling me that a group of them had been at the Purple Pussycat until the wee hours of Sunday morning, then had gone back to Steve Collins's flat in West Hampstead to crash out:

'There were so many of us at Steve's flat,' says Tom. 'That I slept with Maria, Steve's sister.'

BANG! Dad comes barging through the door in a fit of anger, the type of which neither of us had ever seen before: incandescent. He shouts at Tom.

'WHAT did you say? You slept with Maria Collins? You despoiled that child? GET OUT OF MY HOUSE!'

Dad had been eavesdropping outside the door (the indignity!) and had overheard Tom saying he 'slept with Maria.' Without another word Dad grabbed Tom by the scruff of the neck, frog-marched him out of my room, down the stairs, and literally kicked him out of the front door, bellowing one of his dramatic Dickensian phrases:

'Don't – ever – darken – my – doorstep – again!'

I was stunned. Tom knew better than try to argue with Dad in that state of mind, so he slunk off. His immediate destination was his friend Jim Kenny's pad just around the corner, to sleep on a couch. Dad retreated behind his locked door and stewed there all night, leaving me alone in a state of shock. What the *fuck* just happened? To try and put our father's rage into some sort of context, you have to realize who Maria Collins was. Maria was her father Lloyd's favourite child, even more so after her brother Paul's self-inflicted meltdown. Her father's hopes that Maria would attend university were equally shared by our father. And then, eavesdropping outside my door (the indignity of it), my father overhears a snippet of a conversation:

'Last night…. I slept with Maria.' At which point Dad lost his mind. I felt awful, being the catalyst in this latest and most serious confrontation between Dad and his headstrong middle son. This was not just about whether Tom had slept with Maria. This was the culmination of years of spiralling tension between the two of them. Both were very similar in temperament. In essence, it was Dad versus junior Dad.

And the worst part was Tom didn't even sleep with Maria! Or rather, that's exactly what they did: sleep. As he told me two days later when we finally met and went over the events of that horrible evening:

'If Dad had waited ten seconds instead of crashing through the door like a bull in a China shop, he would have heard the rest of the story. Which was that we just shared a bed, a single bed and very uncomfortable it was too! But Dad heard what he wanted, and the rest is history.'

My jaw dropped: to go through all that – and be innocent?'

Tom gave a rueful smile.

'Seems that's my lot in life: damned if I do, damned if I don't.'

The Isle of Wight Festival was the biggest gathering of hippies in the world, a weeklong orgy of music, drugs and, hopefully, sex. The 1970 edition showcased the *crème de la crème* of the rock world: Jimi Hendrix, Chicago, The Doors, Miles Davis, Joan Baez, Joni Mitchell, Jethro Tull, Sly and the Family Stone, Ten Years After, The Who, Emerson Lake & Palmer, and Free. A group of us planned to drive down in two cars and camp out for the week; it was going to be epic. Until Dad said no. 'There's going to be drugs and sex there. You›re only seventeen, no. And that›s final.' I *know* there's going to be sex and drugs. That's why I wanna go! I knew better than to rail against that final no: storming the Bastille would have been easier. My mates came back a week later, raving: they really did have sex, drugs, and rock-n-roll! The music was incredible, topped off by an incandescent performance by Jimi Hendrix. Worse yet: as it turned out, that was Hendrix's last performance. Three weeks later, he died in London from a drug overdose. And all I had to remind me of the gig of the decade was a lousy T-shirt!

Tom and Steve's *Around the World Adventure (as Recounted by Steve)*

It was the Summer of 1968 and Thomas and I were planning to 'travel,' with no fixed destination, abode nor itinerary, and if we went around the world, all the better. The idea was we'd work and save and go off with a decent bit of money. But as it turns out Tom got himself into a spot of bother with the law. He'd been riding an old BSA Bantam motorbike that was falling apart, and got stopped by the Old Bill, so he comes round to my place and says, we've got to leave – now! We packed up and on the way we went to this rock concert in Bath, incredible gig, then Jim Kenny drove us to Dover where our adventure would start. Unfortunately when we got there we found that we only had enough money for one crossing, so we went up to Canterbury and worked on a building site for 3 weeks, sleeping on site.

We took the hovercraft to France where we sold our duty-free fags to make some money. We were hitch-hiking down to Spain, but just couldn't get a lift together, so we jumped a train to Paris, had a great time there then headed south. Jumped another train to the South of France and used the last of our money to take a coach to Barcelona. From there we split up and would arrange to rendezvous at the Town Hall of the next town, it worked a treat and took us about two weeks to reach Malaga. One day this gay bloke picks up Thomas in this flash car. He really fancied Thomas and went hundreds of kilometres out of his way, chatting him up all the way. When night fell Thomas said thanks but he had to look for a spot to sleep the night, the driver got out the car and wouldn't stop following behind. Finally, Thomas legged it in the darkness with the bloke pleading behind him: 'Tomas, wait for me! I love ju!' Amazingly, the following morning Tom and I met up, just a few yards apart on the highway.

Money was always a problem, sometimes we'd get odd jobs but it was never enough. We'd collect empty beer bottles and return them for the deposit, it worked so well that we'd pick up crates of empties from the back of a bar, bring them round to the front and get paid for them!

We had a great time in southern Spain, it was the height of summer so we'd just sleep out in the open. But was during the Franco dictatorship and we had endless hassles from the Police and even worse, the Guardia Civil. These people were diehard fascists and hated us long-haired hippies, we'd be sitting in a café when they'd pounce on us, put us in the back of the car and drop us out of town with a stern warning not to return: 'No 'ippies in Torremolinos!'

Then Thomas got a really bad toothache and didn't have enough money to go to a dentist, so he decided to go back to England, with this right little thief called Eddie. They got to the Spain-France border, then jumped on a car-train heading to Paris. The cars were unlocked so they rode in comfort in a Benz all the way to Paris, but they got caught at the station and arrested. That was when Thomas had to go to the British Consulate in Paris and get repatriated to England.

When I got back to Canterbury a week or so later, Thomas had a car, a Zephyr, which he had 'taken and driven away' from a showroom. He'd taken it for a test drive, in those days they'd just toss you the keys and tell you to be back in twenty minutes. He was back in twenty minutes, but not before he'd gone to a locksmith and made a copy of the key. That evening he just came and drove it away! Lovely car that was, Thomas had a thing for Zephyrs ever since, he even bought a vintage one years later. Me, Thomas and Eddie drove down to Cornwall, and one afternoon in Newquay the Police pounced on us. Thomas and Eddie got arrested for the car, and they sent me on my way with a flea in my ear.

And that was the end of Thomas and Steve's Great Around the World Adventure!

I too got to fulfil my travel dreams, albeit on a less grand scale. In the summer of '70, I'd just turned seventeen, and Dad had finally relented and let me go hitch-hiking across Europe on my own. Gerry had done a similar trip two years earlier, the inspiration for my own trip. But before I could go to Europe, I first had to make the money for the trip, so for a month I worked at my friend's girlfriend's father's factory, hauling transformers out of a burning hot oven, five days a week, overtime on Saturdays. I bought a new rucksack, a one-man tent, sleeping bag, inflatable bed, gas stove, pot, pan, plate, and cutlery. I was primed and ready – *allons-y!*

In those days, hitch-hiking was a common form of transportation for young people. Drivers thought nothing of picking up hikers for the company, especially if she wore a miniskirt. I hitched from

London to Dover, took the ferry to Calais and was in Paris by nightfall. I stayed at the Pax Christie Youth Hostel where Gerry had stayed, beside myself with excitement: here I was – in *Paris!* This was the first time I'd travelled abroad on my own, the start of what would be a lifelong love affair. On the shores of Lac Lucerne, I got arrested for vagrancy, but it wasn't worth their while to do the paperwork, so they let me go with a Swiss flea in my ear. This was early August, perfect weather and plentiful summer fruits. For a week, I'd been living on the cheapest things in France at the time: wine, croissants, and peaches. Big, ripe, sweet peaches; you could buy a dozen for a few centimes: perfect. Then, on the seventh day, in the middle of Geneva, it came: Attack of the Peaches.

Geneva: Financial capital of the world, full of sophisticated millionaires, playboys, bankers, and down-at-heel Eurotrash. The truck dropped me off in the heart of the financial district. I thanked the driver and strolled around, getting my bearings. I must have looked a real sight: this shaggy-headed, grubby, sweaty kid with a rucksack and tent. And then: disaster. Without warning, the solid core of peaches which had been blocking up my bowels for the past seven days gave way. I literally felt it go, releasing a torrent of pent-up poo that my poor sphincter could only hold back for so long. In other words: I needed to shit – now!

Problem: there was nowhere to shit. I was in the middle of the financial district, surrounded by towering banks and gleaming office buildings, not exactly the sort of place where you could just drop in and have a crap. But that's exactly what I did. By now, I'd been on the road for ten days and was, shall we say, a bit soiled (read: filthy). I was also weighed down with rucksack, tent, sleeping bag, pots and pans, plus junk I'd picked up along the way. In short: I looked like shit. Which, to get back to the point, was what I needed: *immédiatement!* I walked into the nearest bank, which looked more like a castle than a bank. The concierge did a double take as I walked through the revolving door, and swiftly moved to cut me off, fluttering his gloved hands.

'Monsieur! Monsieur! Arrete!'

Millionaires in the lobby looked down their Gallic noses at this sweating apparition suddenly appearing in their midst. By this time in the trip, I'd become fairly proficient in Franglais, and with the obligatory hand signals made it abundantly clear to the concierge: *Monsieur, je besoin to use votre toilette – maintenant!!*

He tried to usher me back out the door but to forestall him I dropped my rucksack, pots and pans clanging off the marble tiles, and just stood there, cross-legged, cross-eyed, and pleading: *silvooplay monsieur,* pleeease! The poor concierge didn't have much choice: either he allowed me to use the toilet – or suffer the consequences! He looked around and clicked his fingers, two flunkies appeared out of nowhere and gathered up my possessions. The concierge whispered:

'Come zis way.'

We went through a door marked *Privat,* down a long corridor, me trying to speed up the pace. Eventually, he pointed to a door.

'Zere.'

As usual it was a French flush-and-jump toilette, basically a hole in the ground, but I couldn't care less. I tore off my clothes and then … relief, sweet-sweet relief! And again. And again … It was an unseasonably hot summer and when I finally emerged from the toilette I was pale, haggard, drawn, and drenched. The concierge, who'd taken the opportunity to light up a Gauloise, looked at me kindly and smiled.

'I sink you need a showere, no?' I could only nod: *merci!* At the back of the bank was a whole suite of rooms devoted to the bank's many staff, and very stylish it was too. My new friend the concierge showed me into a spacious bathroom with huge bathtub and fluffy towels – heaven!

'Take as long as you want.'

I had a lovely, long, hot bath – bliss! I emerged an hour later to find they had washed all my dirty clothes, which were still in the dryer. I'd become somewhat of a celebrity in the bank, and while I waited for my clothes to dry, they brought me a hearty lunch on a tray – the first meaty meal I'd eaten in days, with a delicious glass of red wine to wash it down. The concierge turned out to be a great guy, with an accent straight out of a Gerard Depardeau movie.

'I did not know,' he said matter-of-factly. 'Zat zere are les negres, in England.'

Oh yes, we negres are everywhere! He gave me a bottle of fine wine to travel with, and the whole staff bid me adieu. Later that night, as the rain fell gently outside my tent, I silently toasted my friend the concierge, smiling to myself and happy as the proverbial Larry.

This is the life! Little did I know it then, but it was a life that was about to be turned upside-down. Yet again.

11. Brian's Big Year

Everyone's life has their turning point, and mine was the entire year 1972. Late in the previous year, Dad had shocked me out of my comfortable slumber at Harrow Junior College by announcing:

'We're moving to Jamaica!'

Are you shitting me? Unsaid of course, but that's how I felt. Yet another friggin' country? Can't we just stay put somewhere, just for a little while? And Jamaica, really? I was seventeen, and this would be the seventh time I'd be moving country. The thought of yet another move filled me with dread. I'd finally gotten comfortable in my skin in England. I knew myself. I had friends and even a girlfriend – why the heck did we have to leave now? To yet another new country, and be yet another stranger in town? Not only that, but I'd also be moving between lower and upper sixth, to a new school with different examinations boards – who does this kind of foolishness? My father, that's who. But as it turned out, Jamaica was the best thing that ever happened to me.

Joan: Your father was extremely frustrated in 1971, firstly because he could not improve his salary at St George's and even though he applied for extra responsibility this was always denied. He tried for other posts in the area either with no success or he thought them unsuitable. Then he applied to do a degree course at Keele University, and I helped him with his application, but this was turned down as well. This was the final straw which motivated the application for temporary teaching contracts in Jamaica.

Dad and Joan flew directly to Kingston, while I would fly via a two-week stopover in New York, to stay with Dad's old Trinidadian friend Otway Culpepper and his European wife Lena. On August 31, 1971, I was flying out of Heathrow Airport to New York, standing in the Immigration line slowly shuffling forward along with everyone else when I noticed that the man immediately in front of me looked vaguely familiar. He had longish hair, a beaked nose, and those round National Health glasses of the type worn by ... John Lennon! And in front of him, Yoko! My eyes opened wider than his glasses. Lennon smiled, trying to put me at ease.

'So I guess me disguise didn't work then.'

'Sorry? I mean, what?'

'Me disguise, spotted me then, did you?'

Yoko smiled serenely, dressed in a long black gown, John in matching black suit and open-collared white shirt. As we shuffled down the line, Lennon continued to chat with me, about everything and nothing.

'Yeah man, we're leaving England, for good. It's just way too square over here. The police hound us, the press hound us, the fans hate Yoko. Just can't get no peace, man.' Or words to that effect. And then we went into our separate queues. I wish I'd had the presence of mind to get their autographs! That would be the last day that Lennon spent in his native England.

I can't say it was love at first sight with me and Jamaica – *au contraire*. The drive through downtown Kingston from Norman Manley Airport is daunting enough at the best of times, but at night as your first glimpse of your new home, it was positively Kafkaesque: a vision of dystopia. From the back seat of Dad's Hillman Minx, I stared out at a rolling scene of pure chaos as we drove along Windward Road: pushcart vendors, jerk chicken sellers, peanut sellers, rum bars with massive speakers blasting non-stop reggae, mad drivers, bad drivers, honking trucks, belching buses, dallying bikers, hustlers, stray dogs, dead dogs, vagabonds, and beggars. Kingston was an assault on the senses, of monumental proportions. I looked out in awe: Shit, this place is *kray-zee!*

We rented a house in Aylsham Heights, a brand-new housing scheme in Upper St Andrew, treeless and soulless. On my first night in Jamaica, there was a party at the house two doors down, and in true Jamaican style the decibels cranked up as the night wore on. Among the cheek-by-jowl houses without any trees, it felt like you were inside the party, the bass pounding through your bones. Dad was furious: 'This is ridiculous! It's one o'clock in the morning; people can't be so irresponsible!' I looked on, increasingly bemused. He marched over to the party in his dressing gown. I didn't witness his reception from the revellers, but he came back with a worse face than he'd left with. I stifled a chuckle. I was intrigued by the music, how the deejay skilfully moved from one genre to another: reggae to soul, to calypso (briefly), to slow tunes and always: back to reggae. I thought I like this.

At two o'clock, Dad couldn't take it anymore. He looked on the road map:

'The nearest Police Station is Constant Springs, come with me!'

He drove the mile or so to Constant Springs Police Station, marched up to the desk in a state of high dudgeon, and roused the somnambulant sergeant:

'Officer, there is a party going on next door, and none of us can get any sleep for the music pounding in our ears. It's two in the morning, and I demand you send a squad car to put a stop to it!'

The bored sergeant fixed his sleepy eye on Dad: another outraged foreigner. This is the last thing he needed to disturb his peace at this time a night:

Song for My Father

'Come back at four.'

Dad fumed all the way home while I grinned to myself. As predicted, the party turned off the music at four.

Despite my meagre haul of three O-Levels, I was enrolled into Upper Sixth at the same school my father would be teaching at: Excelsior High on Mountain View Avenue – a little nepotism goes a long way. I was aghast to learn that I'd be wearing a uniform again; really? And even more aghast to learn that the English Literature A-Level I'd been studying for in England was under the Cambridge Examinations Council, whereas in Jamaica they were under Oxford. Which meant that the ten classic books I'd been studying in England were now irrelevant, and I'd have to read and study ten new books in one year, rather than the prescribed two. Again, I asked myself: who does this?

The dawn of 1972 found me aged eighteen and not enjoying life. I sorely missed my brothers and friends back in London, with only the snail mail to keep me connected. I sent ten letters for every precious one received; the postman became my best friend, but more often my worst enemy. I found my new Jamaican school peers weren't particularly interested in what went on beyond their borders; when I tried to brag about how I'd met John Lennon and Yoko Ono at Heathrow Airport, I was met with: 'A who dem?' In 1966, when John Lennon had scandalously said that the Beatles were 'more popular than Jesus,' he wasn't wrong – except in Jamaica.

The tiny 1972 pocket diary was a Christmas present from my father's golfing buddy, Mr Wolstenholme, whom I detested because he'd come to Jamaica straight from apartheid South Africa. Having started with the pretentious pledge: *I do hereby swear that this diary is a true account of the life of Steven B. Samuel and that no deliberate falsification has been made.'* I soon found that it wasn't easy to cram everything into its miniscule pages. But I managed, in handwriting so small I needed a magnifying glass to decipher it.

The year 1972 was a year of two halves. In the first half, I was your typical bored high school kid, chafing at the bit and struggling to find my place in this new and different land. But around the middle of the year, three things happened that changed the course of my life. Firstly, I passed my A-levels, and not just passed but passed well. This was the first time I'd ever excelled academically, and it was entirely due to the one year I'd spent at Excelsior High, the 'worst but best' of the five high schools I'd attended between England, America, and now Jamaica. In terms of its physical facilities, Excelsior was a dump, with dilapidated classrooms and precious little in the way of sporting or other amenities. But where it mattered most, in the quality of its teachers and the drive for learning they instilled in their students; Excelsior excelled.

Where are they now?

Song for My Father

That summer I took a rusty old tramp ship, *Federal Maple*, on an island-hopping voyage from Jamaica to St Kitts, Antigua, Montserrat, Dominica, St Lucia, Barbados, and finally Grenada where I fell in love with my ancestral home. The third and most important thing to happen in that seminal year was that I entered University of the West Indies, Mona Campus. In those days, I was a British citizen (I'm not now, but that's another story), and could've gone back to study in England where I would've gotten a student grant. But I chose to stay in Jamaica: after one year, I was hooked.

When I recently uncovered the diary, I hadn't laid my eyes on it since I'd stopped writing it, four decades earlier. On re-reading it, I found myself chuckling at the short, pithy entries to save on space: '*Went to church with Tony. Not good.*' Looking back, I remembered the major events of that year, but I was surprised at how much I'd completely forgotten: who *are* these people?

Another thing I noticed was how different our lives were back then. A telephone was an undreamt-of luxury, so if you wanted to talk to somebody you actually had to go and see them. Every day was 'went here... went there.' Whether by car, bus, beg-drive, or walk-foot; I was a boy in perpetual motion.

Like 90 per cent of eighteen-year-old boys, I was a walking penis: the hunt for girls occupied a large part of my waking life – and no doubt sleeping as well. Having landed with a splash in Excelsior's Upper Sixth Form as 'dat red hippy bwoy from England,' I soon had my classmates speechless when I started dating the school's resident Black Power activist, Antonette Haughton. But it wasn't a compatible political union. We had decidedly different agendas: she wanted revolution; I wanted sex! Naturally, the coalition didn't last. Antonette went on to become a rabble-rousing lawyer and radio commentator in Jamaica, until she was obliged to flee to Cuba, over a matter of missing money. There followed a succession of short-term assignations, one-night stands, near-misses, and reluctant relationships, all in the single-minded pursuit of, well what else do teenage boys pursue?

It took me quite a while to transcribe the diary, hours spent squinting under the light at the kitchen table before my wife Marion wisely bought me a magnifying glass. Every now and then I'd chuckle, look up and bore her with some youthful misadventure, to get the yes-dear nod.

And so, Brian's Big Year begins...

> **Friday 31 Dec, 1971**: *Went to New Year's party with Antonette. Didn't have a good time.*

The year didn't begin brightly, cooped up at home and miserable: '*Bored like hell with this place. Had to make my own way home on the sardine-can buses.*' At school I was studying A-Level Economics, English Literature, and General Paper. And O-level French, but that was a lost cause. Early in the year, I ended my fling with Antonette (she wasn't heartbroken), then cast my eyes around for richer pastures.

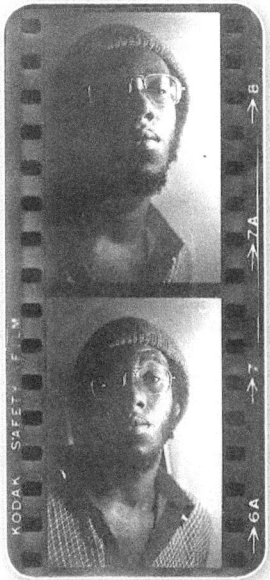

Maurice Wilson

On my very first day at Excelsior, I fell in with two characters who would become lifelong friends: Lloyd Sheckleford aka Shacks, and Maurice Wilson aka Hippo. The three of us clicked immediately and formed the nucleus of the Mango Tree Club, an impromptu lunchtime debating society holding forth on oh-so serious subjects like socialism, capitalism, colonialism, anti-colonialism, imperialism, anti-imperialism, racism, Black Power, and Vietnam. And girls.

Weekends seem to have been one long party: every Friday was a debate as to which 'spot' I'd be going to, and with whom. Plus, beaches on Sunday, concerts, and visiting friends with Dad and Joan, I was a busy lad. For any teenage boy, access to wheels is a crucial aspect of life, and fortunately Maurice had access to his mother's Holden Kingswood, an Australian beast. The three of us would probe far and wide, in the never-ending search for the next spot to crash.

The seventies were the days of that now extinct phenomenon: the no-pay party. People would throw a party for no reason, just because it'd been a while since their last one. It was an unwritten rule that everyone you knew, every distant relative, every old school chum, everyone whose party you'd been to in the past – were all automatically invited, no invitations needed. Gate-crashing was an art form we practised every weekend. Driving through Stony Hill at two in the morning, Shacks would say: 'Stop the car, turn off the engine. There's a party around here somewhere. I can *feel* it!'

Must-have list for any Jamaican fete:

1. Let's start with the single most important ingredient in any fete: the set. The mobile disco that comes to rock your house, literally. In a truck loaded with wall-to-ceiling speakers, mixers, amps, dozens of record boxes, and hangers-on, all thirsty. From reggae to soul, calypso, rent-a-tile slow music and always ending with the highlight of any fete: the oldies session. Get a good deejay, throw a good party. Get a dud, throw a dud.

2. Secondly, you need an inexhaustible supply of every conceivable variety of alcohol. There would be all sorts of grumbling if the beer ran out before the party did. Unforgivable.

3. At around two o'clock, the food must be ready: chicken, curry goat, rice an' peas, salad, fried plantain. And fish, 'cos Rasta don't eat deaders.

4. And a cup of red pea soup to send you home at dawn.

Now *that's* a fete!

My attentions zeroed in on two new cuties at school: Marlene and Michelle, and like any desperate teenager, I had my fair share of heartaches:

> **Sun 20 Feb**: *Michelle came round! Asked me to go over to her house, I went over after lunch – had a great time she's a really sweet girl. Arranged date for next week.*

> **Sat 26 Feb**: *Picked up Lloyd before the party. Me and Marlene split at the party. I'm glad in a way, but sad.*

> **Sun 27 Feb**: *Moped around all day 'cos of Marlene.*

> **Tues 29 Feb**: *General Elections. Driving test (failed, bloody parking). PNP won!! Went to party at the Walker's, saw the results. Great! Saw Manley on the way home and shouted congrats.*

Dad reconnected with his old London friend, Herbie Walker, who was permanent secretary in the Ministry of Commerce and Industry. We spent many a Sunday afternoon relaxing at their pool, and I became friends with their daughter Barbara who was my age. She was a good friend and in possession of one valuable asset: a pale blue Vauxhall Viva.

I was learning to drive, meaning I'd drive the car to school every morning, while Dad read his *Gleaner* in the passenger seat, occasionally glancing up and making some comment. I was champing at the bit to get my license, but motivating Dad to take me downtown to the testing centre on Spanish Town Road wasn't always easy, especially after my mandatory first failure.

In the meantime, the girl-hunt continued:

> **Fri 3 March**: *At Michelle's house all day. No good because her maid was there.*

> **Sat 4 March**: *Did Econ & French. In the evening we went to see the NDTC at UWI. They were terrific, the Kumina and Pocomania were best.*

Fri 10 March: Went to Michelle's house – had a good time but her aunt caught us together.

Tues 21 March: Got filmed by 'Panorama' to be shown in England. About JA & the PNP. Must write everyone. Went to Michelle's, more fun.

So here I was, yet another new country, yet again fitting in. Or trying to; I soon found out that fitting into Jamaica wasn't going to be a straightforward affair: this place was something else altogether: inexplicable and mind-blowing. First of all there was the race thing. On my second day I got a rude introduction into the complexities of Jamaican racial politics. I walking in downtown Kingston when this street urchin shouts:

'Hey white bwoy, gimmie a dollar nuh?'

I looked around: no white bwoy in sight.

'Who you talkin' to?'

'You, white bwoy!'

I wanted to slap the little shit! But he was right; overnight I'd been transformed: from black immigrant to brown bourgeois: oppressed to oppressor. A change I abhorred. Mind you it was a mixed bag: the very next day a Rastaman greeted me loudly on the street with a broad smile:

'Hail, Jet-Black!'

I liked that one.

In 1971, Jamaica had been independent for nine years, but little had changed: Whites and Chinese controlled the economy, browns worked in banks, and blacks lived a life of unending toil. I was amazed at the extreme gap between rich and poor – all living cheek by jowl in overcrowded Kingston. In Aylsham, a brand-new middle-class housing scheme in Upper St. Andrew, I became friends with the kid next door, Kevin Blackman. Like so many West Indian families, Kevin's wasn't quite colour-coordinated: Kevin was Black, his mother brown (despite lashings of Nadinola 'skin-toning' cream), and daddy who clearly wasn't daddy was what Jamaicans call a Syrian. Compared to our modest lifestyle, they lived like kings: mom and dad drove big American cars, shopping trips to Miami, weekends in Ochie, boat in the bay: the good life.

When I saw the source of all their wealth, my jaw dropped. A hole-in-the-wall hardware store in downtown Kingston, selling fridges and stoves to poor people on layaway. THAT little shop can fund such a lifestyle? Back in England, my friend's father owned a factory. I worked there one summer. It employed hundreds of people, but they didn't live anywhere near as lavishly as my neighbours did, from one likkle shop down de lane. How much of each fridge went towards their profits? Probably more than half. Sick. It was then that I started talking about capitalism, exploitation, socialism ...

One night I went with Kevin to a 'spot,' a party in Cherry Gardens, and as we were milling around outside it dawned on me that everyone in the spot, except me and Kevin, was White. I was horrified and told Kevin I didn't want to go in. He couldn't understand my reaction and didn't want to miss this 'opportunity,' but against his wishes I dragged him away, lecturing him about Black Power all the way home.

It wasn't easy, holding onto my Englishness while seeking to assimilate into Jamaica. Shacks and Maurice were mystified when I played my Led Zeppelin records: a wha dat? I had no such problems getting into reggae: Dennis Brown, Toots and the Maytals, Big Youth, and of course Bob Marley and the Wailers were all approaching their prime.

After being in Jamaica for about six months, a strange thing started to happen. Almost without realizing it, my understanding of Jamaica began to deepen, and with it, a new appreciation. With Shacks and Maurice, I explored the nooks and crannies of the island, falling in love with its natural beauty and rich culture. Sure, they still didn't know who John Lennon was, but who cared? There were more important things to get stressed about: poverty, exploitation, politics, crime. Stuff that mattered, stuff that could get you killed.

When it came to Jamaican girls, I was a convert from day one. Compared to the few English girls I'd dated back in London, Jamaican girls were a class apart: confident: bright, sassy – and sexy! And sexiest of all (though not necessarily brightest) was Michelle Davies. This cute little chick was in my Dad's class at Excelsior, the one bright spark in a classroom full of sullen boys and preening princesses. The boys in his class, most of them remedials, weren't used to Dad's stern disciplinary methods, and they nicknamed him 'Sour Hog': Jamaican slang meaning bad-smelling; they even composed a song about him:

Sour shower
Every hour
'Pon de hour
But him still sour!

Being his son, they'd cheekily call out to me as I walked by: 'Sour Juice!,' which took me a while to figure out. After another frustrating day of teaching, Dad would rave over the dinner table about Michelle Davies: Michelle Davies is so polite. Michelle Davies is so lovely. Michelle Davies is so graceful. Thank god for Michelle Davies.

Then I saw Michelle Davies, and thought: has Dad gone mad? Michelle Davies wasn't graceful, polite, or lovely. Michelle Davies was *hot!* The little vixen positively oozed sex out of every pore, in her tight school uniform, tailored to accentuate her plentiful assets, come-hither smile and come-to-bed eyes. I was smitten. She lived in Barbican, a longish walk from Aylsham, but a walk I gladly did many times.

In June, my A-level exams around: pressure drop. I'd been studying hard over the preceding months, but who's not nervous as hell prior to their A's? My biggest fear was English Literature, where I'd had to squeeze a two-year syllabus into one: I wasn't confident.

Mon 5 June: English Paper 2 P.M. Bloody difficult!!! I don't know if I did that well.

Wed 7 June: Driving test 8:45A.M. Bastard examiner failed me on the road test. General Paper exam, not too bad.

Mon 19 June: English Paper 3 P.M. It was gruelling but not too awful. Got various drives home, studied for the Econ tomorrow – I don't know as much as I should. Watched Hawaii 50 last episode.

Tues 20 June: Economics paper 2. Wasn't all that hard, I did all the questions but could have done better.

Thurs 22 June: English paper 8 A.M. Finished English! Waited for Maurice's mother, then me, him & Lloyd drove to St. Thomas. Ate eggs & bread & drove back. Stopped to pick up a crab but it was a female.

Mon 26 June: Economics Paper A.M. Wasn't good at all. NO MORE EXAMS!!

That summer of 1972, Dad, Joan, and I would be going on holiday to Grenada, and instead of flying with them I took an old ship, the *M/V Federal Maple* on an island-hopping trip through the islands of the Eastern Caribbean. This sounded like fun, but the reality was that the old girl was at the bitter end of a long and hard sea life, she weren't no cruise ship. As usual, Dad booked me the cheapest fare possible. Deck passage meant exactly what it said: you tried to find some sheltered place on deck, laid out your foam rubber and prayed it didn't rain. The first three days out of Kingston we headed due East to St Kitts, hard sailing directly into the teeth of big seas and strong headwinds. I was as sick as a dog the entire time:

Sat 8 July: Went to the dock in the morning, the boat left at 2:00 PM. Befriended Kassahun (an Ethiopian UWI student) and others, started to get seasick. Lost sight of JA at 7:00. The boat is nice except for the place to sleep.

Sun 9 July: Still bloody seasick. Spewed up everything I ate. Lay around all day, taking occasional trips to the side of the boat to

vomit. They killed and ate the goat. There's a bunch of girl guides,
but they are perfectly fine. I hate girl guides.

First landfall was St Kitts. I wobbled ashore to be met by a gaggle
of local youths on the dock. They rushed around me:

'You from Jamaica?'

'Yeah.'

'You have ganja?'

'No.'

'You have ratchet knife?'

'No.'

'Cha!' And rushed off to accost the next passenger.

The ship sailed on to Antigua, Montserrat, and Dominica, before
I disembarked in St Lucia where I was to rendezvous with Dad and
Joan. In Dominica, I almost missed the boat because I'd gone with a
Dominican friend to his home, a Carib or Kalinago village a long
way from the capital Roseau. I told them my grandmother had Carib
blood. They hugged me and told me I was Carib too. In St Lucia, I
met some young people my age and was taken to beaches, clubs, and
parties.

This was my first taste of the Eastern Caribbean, and I liked it.
I enjoyed Jamaica's vibrancy, but everyday life in Kingston was
overlaid with a nagging security fear: did I lock the burglar bars?
What's that noise? St Lucia had none of that heaviness; it was way
more chilled. Dad, Joan, and I stayed with his Grenadian friend
Gordon DaBreo, a magistrate. There were huge construction
projects underway at Cap Estate and Rodney Bay, the beginning of a
prolonged tourism boom in St Lucia: an island on the move.

We flew from St Lucia to Barbados, or Little England as per
Caribbean legend. It lived up to its reputation:

Mon 24 July: Mrs. Pilgrim drove us to Bridgetown & looked around.
It looks like a small English town.

We were staying with Dad's old London friend, Torrey Pilgrim, who'd moved back to Barbados a few years previously. Torrey was one of those people who managed to live their entire lives without ever working a stitch. In Barbados, Torrey had reinvented himself as a yoga teacher and lifestyle coach, continuing the same lifestyle he had lived in London, leaving his hard-working English wife Phyllis to feed and clothe the family.

> **Tues 25 July:** *Torrey had a yoga meeting at his house. I listened to an old man who was fascinating. He had a brilliant control over his body & mind. I think I'll take up yoga.*

> **Wed 26 July:** *My 19th birthday. Parents gave me a dashiki & Brut deodorant. We drove around Barbados. It's really scenic especially the eastern side which is hilly & rocky with rough seas.*

We flew from Barbados to our ultimate destination: Grenada. All three of us were looking forward to this trip, each for our own reasons. My only previous recollection of Grenada had been six glorious months in 1960 that Tom, Gerry, and I had spent there when I was seven years old, just before sailing to England. Our father had kept the Grenada flame alive with stories from his own childhood and local folk tales about *La Diablesse, Loup Garoux* and other blood-curdling night creatures. Twelve years after I'd left Grenada, I was super excited to be going home.

The shaky LIAT Hawker-Siddley turboprop landed at Pearl's Airport on the windy East Coast, a nerve-wracking experience in the best of conditions, as these clearly weren't. We took a taxi to St George's, where I learned that Dad didn't have a firm plan as to where we'd be staying that night. Eventually, we found a self-catering apartment just up the road from Grand Anse Beach. I breathed in the air, rich with hints of salt and spice: home.

The next morning, we took a bus into St George's. Those were the last days of Grenada's famous penny buses, old Bedford trucks with covered wooden benches, brightly painted with names like *Hold*

Strain and *Study Your Head*. We met several of Dad's old friends and had lunch in Pointe Salines. Then it was time to make the pilgrimage: Perdmontemps.

My only link to Perdmontemps was Brenda, our older cousin who'd presided over Tom, Gerry, and I for six months back in 1960. It was great to reconnect with her, meet her husband Michael and their growing family. I had great fun playing with her boys, Stanley and Brandon.

> **Sat 29 July**: *Drove around in the morning. Gave the borrowed car back & took bus into town. Met all of Dad's old friends, ate lunch at Sam Graham's in Pointe Salines. Brenda drove us to Perdmontemps. Raining but nice. Grenada is really beautiful!*

Dad hadn't come to Grenada just for a holiday, he'd come to buy land. He was beginning to plan for 'the evening of his days' as he liked to call his retirement, and a nice plot of land in Grenada for him and Joan to build their home on was very much a part of that plan. We looked at a few plots, and they finally settled on a half-acre plot of beach land, right next to the Calabash Hotel, a small upscale resort in Lance aux Epines (pronounced Lansapeen).

> **Tues 8 Aug**: *Went to see Sam Graham. Chatted then went to look at plots of land – one next to Calabash is the best.*
>
> **Wed 9 Aug**: *Tried to contact Brathwaite about the land. Went*

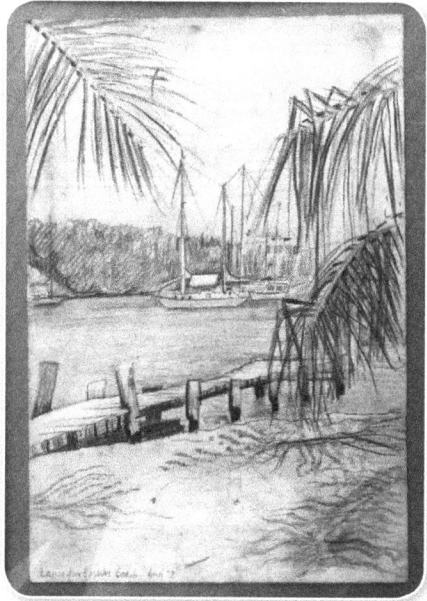

The Land, *by Joan*

> *to Calabash & paced out the area of the land & walked around. Ate at Red Crab, swam, later on went to Brathwaite's house (beautiful) & agreed on the deal. Had supper at the Red Crab, played darts with some fellas afterwards.*

So, Dad got his land. He paid the deposit and received the Title Deed, to be finalized upon payment of the balance of the purchase price. Dad and Joan enjoyed meeting up with his old friends while I delved into island life with gusto: spearfishing with fishermen in Calliste, chilling on Grand Anse Beach with my Venezuelan cousin Gisela, and spending many nights at Mount Rose House. And learning to drink whiskey:

> ***Sun 13 Aug:*** *Denby & Steve called on Dad in the A.M. & I left with them. God I learned how to drink Scotch whisky today! We went to Wendy's and ate, talked & drank. Then for a drive, with more. Went to Blue Danube, ate souse & drank more. Drove back to my house, but nobody was in, then they drove me to Mount Rose, where I stayed the night. Today I got initiated into Scotch.*

Post-script: Sadly, my father died before completing the purchase of the land, and neither Joan nor I could afford to make the balance of the purchase price, after we'd been robbed of his life insurance policy by Island Life. But that's another story. Nowadays, I swim at that same beach and have lunch at the restaurant that occupies Dad's dream spot, and sigh.

Too soon it was time to leave Grenada, and although I'd be saying goodbye to one home, I'd be saying hello to another. We'd lived in Port of Spain up until I was seven years old, and I fondly remembered a life full of fun and fast cars.

> ***Sun 20 Aug:*** *Dad hired a car. Drove up Mt. St. Benedict's, very pretty. Then drove around Port of Spain, North Point, US Base, Fort George. Everything is well organised and clean. The view from Fort George is breath taking. In evening went to a steel band competition. Very good sounds. Then drove up to Lady Young Highway & ate roti. I'm quite impressed with Trinidad.*

Mon 21 Aug: Drove to San Fernando via Pointe-a-Pierre. Then down to Pitch Lake. This is very interesting, then visited Raymond Banfield. Chatted with his children, then went to eat at a Chinese restaurant.

After three hectic days in Trinidad, I took a plane to Barbados, then St Lucia, where I boarded the sister ship to the *Federal Maple*, the *Federal Palm*. Unfortunately, it was identical in every way:

Tues 22 Aug: The facilities on board aren't fit for a pig.

I soon realized that the return journey had none of the romance and excitement of the outward leg; it was just a long sea slog. We'd all been to the same islands just a few weeks before, and all we wanted was to get back to Jamaica, quickly.

Tues 29 Aug: RED LETTER DAY! Woke up 4:00 watched the ship sail into Kingston. Spent a long time clearing Customs & Immigration. Took a taxi home. Results came: 3 passes, B, B & 1! Very shocked about the results. The new house is fantastic – very big. Went & got a TV and saw Barbra. She passed 2 A's. Saw Michael & the James' & phoned Milly. Went back to Barbra's & met Lloyd. Talked a lot & walked home.

If ever there was a red-letter day, as I christened it, Tuesday, 29 August 1972 was it. I vividly remember the heady mix of emotions that danced happily around my mind: shock, disbelief, joy, optimism, and excitement: I'm going to *university!* Specifically, University of the West Indies, Mona Campus, in Jamaica. It had all been arranged. All I needed were my A-Level certificates. But my optimism was premature:

Wed 30 Aug: Went to UWI to give in my grades, but too late, they're full up!! Talked to Lady Phillips about it. Dr. Beaubrun gave me some advice about getting in. I'm on the waiting list. Came home & told Dad & Joan the news about UWI.

Mon 4 Sept: Went downtown to look for a job. Nothing at all. Went to UWI, I'm next on the list.

Wed 6 Sept: *Woke up late, did some more sanding with Dad, then he told me I was wanted at UWI, I'm accepted!!*

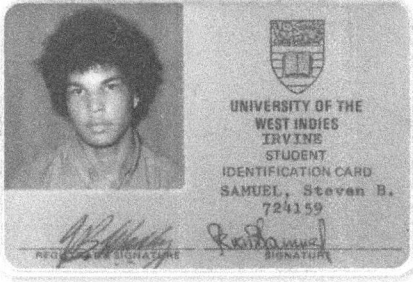

When I got accepted by UWI my father 'suggested' I study law, transferring his own unmet ambitions onto his son in the time-honoured tradition of fathers the world over. But I didn't want to study law – probably just because he wanted me to. I made him suffer for a week, telling him I was going to major in sociology.

'Sociology? What the hell are you going to do with a sociology degree?'

'Um, become a sociologist?'

Eventually, I put him out of his misery and told him I had decided to major in Economics, and surprisingly, he didn't make a fuss.

'Econ-Law: good combination.'

Firebrand lecturers Trevor Munroe, George Beckford, and Norman Girvan filled us with socialist zeal, with their meticulously researched indictments of slavery, colonialism, capitalism, and imperialism. We were young, eager, over-confident, and taking ourselves oh-so-seriously. We knew the faults of every generation that had come before us, but we were different. We had all the right answers. We were the guardians of the New International Economic Order; we were going to *change the world*. No seriously, don't laugh.

The first thing that happened in my freshman year was nothing. Students and lecturers went on strike in support of the UWI workers' demand for higher pay and better conditions. After two weeks, the strike petered out, and we could turn our minds to the serious business of every freshman: partying. Every weekend, there were fetes on the dorms, at the Students' Union and best of all the Nurses' Block. Shacks, Maurice, and I quickly earned the nickname the Three Musketeers as we were, indeed, inseparable.

I loved my freshman year: everything was new, fresh, and fun. I delved into my courses and worshipped my lecturers, intellectual heroes of the struggle. After two years in Jamaica, I began to feel, for the first time in a long time: home. I consciously worked on my Jamaican accent, to rid myself of those pesky English antecedents. I begged Dad to let me live on campus, but he said I had to stay at home – why spend money needlessly? But I made the most of it. I was hardly ever home. Most days were a whirl of activity, squeezed into the margins of the tiny diary:

> **Wed 11 Oct**: *Driving Test 8:45 Spanish Town Rd. Picked up the Viva, went to Sp. Tn. Rd. waited a long time but passed my test at last! Came up with Dad, borrowed the PI (Triumph 2.5 Petrol Injection), went to Shacks, drove with Tony to the garage, then XLCR for Dad, then Tony's, he picked up his mother's car. Dropped Lloyd at Barbra's, drove home, Tony picked me up & went back to Barbra's, had a boring time with her & Milly & Alison. Drove back to Tony's, Maurice got his car from the garage & they ate at my house. Shacks & Barclay came round. Went to Carib for a Wang Yu film (full up), then club near Flamingo (go-go dancers), then High Chapparal (more dancers & thief rum). Then Cottage Club (football not working). Then Fernando's, football, shooting, bowling, wrestling, then drove me home.*

In the early seventies, Jamaica was moving from the rude boy sounds of ska and rock-steady to the slower, heavier rhythms of reggae, and the emergence of a certain Robert Nesta Marley. What foreigners fail to realize is that there were two Bobs: Bob before he became famous and Bob after. Essentially, they were the same Bob, but the music wasn't. Bob re-recorded many of his earlier Jamaican hits, giving them a professional polish lacking on the original versions. The first reggae song I really got into was Bob's *Trenchtown Rock*, his thick patois lyrics explained to me in painstaking detail by Antonette Haughton. *'No waah yu fi gallang so, yu waan come cole I up'* Huh?

As suddenly as my diary started, it stopped:

Fri 24 Nov. *Milly's party. GAVE UP WRITING DIARY TODAY.*

Thus ended Brian's Big Year. My grow-up year, the year that quite literally made me what I am. The Brian of December 1971 and the Brian of December 1972 were two decidedly different Brians, almost unrecognizable. I'd grown by leaps and bounds in just twelve months, from an insecure kid unhappy with his lot in life, to an enthusiastic freshman growing in confidence, thirsting for knowledge and loving his new life in Jamaica. Whoever would have thought?

The rest of my freshman year went by in a blur. I enjoyed a settled relationship, and my social life flourished, on and off campus. But as comfortably settled as I'd become, I was about to follow in my father's footsteps in one aspect of life that has remained with me ever since: Nomadism.

12. Back to America and Back

amaica in the seventies was a hotbed of new ideas and creativity, and I was lucky enough to be there at the right age (young, impressionable, and eager) to hitch a ride on these exciting winds of change. The charismatic Michael Manley had just swept the socialist People's National Party (PNP) into power, ushering in a prolonged radical phase in the island's political history. I enjoyed our lectures, dissecting colonialism, imperialism, and the weaknesses of our post-colonial governments. Political science lecturer Trevor Monroe moved out of the lecture theatre and onto the streets, when he established the University and Allied Workers Union, but when he tried to take on the established and corrupt waterfront unions, he received a hard lecture in realpolitik and got the shit kicked out of him on the docks.

Our socialist bible was Walter Rodney's *How Europe Underdeveloped Africa*. Our heroes were Nkrumah, Fanon, and of course Castro. We followed the anti-apartheid struggles in Southern Africa, castigated the sellouts, went to giant rallies at the National Stadium to welcome African freedom fighters Samora Machel and Julius Nyerere. We were the children of the (armchair) revolution.

It was also a time of rising crime and tension in Jamaica, the beginning of interminable street wars between politically affiliated armed gangs which would soon escalate into full-blown civil war.

Dread days in Kingston

Throughout its history, violence had always been central to Jamaican politics, from slave rebellions and labour riots of the 1930s, politics and violence had gone hand-in-hand. But over time, the nature of that violence evolved, became more deadly. In the sixties, it was rocks and sticks with the occasional cutlass, by the seventies it had graduated to M-16s and AKs. Large sections of downtown Kingston, the so-called garrison constituencies, became no-go areas to anyone with sense, including the police and Jamaica Defence Force.

Song for My Father

But in addition to all that world-changing stuff, we also managed to have a helluva lot of plain fun at uni. My freshman year went by in a blur: lectures, parties, plays, parties, debates, parties, Student Union strikes, parties ... did I say parties? Maurice and Shacks were my inseparable buddies, and in Maurice's mother's big Holden we probed the length and breadth of Jamaica: rivers, mountains, beaches, spearfishing, hiking, and having fun. By the end of my freshman year, I'd been in Jamaica for two years and had become a committed Jamaicaphile. Meanwhile, back in London ...

Gerry Hosts a Double Life-Changing Party:

After Dad, Joan and Brian left England for Jamaica in 1971, I tried the accountancy and just jollied along. I was renting a room in 57 Winchester Road from the Datta family from India. My mate Carlo rented another room. They had an empty garage and we used that opportunity to rebuild a wreck of a minivan that we'd bought for £30. It was great fun stripping it down to the shell and starting from scratch. Pretty much everything I learned about cars was from that summer. The Dattas went to India on holiday for a couple of weeks, so I thought: what better time to host a party? On Tuesday 7th September 1971 I held a party that changed the course of my life, by meeting my future wife! By party, I mean just a venue to snog. I was not providing any food or drink, in fact there was no preparation whatsoever. I'd just said to a couple of friends I knew that 'my place' (yur right) was free that Tuesday. Tuesday? Who holds a party on a Tuesday ferchrissakes? Anyway my friend Ellen Dwyer duly spread the word and Tuesday rolled around. Of course, I wasn't ready. In fact, when the guests started arriving I was still in the garage spray painting the minivan. I finally made it to my own party, rather reluctant to leave the van but needs must. And there was my brother Tom, chatting up three girls, none of whom I'd met before: Valda, Louise and Pat.

Tom and I both hit on the same girl, Pat Long, in her knee length lilac suede boots and black dress with tiny stars on it, although me not remotely in Tom's Lothario league. Somehow Tom inveigled Pat into my bedroom - she has no idea how that happened. Then I came in like Sir Galahad and rescued my fair damsel! For which she was eternally grateful and Tom for the longest while was most miffed! At the end of the night, I borrowed my mate's blue Ford Anglia and took Pat home. I also took a rather puzzled Tom home too. There he was in the back seat, asking 'What's my brother got, that I haven't?' He was perplexed. From that epic evening, I subsequently married Pat, and Tom and Valda became lifetime partners and together had twin sons: Raymond and Toussaint.

For the summer of 1973 Dad, Joan, and I were due to fly back to London, among other things for Gerry's wedding. Two years previously, not long after we'd left England, Gerry had met the love of his life, Pat Long, and now he would be the first Samuel brother to get hitched. I hadn't met Pat and was also looking forward to reuniting with my brothers and friends, after two years away.

As often happens, the bride and groom were railroaded into doing the whole big wedding thing; left to themselves, they'd have probably run off to Gretna Green and done it by themselves. But that would never do, so they had the wedding at Harrow Magistrate's Court, followed by a reception at The King's Head in Harrow-on-the-Hill.

I spent the whole of that brilliant summer of '73 in London. Gerry's friend Pete

10 Downing Street:
I'm watching you

Song for My Father

Bleasdale got me a job at British Tissues in Kenton, and I stayed with my old mate Rob Shepardson and his friends in Wembley. Gerry even lent me his lovingly restored 1953 VW Beetle called Clarissa from time to time. I brought my new-found Jamaican-ness with me back to London, not fully appreciated by my elder siblings.

'All right, Brian,' says a scornful Tom. 'You can quit the fake Jamaican accent now!'

During my freshman year at Mona, I'd become friends with a Black American student called Bill Kirk, who was dating and eventually married my friend Hilary Reckord. Bill went to Swarthmore College in Pennsylvania and had come to UWI on a one-year exchange programme. This sounded interesting; I asked at the UWI Registrar's Office about this programme and did it work the other way round: can I go there? Nobody seemed to know anything about it. Someone found a pamphlet which seemed to say that they did have an exchange programme, but not with Swarthmore, with the University of Michigan – would that do? I didn't know much about Michigan except it was rated among the top ten in America, which was good enough for me – sign me up.

I applied in January 1973 and by March came the reply: accepted. With one proviso: I had to get a minimum B+ average in my freshman year. This wasn't America where they doled out A's like candy; an average B+ was a tough ask, especially for Math & Stats, my weakest subject. UWI lecturers were notoriously stingy in giving out grades. Dr Monroe even told me: 'I never give an A, on principle.' Even though I handed in as he called it, the best first year term paper he'd ever read, he still only gave me a B++. Come on, isn't that the same as an A-minus? No, said the haughty Professor, no undergraduate deserves an A!

Somehow, even counting my dismal Math & Stats grade, I managed to meet the B+ average and was duly accepted for the exchange programme with the University of Michigan for my second year: 1973/74. There was only one problem: fees. I asked the registrar again, and again they didn't have a clue. The hapless administrator said that from what he could read on the pamphlet, 'arrangements will be made concerning payment of fees. The only advice he gave was go up there and see!

So that's what I did. I called Michigan and told them I'm coming. Dad bought me a one-way ticket to Detroit and off I went. I got off the bus in Ann Arbor without a clue what to do. I went to Student Affairs, who seemed surprised to see me. In fact, no one seemed to have a clear idea of what to do with me. Well, I'm here – I told you I was coming! It turns out there was some mention of me being their 'third world exchange student' for the year, so they welcomed me to Michigan, then coolly informed me that I was expected to pay the academic fees for the year, immediately. Including board and lodging, it totalled some astronomical amount. I explained that I was under the impression that since I had paid my fees at UWI, wouldn't that take care of me up here? The counsellor actually laughed.

'Mr. Samuel, our fees are more than ten times yours, so that would hardly be a fair exchange, would it? We are happy to provide opportunities to you third world students (that bloody phrase again); but it's not a free ride: you have to pay your way. And besides, this technically isn't an exchange, because we haven't sent anyone down there, and the first we heard of you was when you arrived here yesterday.'

I shrugged.

'Well, we have a problem, because I was told by my University, based on a pamphlet from your University, that I wouldn't have to pay fees. No problem, I'll just go back home to Jamaica, but could you please give me a return ticket? I've run out of money.'

This was a problem. They'd just announced with great fanfare the arrival of their third world exchange student. They could hardly send him back to the jungle the very next day, now could they?

Song for My Father

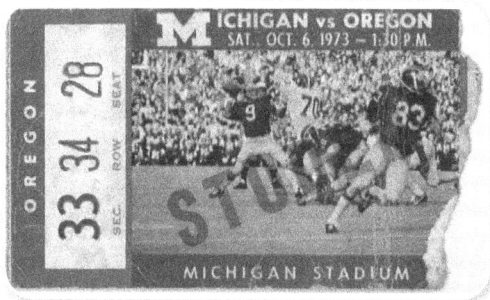

They scratched around and found a solution: they threw money at me. They gave me a full academic scholarship for the year, free board and lodging, plus spending money to boot. Sweet! I was enrolled in the Junior year and studied all sorts of esoteric subjects like Psychology 101 and the Politics of African Liberation. Even though I was on a full scholarship, I also got a job in the cafeteria, so I was awash with dosh.

May you live in interesting times. America in 1973 was all about Vietnam, Black Power, rock & roll, Motown, hippies, yippies, women's lib, and Watergate – a heady mixture. Like everywhere else in America, the University of Michigan was strictly divided along racial lines, most evident at college football games, where everybody of all colours loved their Wolverines.

Somehow all the Black students would contrive to get tickets in one quadrant of the stadium, which would be solidly Black, raising clenched fists to the Star-Spangled Banner. Through some invisible jungle telegraph, everybody knew where to sit. You never saw a White face in the Black quadrant or vice versa. The only things Blacks and Whites cheered together were the touchdowns.

As I was from 'the islands' (a despised term), Black American students took me to their breast, inviting me to join the Black Students Organization, Caribbean Students Club, etc. I had White friends, too, which pissed off my Black friends. They'd call me jungle bunny – which no White person would dare do. I found that Black Americans had a superior attitude to us 'islanders,' which was most annoying because I felt the same about them. They'd tell me:

'You jungle bunnies, y'all just dyin' for that green card, aincha?' Actually, no. One year is quite enough.

White students would at least be willing to discuss America's behaviour as the world's dominant superpower; Blacks weren't interested in that crap. All they cared about was their own struggle. And they all had a huge chip on their shoulder; everything was down to race. I resisted being co-opted into what I called the minority mindset. Most of the help the Black students got was in the form of cash: the university threw money at them. And what did they do with it? They partied.

For spring break, I drove from Ann Arbor in Michigan to Fayetteville, North Carolina, with a Black friend of mine called Mackial. He explained he was supposed to be called Michael, but his parents were poor sharecroppers who couldn't spell. We set out to do the journey in thirty-six hours, taking turns to sleep on the back seat. Mackial warned me that we'd be going into the heart of Dixie; it was only the previous year that they'd taken down the sign on the state border saying: 'Welcome to North Carolina – Klan Country.'

It was a long, boring drive. Just after we'd crossed into North Carolina, I pulled into a truck stop at three o'clock in the morning, desperate for coffee and a pee. We parked among dozens of 18-wheeler rigs and headed for the door. Inside we heard the welcoming hubbub of conversation and country music. We opened the door, and then…

Welcome to Dixie, suhhn

209

Song for My Father

Silence. Absolute, total silence, even the music seemed to stop. A hundred redneck eyes turned our way, under greasy baseball caps with John Deere and Caterpillar logos. It was like a scene from a Richard Pryor movie: Mackial and I sauntering through the door sporting huge Afros, wide lapels, jumbo bellbottoms, and platform shoes – Superfly in da house! Drinks froze halfway to lips, sentences remained unfinished, laughs stifled. Mackial and I sidled up to the counter, trying not to make eye contact with a living soul in the place. The grizzled proprietor wiped his hands on his filthy apron and said, quietly:

'What'n tarnation d'you boys want 'nhere?'

'Er, two coffees please.'

Behind me, Mackial instantly adds:

'To go!'

As we sped away with coffees in hand, Mackial let me have it:

'Nigga, what the *fuck's* wrong with you? Didn't I tell you? You in Dixie now. Stunts like that get a nigga killed!'

And I still needed to pee. The next afternoon, Mackial and I were waiting in line at an ice cream parlour. The woman in front had just bought her child an ice cream sundae. The little girl tugs her mother's dress and shouts, loudly:

'Mommy... mommy! I want some nigger-toes!'

What?? Everyone in the line was stunned into silence. Mommy didn't know where to put her face. She shushed the child and whispered to the server:

'Um, can you sprinkle some chocolate chips on that, please?'

Mackial and I were aghast, glaring at the mother as she and her child scurried away.

Had it been up to my girlfriend in Michigan, Denise Sanders, I would never have left America at all. We'd been an item for most of the year, and although we'd been getting fairly close, it was one of those things that had a definite end date, so it didn't make sense getting too entrenched. I had met her mother and sister in Detroit and found them pleasant if overly religious. A few years previously, her mother had had a botched hip replacement, and naturally she'd filed a malpractice suit. As Denise explained it, the case was virtually won: the hospital had acknowledged liability and the money would be coming though 'within months.' The family would be receiving around three million dollars after legal fees and were beginning to seriously plan what to do with this windfall. Denise told me that she, her mother, and her sister (there was no man in the family) had decided to use a chunk of the money to move to California and buy a horse ranch. A horse ranch? What do you city girls know about horses? Nothing she said, but we could learn. Or maybe ... you could? Huh? She went on:

'Let's just say that if, just if, you and I were to get ... married ... then you would get your green card, and we could all move out to California, and you could run the horse ranch.'

'Whoa, never mind all that horse shit, back up. Did you say ... married?'

'Oh, no!' She says. 'It'll only be for the green card. If you're not ... ready.'

You bet your sweet life I wasn't ready! I had just turned twenty. There's no way I was ready to get hitched. So, for the first but not for the last time in my life, I turned down the offer of a green card – and the noose that came with it. After I returned to Jamaica, Denise became a fundamentalist Christian and bombarded me with letters about how I must be saved before the Rapture. Ten years later, when I was studying in Norway, on a whim I got Denise's number in Detroit and called her up. After the perfunctory chit-chat, I gently prodded her as to how the malpractice suit was coming.

'Oh, great, thanks. The lawyer thinks the money will be coming through any day now. It isn't four million anymore, it's more like ... four hundred thousand? Before fees.'

Phew, dodged *that* bullet!

When I got back to Jamaica in August 1974, I made the mistake of telling Dad that I'd saved up five hundred US dollars.

'Well done, now you can pay your own fees this year.' Me and my big mouth!

There was one welcome addition to the home front: Tom! While I was in Michigan, Tom had continued living the life of a London hippy, going to concerts, parties, and festivals. With his mates Steve Collins and Keith Maniac, they lived a nomadic existence around Northwest London, moving from flat to flat, squat to squat, smoking a lot of dope, and sometimes selling it too. He'd buy cars from breakers' yards for a fiver, without a shred of paperwork, drive it until it died, leave it on the side of the road, then go get another one. In those days you didn't have to drive with your documents, the Old Bill would give you a 'producer': an order to produce your documents at the nearest police station within three days. Then they'd junk the car. They talked in code and used aliases, their favourite being 'Boris Kransmorse.' Once you got a letter for Mr Kransmorse: don't open.

It was a Saturday afternoon on Portobello Road. Tom and Steve were sitting at a café, feeling the effects of the all-night party they'd just left. All of a sudden, they were surrounded by a phalanx of plain-clothed police. The police claimed, outrageously, that Tom and Steve 'looked like they were about to rob an old lady.' Huh? What old lady? Well, there was no actual old lady, said The Filth, but there *could* have been. Tom and Steve had become yet more victims of Britain's notorious 'Sus Law,' giving police the right to arrest people who 'looked suspicious' – and who also happened to be overwhelmingly Black.

This was serious: robbery, attempted robbery, or even looking like you may have been thinking of robbery was way worse than dealing weed: you could get real jail time. As bad luck would have it, Tom's case had been brought up before the most miserable beak (magistrate) in all of England. He didn't like Tom, didn't like his generation, and was set to sentence Tom to some serious jail time. Steve's father Lloyd Collins spoke on Tom's behalf, which didn't move the beak one whit. It looked grim.

Back in Jamaica, Dad had gotten wind of Tom's latest legal entanglement and wrote a letter to the court, via Tom's girlfriend Valda. The letter arrived on the morning of the case, and she took a taxi from her flat in Chiswick to the Magistrate's Court in Watford, arriving minutes before sentence was about to be handed down. In his letter, Dad had laid it on thick: how he was a teacher, lived in England for twenty years, did war service, respected pillar of the community, blah-blah. He profusely apologized to the court for his wayward son's behaviour and offered to bring him out to Jamaica, for 'rehabilitation.' That softened the magistrate's hard heart, and Tom received a suspended sentence provided he flew out to his father in Jamaica, within a week. Tom didn't have much say in the matter: it was either Jamaica or jail. Which, as we'll see, wasn't the best basis for a family reunion.

By the time I got back to Kingston, Tom had been there for six weeks and already things between him and Dad were spikey. Dad had given up teaching by then and was working as a site manager at a company called Modern Partitions Limited. In the beginning, Tom worked as Dad's go-for on building sites, but that lasted all of two weeks before the inevitable clash. Ironically, in years to come, interior partitioning would become Tom's chosen profession, so maybe Dad did teach him something after all. Then Dad 'suggested' that Tom volunteer at the YMCA in Rae Town, one of Kingston's most violent ghettos, where politically affiliated gangs waged pitch gun battles on the streets. Rae Town wasn't a place we uptown people normally visited, but Tom did, every day.

Tom told me how on his very first day in Kingston he was alone in the house while Dad and Joan were at work. Left with nothing to do, he thought to himself: wait a minute, I'm in Jamaica, where the best weed comes from, so let me go and find some! He walked out of the house, down Half-Way Tree Road, and kept on walking until he got to a place called Trench Town. I stopped him right there.

'Wait a minute, you walked from Constant Spring to ... Trench Town?'

'And back! I didn't know where I was going so, I just kept on walking, and ended up in Trench Town. I met a Rastaman and asked him if he knew where I could score some weed. He took me into a tenement yard, lit up a great big chalice, stuffed with pure weed, and I smoked with a bunch of Rastas all afternoon. When I left, they gave me a huge bag of herb for almost nothing, and I walked back home, happily out of my face!'

Tom was always possessed of the common touch, and it didn't take him long to find a closer source of ganja. This was the first time I began smoking weed on a regular basis, under Tom's expert guidance. Just down the road from our house on Devon Road, they were building yet another middle-class apartment block. The site watchman and general leader of men was a contemplative Rastaman called, unsurprisingly, Rasta. Every evening after dinner, Tom and I would go out 'for a walk' to the site, where we would spend an hour or two sitting around an open fire with Rasta, Wet-Up, Indian, Baby-Roy, and the guys playing dominoes, chatting and smoking the finest ganja.

You had to hold your own among the brethren: no weak-heart shall prosper. I was cautious when the chalice was passed my way. I'd take a couple of respectful pulls then pass it along. What's a chalice? 'A chalice is a water pipe used by Jamaicans of the Rastafarian faith, to smoke marijuana or ganja, usually as part of a quasi-religious ceremony.' That's my definition, but it'll do. The base of the chalice, where the water is held, is a hard coconut shell or calabash, with a hole on top into which you fit the kutchie. The kutchie is a cone, made of clay which holds the ganja. An average sized kutchie can hold up to half an ounce of cut and cleaned ganja.

The loaded chalice would be given to the elder dread in the group as a sign of respect. God help you if it was passed to you to light it because to properly light a chalice you need lungs of steel. Before lighting the chalice comes the incantation:

> *'Praises be to His Imperial Majesty, Emperor Haile-I Selassie-I: King of Kings and Lord of Lords, Conquering Lion of the Tribe of Judah – JAH!'*

To which the brethren would respond in unison: Rastafari! Tom had a White Canadian friend who lived in our apartment building, a sociologist working on reform of the Jamaican prison system – God knows it needed modernizing. The Canadian said he too smoked weed and one evening Tom took him along to the building site, to smoke with the brethren. Who told him to do that? The brethren weren't impressed.

'Bombo claat Taam, we no waan' no White bwoy come roun' here!'

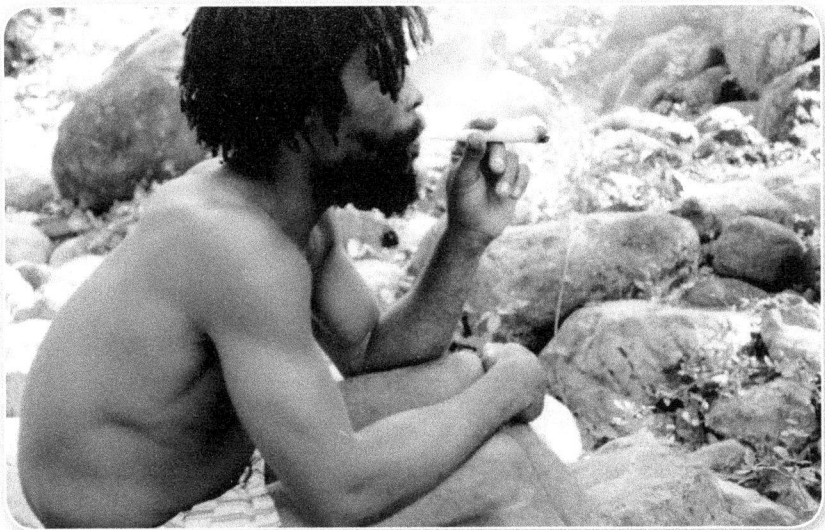

Rasta penetrates on a small one

215

But Tom vouched for de White bwoy, and the brethren grudgingly accepted him into their midst. In the fullness of time, a chalice was lit and passed around. White bwoy gingerly took a few tokes and joined in the general man-talk. After a while, White bwoy goes silent. Rasta nudges Tom.

'Taam, see yuh fren' deh.'

White bwoy was sitting around the fire, staring into the middle distance, with a vacant look on his face. A line of spittle formed, stretching down from his lower lip to the front of his shirt, leaving an ever-widening wet patch! The brethren burst out laughing. White bwoy was oblivious. Tom had to drive him home and put him to bed where he remained for twenty-four hours, comatose! White bwoy never did come back to the yard.

For the whole time Tom was in Jamaica, there was rising tension between him and Dad. It was inevitable: Tom was in Jamaica under duress, a fact Dad never let him forget. In the beginning, we lived in an apartment complex on Devon Road, then we moved to 46 Sandhurst Crescent, Liguanea. Very convenient for me, as I could take one bus to Mona Campus.

Tom's long-time girlfriend, Valda O'Boyle, whom we'd all known since the Kenton days, came to stay with us for a month over Christmas. Even though Tom and Valda had lived together in London for years, Dad refused to let them share a room 'under my roof.' Tom was livid: you can't be serious? But Dad was, and the prohibition stuck. It was the penultimate straw. The ultimate straw broke not long after Valda's return to London. Tom decided to rearrange his bedroom to better catch the prevailing breeze. When he had finished, his bed was directly underneath the window. Dad came into the room, and immediately found fault.

'Tom, don't you think you shouldn't have your bed underneath the window. Someone could put their hand through the window and...' Tom was bemused.

'And what, strangle me?'

Battle lines instantly drawn. The wordplay continued to ratchet upwards, Dad increasingly 'suggesting' that Tom move the bed. Tom resolutely resisting. You know when some disasters are so foreseeable, you can see them coming a mile off? I watched as Tom and Dad moved to the brink, utterly helpless to prevent the ensuing train wreck. The inevitable shouting match only ended when Dad picked up Tom's bed and with one furious motion, flung it halfway across the room, smashing it against the wall.

The only reason they didn't came to blows was because Tom wisely backed down. We had never seen Dad so enraged before – what on *earth* had gotten into him? Rather than be thrown out of Dad's house for the second time in his life, Tom flung some clothes into a bag and left. With nowhere to go, he walked down our long driveway, into the dark night.

Yet again, I had stood silent witness to another of Dad's unfathomable rages towards his middle son. We all have our failings and when it came to Tom, our father just did not know how to handle his headstrong son. They were too alike: Dad couldn't put up with two bulls in the same pen. A couple of days later, Tom came back during the day when Dad wasn't there. He'd been staying at the YMCA in Rae Town, where he'd worked as a volunteer. He stayed there about a week until Valda could organize him a ticket, and he flew back to London. That would be the last time Tom would see his father alive.

A crying, crying shame.

I got on with my final year at UWI. It was strange without my partners-in-crime Shacks and Maurice, both of whom were studying law in Barbados. I studied hard for my final exams but didn't go overboard, like some did. My view was that if you didn't know it by the night before the exam, staying up cramming all night isn't going to help and only make you a zombie the next day. Two weeks after

I'd finished my final exams, the Registrar's Office called me in for a meeting.

'Mr Samuel, we are having an issue with your final grade, that we would like to discuss with you.'

Uh-oh.

'It concerns the grades you obtained in your second year, at the University of Michigan. You got quite a few A's at Michigan and as you know, your final Degree is awarded on the total of both your second and final year grades. Your grades this year are also very good, and if we take your last two years into account, you would be awarded a First-Class Honours Degree.'

I was overjoyed – but what did he mean: would be? He went on:

'As I'm sure you're aware, American universities are a good deal more generous than we are – it's easier to get an A there than here. I'm sure you would agree. Therefore, we feel it only fair that we downgrade the A's you got in Michigan, to our B's. I'm sure you understand. You have still done very well and will be given an Upper Second-Class Honours Degree. In fact, you still narrowly missed a First.'

Oh, thanks a bunch! I protested, but I knew it was useless. I still came second in my graduating class and felt quite chuffed with myself. Now all I had to do was get a job. In fact, I already had one. Earlier in my final term, I had interviewed for a vacancy at the National Planning Agency and been provisionally offered a job. All I had to do was pass and pass well. As I love telling my children (ad nauseum), I started working the day after my final exam. I couldn't wait to start earning that salary, all of J$6,600 per year.

When it came time for my graduation ceremony in November 1975, I decided to tease Dad:

'I'm not going to my graduation; it's an elitist concept.'

'Listen,' he growled 'If you think you're going to deprive *me* of my proudest moment, you're very much mistaken!'

I willingly relented. True to his word, my father beamed at my graduation. He gave me an engraved silver *Caran D'ache* pen set and wrote on my graduation programme: *'To my son Brian: as the first Samuel to achieve an academic degree – I salute you.'* I had never thought about it that way, and it really moved me. Wish I still had them.

For a fresh-faced econ graduate, my job at the National Planning Agency was pretty good, but I hated it. I was stuck inside a windowless cubicle, trying to make sense out of reams of staggeringly boring printouts of monetary data. I would write monthly reports, throwing in a few phrases like 'the velocity of circulation' to sound like I knew what I was talking about. But it didn't matter – nobody read them.

After three months of this tedium, I bumped into Prof. Douglas Hall, my old Caribbean Economic History lecturer. He came straight to the point: did I want a job? The Social Development Commission, of which he was chairman, had gotten East German funding for the establishment of a co-operative rural development project, and they needed someone to do the site selection study. The job was only for a year and paid a generous gratuity at the end of the contract. Then he dangled the ultimate carrot: 'I might be able to get you a car.'

Song for My Father

Chi-ching! I immediately resigned from the National Planning Agency and joined the Social Development Commission (SDC). The government was getting millions in Eastern Bloc money to establish rural co-operatives, worker takeovers, and other socialist-oriented projects, and SDC was the implementing agency. This was my first experience in Jamaican realpolitik, where I would soon learn the ugly realities behind the idealistic rhetoric.

In 1975, Bob Marley and the Wailers returned to Jamaica fresh from their conquest of England, topped off by their legendary concert at the Lyceum Ballroom. On October 4, 1975, the Wailers shared top billing with Stevie Wonder at the Wonder Dream Concert, to be held in the National Stadium. This would be the last time the three founding members of the Wailers, Bob Marley, Peter Tosh, and Bunny Wailer, would ever play together. The American R&B group Harold Melvin and the Blue Notes were also scheduled to appear. I wasn't going to miss this one!

A group of us were lucky to get seats near the stage, and we settled in for the show. The Blue Notes didn't make it, but their replacement the new reggae band Third World ably filled the bill. Between acts I decided to wander around backstage, to see what I could see. I had two cameras slung around my neck, one colour and the other black-and-white, so it was easy to masquerade as a real photographer. Jamaica being Jamaica, they'd parked a smelly old Kingston bus behind the stage and used it as a dressing room. They had to lift blind Stevie up the steps, but he loved the rootsiness of it all.

I waved my cameras at the security guard and breezed into the packed bus. Stevie was relaxing in a gold lamé outfit, with what looked like a dog's skull around his neck. I snapped away and nibbled on vegetarian canapés, drawing minimal attention to myself. After a while, Bob Marley strolled in, and the two superstars disappeared in a welter of hugs and love-you-mans.

As flunkies fluttered around them, Bob and Stevie agreed on an 'impromptu' collaboration, at the end of Stevie's headline set, with a

Stevie Wonder

Bob Marley

Bob and Stevie

joint band playing each of their biggest hits: Stevie's 'Superstition,' and Bob's 'I Shot the Sheriff.' I scooted back to my seat and mysteriously predicted what was to follow, even naming the songs. By this time, the security people had accepted me as a professional photographer, so I strolled onstage to capture the historic moment. Musically, it wasn't the world's best collaboration, and I sold the photos to the *Gleaner* for a pittance, considering their historical significance.

In the summer of 1975, I went to Haiti with a group of students from the Jamaica School of Art. I wasn't an art student, but it was a cool place to hang out and meet arty chicks. We stayed at a low-budget bed and breakfast in downtown Port-au-Prince, and I was stunned by the abject poverty that surrounded us. I'd seen poverty in Jamaica, but this was another level altogether. One evening, the boarding house served fish for dinner. I took one look in that dead fish's eyes and decided: nah. Couldn't say why, but I just didn't want it. The rest of the group were happy to share out my portion.

Even though I was short of money, I walked down the road and ate a delicious meal of what turned out to be *poulet de montagne:*

frog. I returned to the boarding house two hours later, to a scene of utter chaos: every one of my companions who'd eaten the fish had become violently sick, two of whom had to be rushed to the hospital and thence home to Jamaica. Moral of the

tale? Always look a dead fish in the eye!

For the rest of the week, we the survivors visited artists and galleries across Port-au-Prince, but the high point of the trip was a visit to an authentic Voudou ceremony. Or was that the low point? I'm no expert on Voudou, but I believe this was the real deal. We were the only foreigners present, and they definitely didn't like me taking pictures. But when they started biting off chicken heads, I had to.

Life at home was good. I was working, and for the first time in my life had a bit of money in my pocket. Although I didn't have a car, Dad had become fairly relaxed about lending me his – on certain conditions. Chiefly: caddying. He liked having me caddy for him, as much for the company as the money he was saving, and do you think he could splash out and rent a golf cart? After the golf, there was the inevitable and prolonged

With Jamaican artist Albert Huie, right

stop at the '19th Hole' to re-live with his partners each and every frigging shot of the day. To this day, I hate that stupid game.

By this time, Dad had mellowed a lot, and I began to see a different side of my father: infinitely more chilled. He was enjoying his new job plus the extra cash that came with it. Joan had taken up costume designing, and as Dad's unpaid taxi driver, I spent a lot of time with Joan at the Little Glyndebourne Opera House, high in the beautiful Blue Mountains above Kingston. There were quite a few soirées at Sandhurst Crescent.

On January 23, 1973, my father and I went to the Joe Frazier–George Foreman Heavyweight Championship fight at the National Stadium, luckily quite near the ring. What a fight! Harsh, brutish, and very short. Frazier, the Undisputed Champion of the World, conqueror of the much-loved Muhammad Ali, was expected to brush aside this mandatory defence, paving the way for the big payday: Frazier-Ali two. But from the first bell, Big George chased and battered Frazier all around the ring, knocking him down a staggering six times in the fight, which was over halfway into the second round. Like everyone else we just sat there, stunned into silence: what the *hell* did we just witness? Two hours later, at the post-fight news conference at the Sheraton Hotel, I found myself standing next to George Foreman, the new Undisputed Heavyweight Champion of the World. I shook his hand, and my entire fist disappeared inside his giant maw. No wonder he brutalized poor Joe, and many others thereafter.

Nina Simone, Diva of all Divas, also came to Jamaica; that didn't go well either. In the sixties, Nina had a huge hit in Jamaica: 'My Baby Just Cares For Me.' With its catchy ska-influenced upbeat tempo, no self-respecting Jamaican deejay could neglect to play it, to rapturously dancing couples. Trouble is, to Nina herself it was virtually unknown, originally the B-side to a hit song: recorded and forgotten. Not in Jamaica: every single person in that audience at the Carib Theatre in Crossroads was expecting, sooner rather than later, her to get them swinging in the aisles to their favourite tune.

Not so, she ran through her repertoire of jazz-influenced songs, clearly too high-brow for a large and increasingly impatient section of the audience. Inevitably, someone voiced their opinion, followed by another, louder. She stopped the show: what? Someone explained: we want that song. What song? Divas cannot be told what to sing, so she carried on regardless. So did the crowd. Louder. There was only going to be one loser in this battle, and in true diva style she threw an enormous strop and flounced offstage – to the ringing sounds of a thousand Jamaican belly-laughs!

In 1975, the Jackson 5 came sweeping through Kingston like a royal visit. They played at the National Stadium with Bob Marley & the Wailers. We didn't go to the show, but Dad and I along with thousands of others went to gawk at the Jackson 5 at a staged appearance outside the Sheraton Kingston. The police had erected barricades and were manning them with their typical aggressive efficiency. When the Jacksons made their appearance, especially sixteen-year-old Michael, the crowd went wild: cheering, screaming, crying, pleading – the noise was deafening. Dad pointed at Michael Jackson, half-hiding behind his mother's skirt, and shouted in my ear:

'Brian, you see the look on that boy's face? That's not happiness; that's fear. He's terrified, the poor kid. This can't be good for him. Despite all his fame and fortune, when he grows up, he's going to carry an awful lot of baggage from this childhood.' Prophetic words.

Although life in Jamaica was good for us, storm clouds were brewing, as explained in Darwin's letter to his cousin:

46 Sandhurst Crescent
Liguanea
Kingston 6
Jamaica
26 November 1975

Dear Gertie,
I really don't know what to tell you about Jamaica. It's beautiful and ugly at the same time. There is hope and there is despair, social

concern in the midst of appalling violence etc. Yet I suppose it's a bit
exciting – so pleased are you each morning to know you are not shot
during the night. Anyway, it's still in my view better than England
when all is said and done – one just can't have everything.

Over this side we are pleased that Brian did so well in his degree
exams, coming 2nd in the whole West Indies (that's news to me!).
Now he is planning for post-graduate work in Sept '76 which should
take him either to Univ. of Michigan, Yale or Oxford – depending on
how the costs go (ditto!). My Gerry has also graduated (and matured)
while Tommy is still maturing – slowly. I hope Josie keeps in touch
with the boys, and they her.

Love
Darwin

After a few months of earning real money, I started to think about
moving out. I had things to do, and as for girls, I couldn't even think
of bringing them back to my house for any ill-intentions. My modest
salary was enough to live on, and in case Prof Hall didn't deliver
on the semi-promised car, commercial banks were falling over
themselves to throw money at me, so I was good to go. I broached
the subject with Dad.

'So that's how you repay me, by moving out at the first
opportunity?'

Oh lord, now I had Mister Prickly Pear to contend with! For the
next couple of weeks, we sparred gently over the issue of me moving
out, with no resolution. But little did I know that very soon, the
whole matter would be taken out of our hands.

13. Father's Final Words

Saturday, December 27, 1975. We were living at 46 Sandhurst Crescent in Liguanea, a spacious house with an open lot and a horse next door. I was twenty-two and had been working for six months. Dad, Joan, and I each had a wide circle of friends and were comfortable in Jamaica. Life was good. It had been a nice Christmas, lots of friends dropping by for drinks and chats, and vice versa. At around six o'clock that evening, I was relaxing on my bed after a long day. Joan was in the kitchen cooking, and Dad out golfing. Later that evening, we were all due to go to the same party.

Earlier that day I'd gone shopping at Tropical Plaza with Shacks, to spend my Christmas money. I was listening to the album I'd just bought *Family Reunion* by the O'Jays. The title song is a delightfully schmaltzy tune about the merits of the traditional family, songwriters Gamble & Huff clearly hadn't heard of Women's Lib:

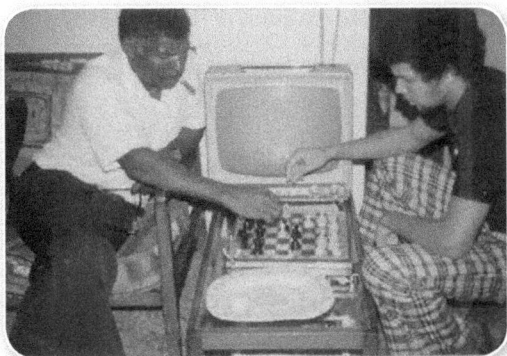

Song for My Father

The Final Morning

Then we have the mothers,
The right arm of the father,
They're supposed to do the cooking,
Raise the children, do the sewing.

I had a chuckle, before additional lyrics caught my attention:

Then there's the son
Most sons are like imitators of their father
So, we're back again to the father
If he is guiding in the right way
The son is definitely gonna be alright

For some reason, I couldn't get the lyrics out of my head. I smiled, thinking about Dad. Sure, he had his faults, principally his failure with Tom. But who's perfect? Prompted by the recurring lyrics in my head, I was feeling particularly well disposed towards Dad at that moment, just as he walked through my outside door from the garage. He'd been playing golf all afternoon, and for a change I'd been relieved of caddying duties.

'Hey, Dad. How was the game?'

'Eh, okay.' He grimaced. 'Not feeling too good. Got gas.'

'I'm not surprised.' I chuckled. 'The amount of Christmas cake you've eaten over the past few days.'

I smiled to myself as he walked down the corridor, towards his bedroom. Five minutes later, I was still ruminating, when I heard my father's voice bellow out:

'BRIAN!!!'

I burst into his room to be met by a ghastly sight. Dad was lying on his bed, his back arched as if defying gravity, mouth agape in a soundless scream. I rushed to his bed. 'Dad, Dad! What is it?' He seemed to have a brief respite. He looked into my face and spoke quickly between gritted teeth.

'It's a heart attack … I'm dying … Goodbye son … I love you!'

He screamed. I screamed. Joan rushed into the room, and she screamed. This was all happening so fast, much too fast. My father gave one huge gasp – then fell back on the bed. Still.

In those days, there were no such things as public ambulances, and we had no phones in any case. Strange but true: I don't know of anyone in those days being taken to hospital in a public ambulance: get yourself there or die on the street! My father was a heavy man and me a slim kid, but somehow Joan and I found the strength to lift him off the bed, down the corridor, out the front door, and into the back seat of the car, our hearts racing. Dad, Dad, just stay alive!

I raced to the nearest hospital, Andrew's Memorial on Hope Road, screeching to a halt at the entrance, horn blaring. Come – now! Nurses and attendants lifted Dad out of the car and onto the gurney. A doctor came running out, stethoscope in hand. They did their best, but it was apparent from very early that it was too late. He was dead. I screamed at no one.

'What do you mean, he's dead? He can't be dead! He's NOT FUCKING DEAD, OKAY!!!'

Joan and I drove home, devastated. In the depths of our grief and tears, Shacks drove up, and we had to relive it all over again as we shocked him to his core. Shacks had been my best friend for four years and had become a part of the family. More tears, more grief. As Joan and I would discover, this would be a constant and painfully repeated aftermath of death: the retelling. Shacks had a commitment to go to the same party that we were scheduled to attend that night, but of course Joan and I didn't. At the party everyone was asking him: where's Gerry, Joan, and Brian? Rather than telling everyone the tragic news and ruining the party, he kept it to himself. He later said that was the hardest thing to do, and he left early to go home and weep.

My world was shattered. My father was my everything, my rock, my refuge. He'd brought us up alone, against the odds. He was my father who mothered me, who comforted me, and yes, who spoiled me. And now he was gone, in the blink of my eye. Just when I was beginning to relate to him as an adult, he was ripped away from me. Why? I felt bereft, cheated. Angry. God, why did you do this to me? *Why?* Why did you rob me of him? Why did you rob him of the one thing he looked forward to so much: the evening of his days?

I looked for answers. I read *Buddhism* by Christmas Humphries and *The Perennial Philosophy* by Aldous Huxley. Nothing worked; no God spoke to me; no one explained. I gave up. I wasn't sad; I was angry.

My father died aged fifty-three of a massive myocardial infarction, his first and last heart attack. His friend Dr Jimmy Munroe performed the autopsy and said he'd never seen a heart so clogged-up with cholesterol, it was a miracle he lived so long. Which was strange, because just two years earlier, at the prestigious Northwick Park Hospital in London, he'd had a complete check-up, including an EKG. He'd proudly boasted, with an obvious tinge of relief, how he had 'the heart of a bull.' I tried not to hide my pride: 'Of course, you passed with flying colours, Dad. You're fit as an ox – no pun intended!' So how come, just two years later, he had the most clogged heart Jimmy had ever seen? Aren't EKGs, not to mention doctors, supposed to pick up on these long-term warning signs? Mind you Jimmy also said that Dad's lifelong diet, aided and abetted by fried Jamaican food, was the chief cause of his death. That rang a huge bell: Dad would cut the fat off our bacon, or any other yucky fat we didn't like, and scoff the lot. Plus, he'd eat black pudding, tripe, pigtail souse – and lots of and lots of oil.

After he died, Joan found a bottle of pain killers in his pocket and believes he may have known he was not a well man, but decided he would not curtail his lifestyle, nor burden his family with the news. That would be in keeping with the man. What I didn't know at the time he died was that huge changes were occurring in his and Joan's lives, and by implication mine.

Joan: Without warning, Modern Partitions ended his contract. This was a massive blow: to be told you were unemployed in his situation was unthinkable. However, he successfully applied for a post at the exciting new venture of the Jamaican government and the World Bank, to establish Sam Sharpe Teachers College near Montego Bay, to provide modern, progressive, tertiary education outside Kingston. So, here was a wonderful fresh start and we were looking forward to purchasing a property there. Sadly, it was not to be.

14. Aftermath

Tom flew out from London to attend the funeral and help Joan and I deal with the tragedy. Gerry didn't come, a disappointment I only discovered when only Tom walked out of the airport. I think Gerry felt that he had his own life to live, and that this would just drag him backwards. Unfortunately, with the rush of the funeral and flight arrangements, Tom arrived a few hours after the funeral, but it was great to have him there to share the grief. One of the worst things about death is dealing with the legal and bureaucratic bullshit that follows. Morbid funerary details to decide, the black-clad director mournfully intoning about velvet linings and brass handles, death certificate, insurance, banks, lawyers, Will, Probate … on and on.

Tom stayed with us for two months, and it was comforting to have him. Without the other side of the incendiary Dad-Tom duo, Tom, Joan, and I got on well, united in our shared grief. When it was time for Tom's return to London, he approached me with the classic Tom opening line:

'Brian, I've got a cunning plan. You know where my British Airways flight stops on its way back to London? Nassau. I can stop off there for a few days, at no extra cost. You know where I'm going with this, don't you?'

I did, and immediately signed up for it: our mother. Although we hadn't heard from her in over fifteen years, the only thing we knew was that Nelleen was living in Nassau. But that's all we knew; we didn't even know her current name. But we knew someone who did: Mark Bethel, Dad's old friend who also lived in Nassau. We got his number, called him up and, after accepting his condolences, asked if he knew where Nelleen was. Sure, she'd remarried, re-divorced, and now went by the name of Nelleen Darville and worked for a company called World Banking Corporation, in downtown Nassau. We told him we were coming to Nassau and asked if we could stay with him for a couple of nights. Sure, said he. For good measure we added: keep this under your hat.

Two days later, at nine o'clock in the morning, Tom and I walked into the cavernous lobby of the World Banking Corporation Building on Shirley Street and asked for Mrs Darville. The receptionist directed us to the fifth floor. As we got into the lift, a middle-aged White woman got in with us. We all faced the door, silently counting off the floors. All three of us got out at the fifth floor, she turned right, we left.

'I think that's her.' Said Tom. I hadn't even noticed. We asked at the reception for Mrs Darville and were shown down the corridor. We entered Mrs Darville's office, and sure enough it was the woman in the lift. She looked up at us quizzically, no hint of recognition.

'Yes, can I help you?'

We stood there silently, savouring the moment. She began to get annoyed.

'What is it? Who are you?'

Then Tom said the classic words:

'We're Tom and Brian. Your sons.'

She looked at us with stunned disbelief. Then it dawned on her: recognition. Then: gush! She disappeared in a welter of tears, hugging us, crying, hugging us again. What's the word ... awkward?

Song for My Father

She may have been our mother, but five minutes ago she didn't even recognize us. She introduced us to her co-workers as her long-lost sons, to yet more hugs and tears. We smiled sheepishly. She took the rest of the day off, and we drove to her house on Norfolk Street in Shirlea, a down-at-heel suburb of Nassau.

Where to begin? How do you start to re-create a relationship, that was dead for fifteen years? Not just dead: buried. What do you say to your mother who five minutes ago was about to throw you out of her office? What does she say, after abandoning us and never making contact? I thought that an apology would have been a good place to start, but I guess sorry really is the hardest word to say – for my mother at least. It was a touchy time. We told her about our father's death, which didn't evoke much response either way. What could she say?

The first day

Nobody said it, but there was an enormous elephant in the room. Our mother felt she needed to justify her actions. She started to defend herself:

'You don't know what it was like, living with your father...' Tom cut her off.

'Listen, here's the rule: you don't say anything bad about our father. He just died a month ago. He's not here to defend himself – *and he never left us.* So please, have some respect.'

She wisely obliged. For a while. But despite those early jitters, Tom and I found that our mother was a clever, witty woman with whom we enjoyed having long chats. She could hold her own in an argument – and then some. She was a chain-smoking, hard-drinking, no-nonsense woman whose favourite beverage was vodka and milk because, as she put it: 'It has everything in it that's good for me!' People would see this little old lady sipping her glass of 'milk' not realizing it was fully charged! She would vary from vodka to rum and back again, but never less than a bottle a day – plus a couple packs of unfiltered Camels. As she would boast, in her raspy smoker's voice: I'm one tough old bird! Despite all our new-found family bonhomie, I could never bring myself to call her mom or mother, as she'd asked us to: she could never be more than Nelleen.

Tom and I were both scheduled to stay in Nassau a couple of days, at the end of which we'd both fly our separate ways, but in the euphoria of the reunion, on a whim Tom decided to stay in Nassau. He cashed in his return ticket to London, moved in with Nelleen and enrolled at the Bahamas Hotel Training College, to do a two-year Diploma in Hotel Management.

But that's another story.

In February 1976, Joan and I moved into a half-a-house on Elmwood Terrace in Red Hills, with a spectacular view of Kingston. I was working at the Social Development Commission, and in July of that year they sent me on a six-week tour of West Germany, sponsored by the Friedrich Ebert Stiftung, a socialist organization promoting worker participation, then all the rage in Jamaica. Part of the tour included a day trip into East Berlin. Going Eastbound through the infamous Checkpoint Charlie was a breeze, and we spent a fascinating day in the East, witnessing a ceremony honouring the twenty-seven million Russian dead of the Second World War. The trouble started when it was time to leave.

The East German border guards, the *Deutsche Grenzpolizei*, were rightly feared in both East and West Germany alike. These guys enjoyed their jobs way too much and had unlimited powers over the people under their dominion – like me. Because my passport picture was of this cherubic sixteen-year-old who bore little resemblance to the bearded hippy standing before them, they decided to have a closer look. I was taken to an adjoining windowless room where I was repeatedly examined by increasingly senior border guards. You could tell their seniority by the size of their caps. They took turns holding my passport up to my face and really, really staring at me, for what seemed an eternity. By this time, our West German minder was nowhere in sight. It was

just me and them. Every now and then, one of them would hurl a question at me in German while others watched my reaction. This was beginning to get scary: people *disappear* in here!

After many, many examinations, they casually handed back my passport and let me leave: *auf wiedersehen.* Yeah, right. As I walked out of East Germany through Checkpoint Charlie with its razor wire, machine gun turrets, and minefields, I got a tiny sense of the immense relief that must have washed over those few East Germans lucky enough to make it safely through this deadly crossing.

At age twenty-two, I was effectively on my own, with no crutch to lean on. Family yes, but no support network: no Bank of Dad. Everything I did from now on – work, study, women, family – I'd do on my own. I remember consciously thinking to myself: 'Okay, Brian, adulthood starts right here, right now. You may not be ready for it, but it's ready for you, so stop crying and man up'!

Joan and I each had our own questions to answer: What now? Where now? Without our father and husband to anchor us, what to do? Joan decided she would finish the academic year at St Joseph's Teachers College, then return to England; there was nothing for her in Jamaica anymore. I decided to stay in Jamaica; there was nothing for me in England anymore. As befitting such a life-changing event, Joan decided to return to England in style and grace and booked passage on the *M/V Jamaica Producer* for a ten-day voyage. Joan and I were two desperately sad, unsure people, sharing the same thoughts with differing details:

> *Joan: I remember saying goodbye at Port Antonio docks and realizing how alone you were and feeling sad that I would not be around to help. I knew I had to leave because I was unlikely to obtain a work permit, as the trend at that time was to limit the employment of ex-patriates in Jamaica. And then, there was my recently widowed elderly mother May, longing for my support back in England.*

I didn't cry on the docks, but somewhere along the road back to Kingston, I pulled over and had a good eye-water. For Joan, for Dad, for me, for every fucked-up thing that happened this past year. I felt angry with myself as well, for not showing Joan the love I really had for her. It just could never come out right. She had been my stepmother, my effective mother, a caring mother, for the past eight years, and Joan had an enormously positive impact on my late adolescence. But did I show it? No. She was also hugely brave, moving into a family of four confirmed cavemen, devoid of a single civilizing female influence in their lives, and somehow, slowly, wisely, patiently … civilized us! Well, me at any rate.

My only excuse for not embracing Joan as I should have done is that when she came into our lives, I'd just turned seventeen, already burdened with more than my fair share of mommy issues, just like Tom and Gerry. I never said anything emotional to my own mother, except for condemnation, and I found it difficult to emotionally bond with Joan. Was I angry? Rejected, dejected? All the above, and Joan bore that brunt. *Joan Samuel: I love you.*

After Joan returned to England, Shacks returned to Jamaica from studying law in Barbados, and moved in with me at Elmwood Terrace, a house we shared for three epic years. The third musketeer, Maurice, was also back in Jamaica, so the triumvirate was re-formed. Not long afterwards, who joined us three reprobates? Tom! As young men will do, the four of us had a ball, getting into quite a few escapades.

But that's another book!

15. Killing Ghosts

My mother was a complete and utter bitch: selfish, mean-spirited and without one shred of empathy, affection, or motherly love. There: that only took sixty years to get off my chest – and it sure felt good! Sixty years of the Big Question: *Why?* Why did you leave us? Not just leave, abandon, forget, ignore us – why? Never mind why; how? Even when our father flew to Nassau and begged you to come back, for your sons' sake, because they needed their mother, you couldn't reach out, send us a letter? You even forgot our faces, for fuck's sake! Don't all females have that motherly instinct to protect their young? Can a mother just abandon that primal urge? Evidently yes. She was one of a kind, our mother.

At which point Tom and Gerry would chime in with two hard slaps to my head-back: Oh, fafucksake Bri-Bri, stop whining you little wuss! We've all heard your mommy-left-me stories, ad bleedin' nauseam! You think ours are any different? Although we didn't have our mother, we sure as hell had our father! Especially you, Golden-Bollocks! So enough of all this angsty mommy-shit, okay? Save

Happy new mommy and nonplussed sons

that for Oprah. After all these years, how about cutting your dead mom a little slack? We both did; you need to as well. If you can't forgive, then how about forget? Ignore? Whatever, just move on!

Yeah, yeah, I did all that. I didn't forgive nor forget, but I moved on, made my peace with Nelleen. For years, decades. Although I never got to know her as well as Tom and Gerry did, both of whom had lived in Nassau. At age twenty-two, my mother had become part of my core family. But can you create love out of a vacuum? No, at least I couldn't. She sensed, rightly, that of the three of us, I was the one she should tread most carefully with, so we came to an understanding. We enjoyed each other's company, had great conversations about books, movies, scandals, everything, and everybody. Except… there. No family talk, which in her case meant: Don't you *dare* bad-talk my father to me. Agreed? Agreed. Good: all is happiness and light.

Until, even for her, she did the unthinkable.

It's funny how the Samuel herd migrates. One of us branches out, gets a toehold in some far-flung pasture. He then gives the call and soon enough others follow. After Tom moved to Nassau and enrolled at the Bahamas Hotel Training College, within a year he was joined by Gerry and Pat, both of whom went to Nassau on teaching jobs from London. Tom was delighted to vacate Nelleen's house and move in with them, and the three of them got along like a house on fire.

I was living in Jamaica at the time, branching out and raising a family, but I spent many an Easter and Christmas holiday in Nassau, laughing, storytelling, partying, and bonding – all good family fun. But after Tom, Gerry, and Pat had left Nassau for various destinations, my only connection was Nelleen.

Still, I persevered, maintained the family tie with my mother, made efforts to grow it. With wife Marion and children Tanisa, Zachary, and Dylan, we went to Nassau to stay with grandma Nelleen for a week. We lasted four days. When she got in a snit because my four-year-old son Zack broke some piece of shit (sorry, some rare and precious *objet d'art*), we rebooked our flights. My mother was the most unmotherly woman I have ever met or heard of. Ever, ever, ever.

In 1994, I was living in Washington DC, working for the World Bank. Nelleen was in Nassau, keeping her head down. Her legal status in the Bahamas, tenuous at best and fraudulent at worst, had long since expired after she'd divorced her Bahamian husband, and she lived a life under the radar, never travelling, never making a fuss. Best friends came and went: Edie, Faithie, and Peaches, all similarly sozzled expats, clinging onto their fading lives of White privilege in Nassau. Nelleen fell in the shower, drunk of course, and broke her arm. While still in a cast, she fell again, breaking the other arm. I sent crutches by FedEx.

At this time, I had reconnected with Grenada and would make frequent business trips, always with a few personal days added on. On one trip, I was staying with my friend Leon Taylor and on a Sunday with nothing to do, decided to find the house where I was born: Eden. I knew it was somewhere in Belmont, overlooking the beautiful Lagoon. Grenada doesn't do silly things like street numbers, a typical address could be: 'de green house, wid ah big mango tree in front, yuh can't miss it, man.' So, what do you do? You ask someone, everyone knows everything. I see some fellas sitting on a verandah, bottles and glasses littering the table. I get out the car and walk up to them.

'Hey guys, anyone know a house around here called Eden?'

They look at each other, smiles break out. One of them asks:

'Are you a Banfield?'

'Me? No, I'm a Samuel, but my godfather was a Banfield, Linton Banfield, and I was born in his house, Eden, which is why I'm looking for it. Any of you know of it?'

Song for My Father

More looks, more smiles. I'd hit the jackpot: they were all Banfields; it was a family reunion. Linton was their great-grandfather. In true Grenadian style, they invited me in for a drink, which in equal style I readily accepted. Half an hour and two rum-and-gingers later, I said my goodbyes, with instructions how to find Eden: 'is just around the corner, man' And so it was, a smallish wooden house that had been derelict for some time. I took the obligatory picture and flew back to Washington the next day. A few days later, I called Nelleen and told her about my encounter in Grenada.

> *I found Eden House. Coincidentally, I bumped into a group of Banfields, and they gave me directions to the house. They even asked me if I was a Banfield too, ha-ha. I'll send you a picture of the house. It's derelict now, but what a beautiful view you had, over the Lagoon. By the way, what time of the day was I born? You should've given birth to me in the garden of Eden, ha-ha.*

She expressed mild interest, made no comment about the house, and couldn't remember what time of day I was born. Really? We hung up: bye son, bye Nelleen. That was at eight o'clock. At one o'clock in the morning, the bedside phone rings, jolting me awake.

Ruins of Eden

Oh shit, what's this now? No phone call at this time of night is good news. I composed myself and picked up the receiver.

'Hello?'

'Hello, Bhian.'

Oh, for god's sake, it's Nelleen, drunk again. She had that voice that was instantly recognizable from her first slurred syllable.

'For fuck's sake, Nelleen! It's one in the morning. I'm going back to sleep, and don't call again!'

'No wait! I have something very important to tell you.'

My hand hesitated.

'Okay then, what is it? And be quick.'

She paused. I could hear the sobbing as she slurred her words.

'I've been thinking about what you told me, about meeting the Banfields. I'm not surprised they asked you if you are a Banfield ... because you are. Your father isn't your father. Your father is Linton Banfield.'

My world stopped. A battering ram hit me. I couldn't breathe. My head pounded.

'WHAT did you say?' I screamed into the phone, startling Marion lying next to me. Nelleen blubbered on:

'Well, at the time you were born, things were very bad between me and your father, and, well, I needed Linton for ... comfort, so ... he may be your father.'

'MAY be? You don't know who's the father of your child? You fucking bitch! WHY did you tell me this? Me of all people, who idolizes my father? Why couldn't you take that piece of knowledge to your grave? I want nothing to do with you from now on, you hear me? No calls, no visits, nothing, and that goes for my children too. You are dead to me; dead!'

Or words to that effect. I was in pieces, collapsed in a welter of shock and tears, rocked to my core. Marion hugged me, comforted me as best she could, assured me that that was just the result of my mother's drunken guilt and uncertainty, that of course I'm my father's son, just look at the photographs! Which is what I did. I went down to the basement, hauled out the box containing my father's papers, and tears streaming down my face and a bottle of Appleton Rum for solace, rummaged through it until I found what I was looking for.

Two photographs: of me and one of my father, at about the same age, that bore a striking resemblance, that screamed a genetic link. Father and son: cause and effect. I sat there, rocking back and forth, one picture in each hand, looking at them, staring at them, wiping away tears, repeating over and over: This is me; he is me. I am him, it's obvious...

This is me ... this is me ... this is me ...

I desperately needed Tom and Gerry, but with the time zones I had to wait a few hours. Those were the worst few hours of my life. I sat there in the basement, racked in an emotional roller coaster. Just the ramblings of a drunk, guilty, lonely old woman who wants to offload her guilt onto me. Of course, she's wrong. Of course, I'm my father's son. Just look at those two pictures, look! But ... what if ...? Does it matter if he's not my biological father? Of *course*, it matters! What time is it in London? I got hold of Gerry first. He shocked me with his response.

'Oh, god. She didn't tell you, did she?'

'What?? You *knew* about this?'

He did, both he and Tom.

'Years ago in Nassau, she'd drunkenly blabbed the same story to both of us. We told her this was just the ramblings of a drunk, guilty old lady. *Of course*, Brian is Dad's son. Just look at him! But your guilt is eating out your stomach. Well, you'd better leave it right there, where it belongs. If there's one person you *never* tell this to, it's Brian! You got that?'

But, of course, she couldn't keep that inside her: guilt is like a cancer; it eats you from the inside. But in the end, she didn't win. None of her guilt was assuaged, and I recovered from the shock. I know who I am. It's gone. And so was she. Ha, if only.

I never laid eyes on my mother after that, which is not to say I never felt her malignant presence. One huge presence concerned my father. Years ago, she'd told Tom and Gerry, also drunkenly, that our father was an abuser, and that was why she ran away. She couldn't take it anymore, playing the ultimate victim card. I didn't believe her, but for twenty years I lived with this gnawing shadow over my father. He beat us kids, for sure, but I could never imagine my father putting his hand on a woman, ever. I thought she was outright lying or at best exaggerating, desperately seeking excuses for what she had done. But I had no proof.

Then I got proof. In around 1995, I was on a routine visit to Grenada, and before heading to the airport on Sunday afternoon, I made the mandatory pilgrimage to Mount Rose House. After ole talk with cousin Brenda and playing with the kids, I was about to leave when Brenda's husband Michael Ferguson approached me, with a hesitant look in his eye.

'Brian, ah had this thing here for a long time, but ah never know if you ready for it. Well, now you ready, here.'

He handed me an old manila folder, filled with yellowish sheafs of paper. I glanced inside and saw dozens of letters, some in handwriting, others carbon copies of typewritten letters. Michael was right: this was huge. I thanked him and headed to the airport. Coincidentally, I was flying to London that night, where I planned to make copies for Tom and Gerry. On the plane, I started to read them. And wept. After the flight attendant had cleared away the dinner tray, I retrieved the manila folder, turned on the overhead light and started reading. After two decades in the grave, my father spoke to me. I could almost hear his voice as I read his letters. And what a story he told: exoneration. Did he put his hand on her? Yes, he did, once. As he himself admitted:

> *Nelleen, be truthful to yourself and stop telling people I beat you up. Yes, I laid my hand on you, once, and we both know why. And as you yourself said, you weren't hurt in the altercation, and you gave as good as you got. If you persist in telling these lies, I shall be forced to tell people what caused the altercation between us.*

What was the reason for the altercation? Because she slept with her husband's best friend. In 1958, when Darwin's father died, he flew up to Grenada to attend to the funeral. At some point while Darwin was burying his father, Nelleen brought her lover, Linton Banfield, into her bed, where he stayed the night. As Darwin wrote with obvious bitterness:

> *When little Gerry came into our bedroom in the middle of the night complaining of nightmares, you had Linton carry him back into his room and put him to sleep.*

To fully appreciate our father's sense of betrayal, Uncle Linton was his best friend. They were inseparable. Both men had moved from Grenada to Trinidad at around the same time. With wives Nelleen and Babsie, they were a popular foursome. In Grenada, we had lived in Linton's house in Belmont. Dad bought Linton's car, and Uncle Linton was my godfather. Both men shared everything – including, evidently, our mother. Hence on that night, little Gerry wasn't perturbed to be put to bed by his Uncle Linton.

Another letter revealed that Nelleen had planned her flight well. Her husband had no clue as to her whereabouts:

> *Radio Guardian 610*
> *17, Abercrombie Street,*
> *Port-of-Spain*
> *September 2, 1960*

Dear Mr. Samuel,
With reference to your letter of September 1 regarding the whereabouts
of Mrs. Samuel, it is my understanding that she is in the employ of
ZNS, a radio station in Nassau, Bahamas …

Having caught up with Nelleen, Darwin was not about to let his wife of ten years and three children slink off quietly into the night:

At home
Gerry's birthday, (17th January)

Dear Nelleen,

When are you going to realize that the whole circumstances surrounding your leaving are abnormal; with all your possessions – including some things that must be dear to you, still in this house, with your not having 'looked back' at the children who you bore for nine months – three times. Everything, everything pointing to your having made a very tragic mistake.

For the love of Mike, Kid, get wise to yourself, wake up and pull yourself together and realize that in one fell stroke you are ruining what till now has been a fine existence – with the promise of greater things to come. I am, naturally, looking into the possibility of life alone with the children, our children. But it is because I so well know that once I start there'll be no looking back that I am constrained to write to you as I am doing. There's no doubt that in time I'll be okay but on account of the children, on account of you, on account of my faith in the future, that that I write with a full and aching heart. Please do not think that I want you back at all costs. It is simply that I believe you are good and worth retrieving – in the name of God.

Be woman enough to return as you left – I'll have you. Return and take care of your children, motherless at present, as you have not done since they were babies – even at the expense of your precious Radio Guardian. Your children will grow up to be your honour, your glory, your credit and your joy.

At least, if you must have advice, talk to the persons you admire for respectability and Christian living – not to those you know you really detest; fly-by-night saggaboys and saggagirls, the flotsam and jetsam of this world who are anxious for you to join them in their meaningless existences. AMEN.

I sat up for the whole night in that darkened plane, reading letter after letter, taking time to decipher his handwriting. More than once I cried. The man in the seat beside me stirred, but wisely pretended to sleep. My father kept carbon copies of the letters he sent to Nelleen, for precisely this moment: to defend himself. From the grave if necessary. The defence may now rest. As may he.

Nelleen settled in Nassau, working at ZNS Radio. Soon afterwards she met and wanted to marry a Bahamian, Mack Darville. But there was one problem: she was still married to Dad. Rather than go through the time and expense of a proper divorce, Nelleen took shortcuts. She and Darville flew to Nevada where she got a quickie divorce, then onto Mexico City where they got a quickie marriage; returning to Nassau as the new Mrs Darville. But you know what they say about Mexican marriages? Looks great on paper, but it ain't legal tender, a fact which would come back to haunt her.

Neither Tom, Gerry, nor I ever met this Mack Darville. He was long gone by the time we came on the scene. He was what Bahamians call a Conky-Joe, a local White from one of the Outer Islands. Small, interbred communities where a lot of people have eyes just a tad too close together, if you get my drift. He owned a gas station in Shirlea, and for a while everything was good. In 1968, when we were living in Illinois, Dad flew to Nassau for a weekend to meet Nelleen. The objective of this mission remains ambiguous: I was told he went to ask her to come back; Gerry was of the impression he went to ask for a financial contribution. Or probably both.

Whatever the reason, he failed on all counts. Nelleen and her new husband were living high off the hog, with the gas station, a sprawling house with a pool, and a yacht moored in the bay. When Dad was returning to La Grange, he asked Nelleen if she'd like to send letters to her children; she declined. But appearances are deceiving. Mack Darville's evident financial success was a sham. He and Nelleen soon lost the gas station, followed by the house, and the last they saw of the yacht was watching it sink beneath the waves in a hurricane. Then she divorced him. Actually, she didn't have to divorce him because they were never legally married.

Our father's prediction proved correct: guilt is a bitch. In her later years, Nelleen cast a forlorn figure: forever alone, living out her life with fake friends and the ghosts of past lives. Although she lived in Nassau for thirty years, for the last twenty of those years, she was an illegal alien. She had no status, no passport, and could not travel, living in constant fear of being deported, which had happened to several of her expatriate friends. She was terrified of that threat: she had nowhere else to go.

Then, out of the blue, she found somewhere to go, or rather, someone. She and her younger brother Steven had long since lost contact; and by an amazing coincidence she met a British Airways stewardess who knew her brother, then living in Spain. They re-connected, tears over the phone, and a year later Nelleen sold her house in Nassau and joined him in Spain. In the coastal town of Mojacar, she bought a small flat, two doors from his.

To close the book on our mother, Helen-Nelleen Hogan-Samuel-Darville died of cancer aged seventy-three, in the village of Mojacar, Spain, on January 29, 2002. A long life, considering the rigours she'd imposed upon her long-suffering body. Gerry had been doing yeoman service in her final days, flying out from London to help her out, and when I got the call at two in the morning, I sat in the living room and wept. Not for the mother I'd lost; for the mother I'd never had.

Gerry and I flew out to Spain to take care of business. Tom had a pre-booked ticket to go to Trinidad Carnival with his partner Valda O'Boyle, which obviously took precedence. Her cremation was a sparse affair: just me, Gerry, her brother Steve, and some strange woman. Two hours later, on the way to the airport, Gerry and I emptied her still-warm ashes into the Mediterranean. It was only then I could exhale, feeling a physical weight lift off my soul. Finally, I could lay her malevolent spirit to rest.

16. Song for My Father

The first time I heard 'Song for my Father,' a bluesy jazz instrumental by Cape Verdean pianist Horace Silver, I immediately fell in love with it; as much for the music as the message. And so, five decades after his death, what was my father's song? His legacy?

Our father had a VW budget, with a Rolls-Royce appetite. 'Best is cheapest in the long run,' he'd say on our shopping trips to high-end retailers on Oxford Street. The dark green Selfridges van was a frequent visitor to our house in Kenton, far outside their normal routes around Mayfair and Maida Vale. Dad was also a patron of the White Knight Laundry Service, a bespoke valet company that delivered his starched white shirts (never ours) in distinctive blue-and-white cardboard boxes. At some point, he liberated one of these boxes and used it to store his important documents, letters, and clippings.

After our father died in 1975, the White Knight box fell into my hands, and for decades I carried it with me: Jamaica, England, Norway, Barbados, America, Zimbabwe, South Africa until, finally, home: Grenada. I'd flipped through its contents a few times, chuckling at the reams of court notices and threatening letters, but perhaps subconsciously fearing what I'd find therein, I never went through his personal letters. Until …Until I decided to write this book.

Song for My Father

Our family's story is an uncommon one, and over the years many people have said that we should write it down. As the self-appointed family scribe (or as my bastard brother Tom put it: Brian, king of turgid prose!), it was a challenge I readily accepted. It has been a long time in the writing, an on-again off-again love affair for the better part of a decade. With the luxury of my latest semi-retirement, I decided to finally *finish the damn book!* And to do so, I turned to the White Knight box.

After wiping away decades of dust, I emptied its contents onto the dining table, flipped through every letter, every document, every faded photograph. Some I read straight away, some I saved for later, some I paused at, some I cried at. It made for riveting reading; answering so many questions and shedding new light on the complex personality that was my father.

I also found a gold mine of information about us: school reports, letters from teachers (never good!), and handwritten letters from relatives, some known, others stirring hazy memories. I found a pile of negatives and got them developed, revealing grainy black-and-white photographs going back to our babyhood and beyond. In addition to being a hoarder, our father was also an amateur photographer (plus amateur writer, amateur actor, amateur sportsman, amateur ...) and made sure to document his growing family as we travelled from pillar to post. Some of these photographs brought back instant memories of family stories that resonated from childhood, while others whispered at mysteries that had lingered in the air for decades.

As a single father bringing up three boys on a tight budget, our father did his level best. Children live a charmed life, oblivious to the struggles our parents go through just to put food on the table and clothes on our backs. Even though we knew that times were tough, we had no idea just how tough: everyone wanted a piece of Darwin Samuel's wallet!

He was a financial juggler, attempting to keep several balls in the air at once. In Trinidadian parlance, this is known as 'scrunting.' And as with all scrunters, balls will fall. The creditor list was long and recalled many things that we took for granted, never dreaming how much of a struggle it was for our under-funded father. North Thames Gas Board, London Borough of Harrow, Dartmouth Travel, Selfridges – to name but a few – they all had him in court at one time or other. I don't know how he survived but survive he did.

My father said you cannot judge a man outside his time. Darwin Fitzgerald 'Gerry' Samuel was a product of a time vastly different from today. In some ways, he was typical of his time, and in others far ahead. In his attitude to England, for example, not just him but for entire generations of West Indians, England represented the epitome of learning and culture. In 1954, Darwin wrote for the *Argosy* Newspaper in British Guiana:

> *Westindians (a term that was en vogue around Federation) emigrate to England not for economic reasons though naturally they are influenced by these factors, the Westindian emigrates to England because they have England in their blood and have to make the pilgrimage for a sort of inverted expiation, because simply 'going to England' constitutes the fulfillment of a deep-seated desire that goes right back to childhood.*

> *The East Indian identifies himself with 'Mother India', the Chinese with China etc. but the black Westindian has, in a certain way unfortunately, only 'Mother England'. Like the Englishman his native*

tongue is English, his education English in concept and even though he looks very different it is no surprise how much the Westindian is, despite himself, every inch the Englishman.

He was a proud Black man. He never straightened his hair like many did. He wore an Afro before Afros were invented. He was colonialist in culture, but anti-colonialist in politics. He would proudly relate how Kwame Nkrumah used to sleep on his floor during their student days in London. At home we were kept abreast of world politics: the Kennedy assassination, Berlin airlift, Sharpeville, Paris riots. Once he yelled at Gerry in frustration: 'Why don't you join a demonstration or something?'

Yet for all that, he was a staunch monarchist and celebrity stalker. He would frame his Buckingham Palace invitations and photographs of him with the Queen Mother, Prince Phillip, Yuri Gagarin, Coretta Scott King.

Joan: This photo was taken after a service in St. Paul's Cathedral which DFS and I attended, invited by Sir Michael and Dame Ann Dummett. Coretta King gave the address from the pulpit and was the first black woman to do so and also the first woman. I recorded the momentous event in a painting which DFS presented to the anti-racist campaigner Father Trevor Huddlestone, who was also present.

Our father had a passion for learning, a passion that was, sadly only partially fulfilled. His big disappointment was not being able to pursue his dream of studying law. But that didn't stop him pursuing other academic goals. He was always studying something, formally or informally. As I never fully appreciated until the night of my UWI graduation, despite all the night school classes he attended, our father never attained his bachelor's degree. Although our academic results didn't always show it, his passion for learning did rub off on us – through osmosis if nothing else.

After his wife abandoned us, our father went above and beyond the call of duty. Most West Indian men in his predicament would have parked his children in Grenada and gone off to make a new life elsewhere, showing scant regard to his children back home, save for Christmas calls and the occasional birthday box. Not so our father; he lived by his own words, written weeks after the departure of our mother: *'Where children are involved, it is the duty and responsibility of the parents to stay behind and dedicate their lives to their children.'* He made a conscious decision that he would raise his sons on his own. Apart from Auntie Phyllis, our father rarely brought his lady friends into the house, until we were much older.

That he loved us was beyond doubt; that he always showed it wasn't always so clear. In this regard, I speak primarily of Tom, Dad's Achilles' Heel, his *bête noire*, his ultimate adversary. Dad just had no idea how to handle his headstrong middle son, who was identical to him in so many ways. Both my father and mother told me this story, almost verbatim:

Song for My Father

Port of Spain, Trinidad, 1957: Sunday afternoon and the Samuel family was strolling in the Botanical Gardens, an oasis of green in the middle of the city. Gerry and I were off romping somewhere, and Dad and Nelleen were walking along the path, with Tom ahead of them. From babyhood, Tom was always a robust boy, built like a mini brick house. Both troubled parents watched as their beautiful middle boy went forging ahead on his tricycle, clearing a path. They both looked at each other and Nelleen said:

'We may have our problems, but we can thank god for one thing: we've both created one beautiful child!'

And yet she would abandon him, six months later.

When we were kids, Tom was the Golden Child, strong, handsome, apple of his father's eye. Fast forward seventeen years, to that awful night in Kingston in 1975 when Dad flung Tom's bed across the room in a fit of fury, one has to ask: where did it all go so wrong? The younger we were, the more fun our father was. He knew how to play with us, make us laugh, make us love him. But as we grew older, he didn't seem to have all the right answers anymore. He found it easier to relate to us as adoring boys rather than as questioning adolescents. Particularly obstreperous adolescents with a cheeky grin!

We all loved our father, to distraction. He need not have been afraid of opening up to us as we got older. To this day, so many parts of our father remain a closed book – such as the twin taboos of women and sex – areas where his sons could have benefited from his wise council. My only lesson from him on that subject was '*Hell hath no fury, like a woman scorned.*' I wonder where he got that from? I'm still laughing at him, playing a record to explain the facts of life to us. Dad why couldn't you just *talk* to us? We were older than you thought.

And as regards Auntie Phyllis and our lost sister Jacqueline – the less said the better.

'Brian, it's not your fault you're a heartless bastard. It's because of your mother!'

The number of times I've heard those or similar words, I can complete the diagnosis by heart: (a) I'm a heartless bastard; (b) my mother left me; ergo (c) it's her fault. Psych 101 was never easier. If only life were so simple. Was I emotionally affected by the departure of my mother? Of course, I was, who wouldn't be? All three of us have in our own ways been negatively impacted by Nelleen's abandonment. I, Tom, and Gerry have all, at various times by various women, been accused of being emotionally distant. What caused that, I wonder? But we needn't dwell on the negatives; it's all part of life's rich mélange that makes us what we are. There are no perfect families; perfect families are boring.

I can only imagine the emotional pain our father must have suffered, after our mother left us. His letters show he was devastated, and his subsequent actions reveal the effect it had on him. He decided he would raise his sons on his own; there would be no replacement mother. Until he got married to Joan, the longest relationship he had was with Auntie Phyllis: three years. We do not know the ins and outs of their breakup, but in hindsight it's almost as if her time was up. She was in danger of becoming a permanent fixture. He never hid the fact that he had girlfriends; he just never let them get too comfortable. Our father became an emotional island.

It was only in his later life that Dad emerged from his self-imposed emotional cocoon. Given his previous history of short-term encounters, our father's courtship and subsequent marriage to Joan Danby was nothing short of unique, heartfelt, and just plain romantic. They met on the *RMS Sylvania* for the seven-day voyage from Southampton to New York in August 1966. It must have been quite the shipboard romance, as it spawned a year-long correspondence while we were in La Grange and Joan in Hawaii. Again, we don't know the ins and outs, but I believe Dad made up his mind when we were still in America that he would marry Joan. As he said: 'She is the right woman for me.' And indeed, she was. Not only was Joan right for Dad, but she also changed him. Thanks to Joan, we came to see a different Dad, infinitely mellower. He really did change after his marriage. This probably coincided with the fact that his sons were now older and, apart from me, about to fly the coop. It was touching to see this new, improved 'Dad-Light'!

Dad took me from England to Jamaica in 1971: just in the nick of time. England in the seventies was a difficult time for the children of the Windrush generation. The West Indian and Asian immigrants who came to England in the fifties and sixties ultimately did well. They worked hard: on the buses, hospitals, factories. They raised children, bought property, became a settled, identifiable community. They assimilated, though maintaining a strong sense of cultural identity. Sadly, their children didn't have such an easy time of it. Several forces combined to put pressure on the new generation of young Black British, chiefly the Police Force. The first generation of immigrants had the benefits of a booming economy; there were plenty of jobs for all. By the seventies, the tide had turned, and with the recession came competition for jobs – and increased racism. This cultural change in Britain is typified by one word: skinheads.

In their first incarnation in the late sixties, White English skinheads were the antithesis of racists: they adored and imitated everything Jamaican: clothes, culture, and most of all music. They aped the Jamaican rude-boy combination of badness and style, wearing the best quality Crombie raincoats, drainpipe trousers, Clarks shoes, and button-down Ben Sherman shirts. In 1967, my skinhead friend Kevin Corrigan introduced me to ska and reggae. Fast forward ten years and the skinheads had transformed themselves into a violent far-right cult of racist thugs, most of whom were members of the National Front. I'm not qualified to say what caused this radical and unwelcome change; I'm just glad I wasn't there to witness it.

Along with skinheads and the National Front, Black British youths had another enemy to contend with: the police. When I left England in 1971, I had no particular feeling about the police, one way or the other. But immediately upon my return to England in 1980, at Notting Hill Carnival no less, a uniformed policeman left me in no doubt as to his view on race relations, screaming into my face: '*Why don't you go back where you come from, you Black bastard!*' Huh? What did I do to deserve that? And so, it proved to be that as a twenty-seven-year-old Black man in London, I got tired of being stopped by the police, especially after I acquired a brand-new car. The first question was always: 'Who's car is this then?' In just one decade Britain had changed, significantly and for the worse. Thanks, Dad.

By a happy coincidence, 1971 was also a pretty good time to move to Jamaica: a brash young nation chomping at the bit to make its mark on the world stage. The victory of Michael Manley's socialist People's National Party (PNP) heralded a radical break with the stuffy post-colonial politics of the sixties. Out went jackets and ties, crimplene pants, and white shoes; in came denims, afros, bush jackets, and flares. Music and fashion were but outward manifestations of the huge gulf that existed between us and previous generations; in music, fashion, values, morals – pretty much everything. With all these changes came a tremendous sense of optimism: we were the new generation, out to change the world! Sadly, it wasn't to last. By the time I fled Jamaica ten years later, the dream had turned into a violent nightmare. Nevertheless, Jamaica still had a hugely positive impact on the trajectory of my life. Thanks again, Dad!

My father died when he was just fifty-three years old – still a young man. He was robbed of 'the evening of his days' that he'd looked forward to so much; barely making it into late afternoon. But at least it was a very pleasant late afternoon. After he married Joan and moved to Jamaica, our father became noticeably less stressed, mellower and, in a word: happier.

Song for My Father

For her first birthday after they got married, Dad gave Joan a budgerigar in a cage, wrapped with a big red bow. One day the budgie escaped and flew into a tree in front of our house in Kenton. Birds of prey began to hover, Joan was distraught. Dad and I moved into rescue mode: I climbed the tree with the cage, and with Joan gently cooing from the pavement the budgie flew back into its cage. The whole street applauded: aww. They played a lot of Scrabble and on the score sheet he would draw a 'Bird on a Wire' for her and an 'All-Seeing Eye' for him: aww.

Of his three sons, I undoubtedly had the closest relationship with our father, certainly the longest. I don't know if I was his favourite, but he was certainly mine. He summed it up himself: *'All three of my boys have been emotionally scarred by the departure of their mother. Gerry the eldest has become distant and aloof from me; Tommy the middle boy is headstrong and rebellious; while Brian the youngest clings to me overmuch.'*

Never a truer word spoken. I vividly remember clinging to my father, cuddling up to him in bed, squeezing myself under his armpit. For weeks after he died, I'd go into his wardrobe and bury my face in his clothes, breathing in his essence. Forgive the overworked reverse cliché, but he was truly my father who mothered me.

Tom used to tell me:

'I softened Dad up, so you could walk all over him, bloody ingrate!'

But he's right. Dad blunted himself on the Rock of Tom, and by the time I entered my rebellious stage (tame by comparison), Dad didn't have the energy to fight anymore. Or maybe he'd learned a better way. The first time Tom stayed out all night, Dad went mad. The first time I stayed out all night, Dad said I should've called. This mellower approach clearly worked better than confrontation. After we moved to Jamaica and particularly after he stopped teaching, it was as if my father exhaled. Finally.

Dad enjoyed the last four years of his life in Jamaica. He fitted into the middle-class milieu of Kingston: golf, parties, beaches, weekends on the North Coast. He was back where he belonged: the West Indies. Financially he was secure. He played a lot of golf and made new friends. In short, he came into his own. And then: gone. Just like that. I still get sad sometimes, still cry sometimes, usually when December 27 rolls around.

With every mistake we must surely be learning – George Harrison

If that is true, then what about us? Did my brothers and I learn from our father – warts and all? Did we grow? Are we 'better'? Far be it from me to be so presumptuous as to try and answer such weighty questions, except to say that of course we learned from our father. How could we not, from the man who single-handedly raised us? I continually find myself 'doing a Dad': recycling his phrases, telling his corny jokes, re-living his frustrations. And every time I do so, I smile.

People die, but their spirit lives on. The essence of my father is still here, embodied in us his children, and his children's children. At this rate, it will take a long time for the spirit of Darwin Fitzgerald 'Gerry' Samuel to fade away.

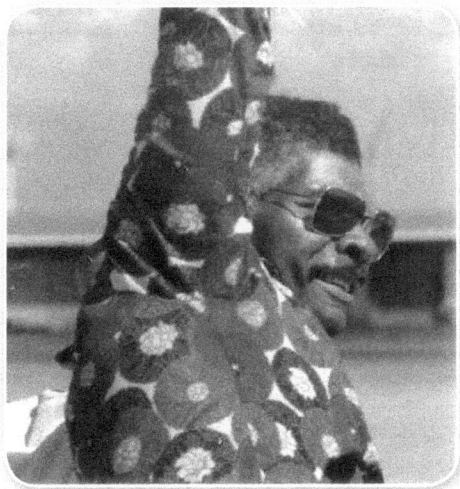

Postscript

My elder brother, Thomas Dougald Samuel, died on February 8, 2014, aged sixty-three. On that same day, his beloved Arsenal Football Club lost to Liverpool, 5-1.

Brother, protector, friend – he leaves a gaping hole. Walk good, my brother.

Milton Keynes UK
Ingram Content Group UK Ltd.
UKHW041018081024
449420UK00001B/38